EAT
PRAY
DIE

EAT, PRAY, DIE is a work of fiction.
Names, characters, places, poisons, and incidents
are products of the author's imagination or used
fictitiously. Any resemblance to actual events,
locales, or persons, living or dead, is purely
coincidental.

Published by JFP Trust
2018 Third Print Edition

ISBN 978 0 9945756 0 9

Printed in the United States of America.

www.chelseafieldauthor.com

For my husband.

I got stupidly lucky the day you first
checked out my ass.

Thank you, for everything.

1

I STEPPED INSIDE one of Los Angeles's high-rise buildings for the chance to turn my life around.

It was a sweltering day in September, the kind that had my clothes clinging in places they weren't designed to cling, and I should've been thinking about the job. About what I would be doing. The honor of protecting someone from harm.

But facing my fears didn't come naturally to me, so I was thinking about my hair instead.

I crossed the lobby and entered a waiting elevator. I wasn't equipped like someone in the protection business. No gun. No Taser. No combat or defense training. I didn't even have any muscles worth acknowledging.

I did have a hard knot of nerves in my stomach though. Would a bad guy be intimidated if I threatened to release the butterflies?

The elevator shared none of my misgivings and shot skyward.

I patted my unruly, shoulder-length hair—a nervous habit I'd developed over twenty-nine years of experiencing it having a mind of its own. Some strands were stuck to my neck, subdued by sweat, but the rest was likely poking in all directions. I watched the golden numbers light up one by one. In typical Los Angeles fashion, even the damn elevator was more glamorous than me.

The nagging concern I might be underdressed rose with every floor I passed.

I patted my hair some more.

Twenty-three lit up, and the doors slid open with a quiet whoosh, reminding me of one of Aunt Alice's disapproving sighs. Aunt Alice and her perfect children never had problems getting *their* hair to behave. They were probably above sweating too.

The corridor ahead of me didn't look to be any more sympathetic. It was insulated and silent, far removed from the heat and bustle of the street below and untouched by my mounting tension.

Ignoring the way anxiety had me projecting my feelings onto an inanimate building, I squinted at my palm. The number I'd written there when my handler set up the meeting had faded from an embarrassing number of bathroom breaks in the hours since. But I could just make out the smudgy figures: 2317. I walked until I found the matching plaque and made sure my shaking hand gave a firm, audible knock.

"Come in."

I took a moment to steel myself, then shouldered my way through the heavy door.

The room where my fate would be decided could've been plucked from a European design magazine. Floor-to-ceiling windows filled the space with natural light, all the better for calling attention to the distinct lack of furniture. Despite the generous square footage, it was furnished with only two expensive-looking chairs and a sleek rosewood desk with nothing on it but the token MacBook Pro.

I fought back a smirk. *Where did this guy keep his stuff?*

The man in question was seated behind the desk and looked so unenthused to meet me that I wondered if I'd misread the smudged ink after all. He was dauntingly handsome, with none of my insecurity, and dark hair that was cropped far too short to even think of misbehaving.

The no-nonsense style seemed at odds with the swankiness of his office, hinting he might be more practical than the decor suggested.

My gaze dropped to his eyes. They were the stern gray of an overcast wintry morning—the likes of which I hadn't seen since moving to California—and just as unsympathetic. The clean-shaven square jaw and broad shoulders did not soften his image.

I finished admiring his jawline and noticed his gaze was roaming over me as well.

For a fleeting second, I wished it was his hands doing the roaming. Then I remembered why I was here.

This was the guy I would be endangering myself to protect. If he hired me anyway. If he didn't, maybe I could talk him into pushing me down the elevator shaft on the way out.

Judging by the cool expression on his beautiful face, he might be amenable to the idea.

My concern had been warranted. I was underdressed. The conservative navy-blue dress and heels I'd chosen to make the most of the slim build and blue eyes I'd inherited from my mother seemed drab compared to his sharp, tailored suit. Sure, I'd inherited the dress and shoes from my mother too, but I *had* been hoping they were old enough to pass for vintage.

By the time we'd finished our mutual assessment, his mouth had formed a hard line.

I forced myself to meet his eyes.

"Isobel Avery, I take it?" he asked.

"That's right."

He didn't react to my Australian accent. Some Americans found it charming. My potential client wasn't one of them.

Actually, he didn't look as if charming was even in his dictionary.

Nor did he look like he needed me to defend him. A notion intensified by the fact that my knees were wobbling, and I was betting his weren't.

He didn't invite me to sit, and I wondered if that was so he could gauge my competence level by my traitorous knees. I sat down anyway, lifted my chin, and put on my best impression of professional indifference.

"What experience do you have?" he asked.

I resisted the urge to lick my lips before answering, leaving me acutely aware of how dry they were.

That seemed unfair when the rest of me was still damp with sweat.

"I've been selected for you by the Taste Society," I said. "That's as much as you need to know."

In other words, none, zilch, nada. I'd just finished eight months of intensive training, and aside from that, I was as green as a queasy leprechaun.

This job would either be my saving grace or the final rut in a long road of potholes.

One step at a time, I told myself. *First get the job, then concentrate on whether you can pull it off.*

I stared at him, willing him to say yes.

"I'm not in the habit of trusting others' judgment," he said instead. "Why should I start now?"

Good question. Especially since the Taste Society had sent him a rookie. But I couldn't tell him that, so I took a stab in the dark.

"Because it's efficient, and you're short on time."

This guy would prefer to pull out his fingernails than ask a girl for protection. Which meant he'd postpone asking until there was no other choice. Until he couldn't afford to delay any longer. Or so I hoped.

Waiting to learn whether my guess would pay off was almost as painful as the job training.

He relented at last. "You'll have to do, I suppose."

I let out the breath I was holding. It wasn't the most affirming offer I'd ever received, but desperation is a wonderful substitute for rose-tinted glasses.

It turned out desperation was a wonderful substitute for self-respect and self-preservation too.

He stood up and withdrew two envelopes from his inner breast pocket. I took them from him and caught a whiff of cold, biting citrus and sun-warmed leather. It figured he smelled good. The envelopes were toasty from being against his chest, and for a brief second, I imagined slipping my hand under his jacket to the place they'd vacated.

I needed to get out more. But entertainment hadn't been high on my priority list of late.

"The first envelope is from the Taste Society," he said. "They asked me to give it to you if I approved you for the job. You'll start at breakfast tomorrow. Before that, have my stylist give you a makeover." He scanned me again. "A big one."

Jerk.

He didn't pause to let the insult sink in. "The stylist's number and my schedule are in the other envelope."

"Anything else?" I asked, not keen on hearing his answer.

"Get a tan."

"Sorry, I don't tan." Also compliments of my redheaded mother.

"You do if I say so, sweetheart. You're in LA now, and I've got a reputation to maintain."

Ugh. Sweetheart. "No, I mean my skin goes bright red, then white again. So your options are beetroot or potato."

"Then get a spray tan."

"I'm allergic," I lied. He'd already given me the envelopes, and I figured it'd do him good to broaden his horizons. I smiled sweetly. "So if it's all right with you, I'm gonna go ahead and live to a ripe old age as a potato."

I couldn't tell if the barely perceptible shift of his eyebrows was from anger or amusement.

"You chose an interesting profession for that."

I brushed aside his comment and headed for the exit. He was probably just being funny, right? Sure, that was the interpretation I'd go with. Never mind that nothing in the past few minutes had pointed to him having a sense of humor. All the same, recruitment had told me the job wouldn't affect my chances of longevity too much, and despite rumors to the contrary, I was taking their word for it.

I was broke, not suicidal.

In a last-ditch effort to resuscitate my dreams of leaving a positive impression, I paused at the door and gave my new client a wave. "See you tomorrow."

He didn't reply, but when I glanced back, I saw his contempt for my appearance hadn't stopped his eyes from following my ass on the way out.

I GAVE THE SNOBBY ELEVATOR a smug smile as I stepped inside. Like we were equals now. But by the time I returned to earth—a.k.a. the ground floor—the reality of my situation had drained away my sense of triumph. Yes, I'd landed my first assignment, but it was a job I would have run from under ordinary circumstances, and I had no one to share the dubious victory with. No one I was *allowed* to share it with anyway.

The elevator released me with another of Aunt Alice's sighs, and I set off across the lobby. My new career was classified, and that was all I could tell my loved ones about it, including my poor mother.

Sometimes the classified thing came in handy—"Have you met any nice men?"—but mostly it was hard. My family and best friend in Australia knew only that I'd flown to California for a secretive job opportunity. Everyone else thought I was here to get as far away from my ex-husband as was geographically possible.

There was some truth to that version too.

I fought off the familiar pang of homesickness and fingered the two envelopes I'd received. This was it. My last chance to back out. The client had given his grudging approval, and now I would learn the details of the assignment. After that, a single phone call to my Taste Society handler would seal my fate.

You could argue I'd already committed when I hopped on a flight to the other side of the world. Or when I'd stuck out the eight months of awful training even once I learned the truth around what the job entailed. But this felt different. The reality of what I'd been trained to do sat heavy on my chest.

Not wanting to hang around in case Mr. Jerkface came

down for an early lunch, I rejoined the people sweating on the street and tried to recall where I'd left my car.

Parking in Downtown LA was a competitive sport that only the mean, skilled, or lucky won. None of those applied to me, so I was in for a long trek.

On the upside, I had some reading material for the journey.

I broke the seal on the Taste Society envelope and pulled out the two sheets of paper within. The first page was a photo of my new client, Connor Stiles, and his stats. He had some years on me at thirty-six, and he worked in "Private Security and Investigation." In addition to his PI license, he held permits for firearms, tear gas, and concealed carry.

No wonder he didn't look like he needed protecting.

He was also a millionaire, as expected. Only the rich, famous, and influential required the Taste Society's special brand of services. Which was fortunate because they were the only ones who could afford them.

The reason those special services existed was the most shocking revelation I'd learned since landing in LA.

The world's powerful elite are hiding one great big dirty secret.

Reports of a celebrity or political figure doing something stupid under the influence are so commonplace that sometimes they don't feel like news anymore. Often the individual in the spotlight sabotages their own career. Other times it's the last thing they ever do—a fatal drug overdose. The general public takes the stories at face value, as I had until a few months ago.

Now I knew better. The climb to power and fortune is a war zone, and poison is the weapon of choice.

Of course, not every drug-related story is a sabotage or murder attempt. The culture of recreational drug use just provides the perfect backdrop to get away with those that are.

My new job was to stop them. A bit like a canary in a coal mine. Except I wasn't supposed to die.

My ex-husband might've considered me expendable, but I was trusting my new employer was different. Certainly, they'd invested more in me than he ever had. Eight months of all-expenses-paid job training teaching me to memorize the taste and smell of relevant poisonous and psychoactive substances so I could detect them in food. Without dying.

Theoretically.

I swallowed hard, reminded myself that I'd be paid better than those canaries, and focused on the paper in front of me. Connor stared back as unimpressed as he'd been in the flesh. I didn't want to speculate about what he'd secured and investigated to become a millionaire. Or what he'd done to attract someone's lethal attention.

Instead, I flicked over to the second page. According to his Taste Society application, he wanted one of their elite food tasters—known as Shades to those who knew of our existence—to protect him from "criminal and rival entities." I hoped these entities favored using poison because I had nothing going for me in the surviving-physical-violence department. Otherwise, I wouldn't have been desperate enough to become a Shade in the first place.

I made myself keep reading.

Shades need a plausible reason to spend every day with a high-profile figure and taste their food in public. So they're given a cover story for each assignment. This could be personal assistant, life guru, personal fitness coach, or any other fabrication that fits the individual needs of the client.

My cover was to be Connor's girlfriend.

Not good.

I flicked back to the picture of Connor's unsmiling face. His disagreeable attitude hadn't concerned me until now. I could handle condescending jerks. After all, I'd perfected the suck-it-up-and-smile routine over years of customer-service roles. However, none of my previous professions had required allowing my customers to grope me.

Not that some of the customers hadn't tried, but I'd never needed to pretend to enjoy it.

Maybe I should've taken acting lessons as part of my job training. Or stuck with selling sticky buns for a living.

I rounded the last corner and spotted my new company car waiting for me by the curb. It was a beautiful, twelve-years-young silver Corvette, and a far cry from my former rusting hulk. I went to the wrong door before remembering what country I was in. While I'd been in LA for eight months, this was my first week out of the sheltered confines of the training facility, and it was taking time to adjust. Hoping no one had seen my blunder, I strolled casually around the car and slid onto the leather seat.

My phone rang as I was clicking my seat belt into place.

I rolled the car windows down to keep from cooking and answered it.

"Darling." My mother's soft voice floated down the line. "Is now an okay time to chat?"

"Always." I meant it. There were few people I'd prefer to talk to.

"Oh my, that's nice of you to say. Angling for a favor?" The humor was audible in her tone, and another wave of homesickness swept over me.

"Ha ha, very funny."

She was uncomfortably close to the truth. I did have one alternative to risking my life and sanity by taking on this new job—I could fess up to my parents. They would sell their house in a heartbeat to pay off the debt and save me from the mess of my own making.

Which was exactly why I hadn't told them.

"I was ringing because a nice man from the bank dropped by to ask about you last night," Mum said.

Her innocent words landed like arsenic in my stomach. I didn't have a bank. I didn't have enough money to warrant one. But the loan shark operation I owed money to had a respectable lending branch as a front for their illicit activities.

She called him a nice man, I reminded myself. He couldn't have told her the truth.

"He said you'd forgotten to give him your new contact details. So I gave him your number, but I didn't have a current address for you. Have you found a place to live yet?"

I tried to answer, but my mouth was as dry as my former

boss's dandruffy scalp. *What if he'd hurt her?* I knew firsthand those guys were mean.

"Are you there?" Mum asked.

"I'm here."

"Well, what is it then? Your new address?"

The loan shark would find me no matter what continent I was on, but by "forgetting" to notify them of my whereabouts, I'd hoped to buy myself enough time to start earning paychecks before they sent some guy called Bruce-the-Bruiser to hunt me down.

Looks like my time had run out.

"Uh, sorry, Mum, something's come up. I've gotta go, but I'll call you later. Love you." My voice wobbled on the last words, but hopefully she'd chalk it up to the overseas connection.

I threw the phone back in my bag and pressed my forehead against the hot, hard steering wheel. At the end of the day, my choices were: die at the hands of Bruce-the-Bruiser; run home and be rescued by my parents (they'd have to front me the plane ticket first); or ignore my misgivings and take on this job.

I couldn't live with myself if I made my parents lose their house, so it was no choice at all really.

Taking a deep breath, I removed my head from the steering wheel, picked up the phone again, and dialed my handler's number.

2

MY LEGS WERE STICKING to the leather seat, so I turned over the ignition and cranked up the air-conditioning while waiting for my handler to answer. It was the first week of September and eighty-six degrees outside. In my hometown of Adelaide, it would be curl-up-in-front-of-the-fire weather.

He picked up on the fourth ring. "State your ID."

"Hi, Jim. It's me, Isobel Avery."

"No names remember? I only told you mine because you got so worked up about it."

I hadn't actually gotten worked up. Fraternizing amongst Shades was discouraged, so Jim was my sole contact at the Taste Society, and I wanted him to think of me as more than a number. When he kept answering all my getting-to-know-each-other questions with "it's classified," I'd resorted to pitching my voice higher and higher and crinkling tissues near the phone. Jim then admitted disclosing his name and one little-known fact about himself was within regulations. It gave Shades the ability to verify their handler's identity if they needed to.

He'd also felt the need to point out that no one else had ever asked him to do this.

"That was very sweet of you," I said.

He muttered something about how he must have been a dictator in a former life to be punished with fresh Shades in this one.

"Let's get a few things straight," he said. "I am not sweet, and you will not address me by name under any circumstances. If I ask you to identify yourself, use your ID number and nothing else."

"Sorry. Let's start again." I cleared my throat. "This is Shade 22703." It had taken me ages to remember that.

"How did it go?"

"Connor—"

Jim cut me off. "No names."

"Right. Sorry. The client agreed to work with me."

"Good. Are you willing to take the assignment?"

"Yes, although the brief didn't say how long he expected to need protection."

"I'm not supposed to give out that information over the phone."

Boy, was this guy a stickler for the rules. Aunt Alice would love him.

"Oh, come on," I pleaded. "It's not like anyone listening in would know who or what we're talking about."

"That might be true if you'd kept to the no-names policy."

Touché. "Please? It's my first case, and I'm nervous, and I bet there's a loophole in the rule book about it somewhere…"

I watched eleven cars crawl past before he caved. That may not sound like a long time, but traffic in LA is terrible.

"Fine. But this is the last rule I stretch for you, and it's only an estimate anyway. At the time of the application, the client thought it would be about two months."

Wow. Two months in a fake relationship with the charming Connor Stiles. Two months of spending every day together, tasting every morsel that passed his lips.

It would be my longest relationship since my divorce.

"Okay," I said, keeping my voice even, "and thank you."

"Don't mention it," Jim said. "And by that I mean, *don't mention it.*"

"Got it."

"I'll enter you into the system now, so your salary will start today."

The Taste Society provided room, board, medical care, and all other necessities, as well as a modest allowance during the months of training, but the hundred-grand salary only kicked in with the first assignment.

Today.

Despite the two-months thing, I smiled wider than I had in weeks. "Great, thank you so much!"

"No need to thank me. It's not coming out of my pocket."

"I take it back then."

I heard a noise that might have been a pencil snapping. "Goodbye, Shade 22703."

"Wait. Before you go—have you had that bite looked at?" This was the "little-known fact" he'd entrusted me with: that he'd been bitten by something on his belly button. It was oozing yellow discharge, so I'd told him to see a doctor.

The dial tone sounded in my ear. The stubborn old goat hung up on me. My finger hovered over the button to call him back, but I hesitated. Maybe I shouldn't push him any further today.

Without talking about his belly button, however, I had no more excuses to procrastinate calling the stylist. It was makeover time.

———

"MAKEOVER TIME" lasted seven painful hours. Even the stylist looked weary by the end of it. In contrast, I'd made it just ninety minutes before I was hobbling so badly in my interview heels that she relented and purchased a pair of flip flops for me.

The footwear substitution only cost five dollars, but the concession in style cost her a great deal more.

Part of the problem was that Shades need to use low-scent products on the job that don't interfere with our senses of taste and smell, so I told her fragrances of any kind gave me migraines. That meant she had to hunt down fragrance-free alternatives to all her favorite products, and I had a sneaking suspicion she'd dragged me around with her while she did it out of spite.

The one silver lining was that we passed a food truck on the way in, and I snagged the special of eight churros for three bucks. Comfort food. My extravagant purchase left me with thirteen dollars and twenty-five cents to my name. Still, with the current exchange rate, it was equivalent to eighteen Australian dollars, so I wasn't *that* broke. Plus I had a credit card, but it was reserved for emergencies. The last thing I needed was more debt.

The stylist had wrinkled her pert nose in disgust. "Do you know how many calories are in those?"

I'd smiled a blissful smile. "The perfect amount." Then, mouth watering like one of Pavlov's dogs, I lifted the precious paper parcel to my nose and inhaled the scent of cinnamon, sugar, and hot oil. It was mostly in appreciation, but I automatically checked for harmful substances too. Smelling nothing untoward except that the oil should have been changed a week ago, I pressed the first churro against the tip of my tongue and sampled it all over before swallowing.

Then I devoured the rest with obscene pleasure.

Come to think of it, maybe *that* was why she'd been so snotty.

I found a parking space for my heavily laden Corvette only a block down the street from my new rental. My apartment was on the top floor of a three-story slab of concrete built during the affordable-housing boom in the 1960s. Unlike most of the apartments in the area, mine hadn't been renovated since.

I hiked up the outside stairs and opened the door to musty green carpet, which gave way to the dizzying geometric pattern of the linoleum as I walked through the kitchen. Some enterprising soul had painted the wood paneling and walls white in an attempt to open up and modernize the cramped quarters. Although, for some unknown reason, they'd left a feature wall in the living room of original 1960s wallpaper depicting flowers, bananas, and pineapples in green and yellow. My housemate, Oliver, had taken it upon himself to draw eyes on the pineapples, which gave it a creepy feel, especially late at night when shadows played on the walls. The whole apartment was fitted out with mismatched furniture from secondhand shops and pieces previous tenants hadn't bothered to take with them.

Home sweet home.

I cherished each piece of ugly since it meant I could afford to live in the safe neighborhood of Palms, minutes from Beverly Hills and Culver City. The fully furnished aspect had also been a big factor in my decision. The only thing I'd spent money on was some fresh bed sheets.

It took me seven trips to carry my new wardrobe, makeup, and hair products up the two flights of stairs. I cheered myself by thinking of how much exercise I was getting without paying for a gym membership—and when that wore thin—by imagining Connor Stiles's credit card statement. Shades are obligated to cater to the particular tastes of their clients, but the clients foot the bill. Maybe I should've snuck in a new duvet cover while the stylist was distracted by twelve indistinguishable hues of lipstick. Mr. Stiles wouldn't have noticed the extra charge.

I took a lot of pleasure in washing the makeover off me and changing into my comfy sweats. Meow, my house-mate's cat, twined herself around my ankles as soon as I emerged from the bathroom. One week of living together and she already knew I was a soft touch. I gathered her lithe body into my arms, carried her into my room, and flopped backward on the bed.

She blinked her gold-green eyes at me and began knead-ing my stomach to make the perfect nest. I gave her free rein. She was a light little thing without an ounce of fat on her, and her sleek, short hair didn't add any weight. But she didn't let it hold her back. The bold, black tiger stripes on her gray coat suited her to a T. I petted her until she lay down, one paint-dipped black paw rested by my chin and her purr sending pleasant rumbles through my body.

We stayed like that until the front door creaked open and Oliver moseyed in.

"Izzy? You home?"

Whenever things had gotten too much while I was board-ing and training at the Taste Society facility, I'd escaped to the Fox, a nearby pub that reminded me of home. It was there I met Oliver tending bar. He was intelligent, funny, and absent of any ambition to become famous. He also had wholesale access to alcohol. That and rental prices convinced me he would be the perfect housemate.

To convince him in return, I promised to cook.

Seeing as I love all things food related, including its preparation, it wasn't a hard bargain.

"In here," I called, mentally getting ready for the homework I'd set for myself on the drive home. I had to work on my acting skills, and Oliver was the perfect guinea pig.

He came to my room, leaned his lanky frame against the doorjamb, and took stock of the shopping bags scattered all over the floor. "Looks like someone's been on a shopping spree, love. No wonder you can't afford better accommodations." There was no disapproval in his tone, only cheerful amusement. "Wanna beer?"

I eased Meow from my stomach to my lap and sat up to take his proffered drink. Oliver used his newly freed hand to tickle a sleepy Meow under the chin. He moved with a deftness and grace that seemed at odds with the careless way he drifted through life, but I was guessing it was useful in dealing with drunkards and glassware all day.

"At least I'm not always drinking," I said, putting off my announcement until I'd had some beer.

My confidence in my acting ability was low since failing drama in high school. I used to believe I'd only failed because I'd cut a butt flap in the class bully's costume and the teacher hadn't seen the humor in it. Now that my new job depended on believable acting skills, I was less sure. Hence, the homework I'd set for myself.

Oliver smirked at me and shifted a dark blond lock of hair out of his eyes with the neck of his beer bottle. "You know I'm still heartbroken over Adele. I have to drown my sorrows somehow."

"That was over two years ago."

He gave me a hurt look. "I left England and came to bloody California for her! It was true love, and you of all people should be sympathetic."

I eyed his sun-bleached hair and golden tan, both testaments to his love of the sun which was in short supply in freezing England. "You might have come to California for Adele, but you stayed for the weather."

He took another swig and shrugged. "Eh, guilty as charged."

"Besides"—I kept my voice relaxed even as my heart rate skipped ahead—"I've moved on. I've got a new boyfriend."

Oliver beamed at me. "Really? That's great. What's his name?"

So far, so good. "Connor."

"Where'd you meet him?"

Oops, didn't think of that. "Um, in town. While I was going to a job interview."

"Uh-huh. Is he your new boss or something then?"

I spun to see if I'd left the file on Connor out in plain sight. Meow was not impressed. "What? No. Why would you ask me that?"

Oliver held up his hands. "Sheesh. I was joking. If you were that desperate for a job, I could've hooked you up without er, hooking up, if you know what I mean."

There was no file in view. "Yes, of course. Sorry. It's been a long day."

Oliver was staring at me, all humor gone from his face. "Geez, Izzy, you weren't that desperate were you?"

"No!"

Oh dear, this is going just like that improv skit in high school.

Even Meow sensed it was a sinking ship. She leaped off my lap and sprinted out of the room.

Oliver sat down next to me on the bed, keeping a careful distance between us. "I don't want to overstep here, but you seem pretty wound up and unhappy for someone who just started a new job and a new relationship…"

I shook my head, unable to think of anything I could say to salvage the situation.

"And I know you must need money to pay the lease on your Corvette and support your shopping habit. So I won't judge. But if you need help, I'm sure I can get you a job at the Fox." He patted my shoulder awkwardly and stood up. "Sleep on it, okay? And don't worry about cooking. I'll eat leftovers tonight."

He let himself out, and I flopped back onto my bed.

This did not bode well for tomorrow.

———

AT SEVEN THE NEXT MORNING, I was cruising

along Santa Monica Boulevard with my windows down and the music loud, trying to pluck up some courage. My copper-brown hair had been subjugated into an elegant updo by a third of a bottle of flashy hair serum that cost as much as a week's rent; my makeup had been applied with painstaking precision using the stylist's paint-by-numbers system (rather than my usual half-assed one); and my wardrobe had been updated to the twenty-first century. Today's ensemble was a mid-waisted, yellow pencil skirt ending a few inches above my knee, topped off with a soft-fitting, silky black blouse and peep-toe heels.

Annoying as it was to admit, I looked good.

I couldn't decide whether it would be worse if Connor was pleased or displeased with the result of his mandated makeover.

Either way, now I just had to bluff the world with my D-grade acting skills and convince myself Connor Stiles was worth risking my life for.

It was easier to be persuaded if I thought of Bruce-the-Bruiser at the same time.

The address in Beverly Hills Connor had given me was claimed by an old Tudor-style mansion on a half-acre lot. The grounds were plain—well-kept green lawn with a few ancient maple and oak trees scattered about—encircled by a low stone wall. It was pleasant. Tranquil even. A stark contrast to its owner.

The gate was open, so I parked in the circular driveway, left the safety of my vehicle, and banged the bronze lion-head knocker against the massive wooden door. I busied myself by tugging the skirt farther down my legs while I waited for someone to answer. Connor opened the door himself.

I took a step back.

Gone was the intimidating, dispassionate man from yesterday. He wore a T-shirt and jeans, with his hair wet from the shower and stubble softening the edges of his jaw.

His voice softened to match. "Good morning, gorgeous."

I was overdressed. Yet I still felt like a cheap knockoff on his fancy doorstep.

He leaned in to kiss me on the lips, and I stood there like a stunned mullet until I remembered to flinch away. Then I remembered I was supposed to be his girlfriend. Then I remembered the Taste Society contract stipulated:

Lip contact is permissible on the hands, cheek, and neck but prohibited elsewhere unless explicitly agreed on by the two parties.

"Cheek only," I hissed.

He aborted the kiss and moved his mouth to my ear instead, his stubble grazing my skin. I stifled a shiver.

"Get in character," he said. "My maid is here." Stepping back, he looked at me in a way that would've made my heart work double time if it had been real. My ex-husband used to look at me like that. I wondered if it had ever been real. "I'm so glad you could make it for breakfast."

I reminded myself I was on the job and matched his soppy pretense. "Of course I came, schnookums." His jaw tightened on hearing my chosen term of endearment. "Wouldn't miss it for a year's supply of donuts."

Okay, so my act was more soap opera than reality TV, but at least I hadn't run home to Meow yet. I was proud of myself.

His acting was better than mine. "Come in then, and let me introduce you to Maria. She's prepared a feast for us."

Before turning, his eyes flicked over me and my make-over, and I thought I saw a hint of desire. He reached out and caressed my face. "You clean up nicely."

My stomach tingled.

"But I suggest you rethink that nickname."

I decided my stomach was hungry. For food.

I followed Connor through a wide hallway artfully renovated in a modern, minimalist style that somehow retained the character of the original structure. Exposed dark timbers contrasted with bright white paintwork, and the timber was picked up again in the floating shelves and art frames that created points of interest along the walls.

The hallway led to a kitchen that made me want to bust out my apron and cook up a week's worth of meals for Oliver. Aside from the beautiful antique wood stove, the cooking area had been modernized too and boasted everything a food lover could wish for—except for the disappointing absence of a decent espresso machine. It took me a minute to drag my eyes away to focus them on Maria.

She was so short I wondered how she could use the

kitchen counters comfortably, but authority oozed from every inch of her small frame.

She'd kick my ass in a brawl.

Just as well I wasn't supposed to be protecting Connor from fisticuffs with stout little women.

Maria's bright floral dress was perfectly pressed, her apron straight, and her shoes polished. Her age was difficult to determine, though the silver threading through her black hair and the wisdom in her sharp eyes made me place her somewhere in her fifties. I liked her at once.

"Señorita, I hope you are hungry," she said. My stomach confirmed my earlier theory by rumbling loudly, and she looked pleased. "Good."

She led us to the dining table where fruit, yogurt, muesli, baguettes, and cream cheese were laid out in an orderly fashion.

In fact, everything I'd seen of the house was laid out in an orderly fashion, and this, along with Connor's empty desk in his Downtown office, was making me wonder if he was a neat freak.

"These are only the cold options," Maria said. "I make you whatever you like, toasted baguette or croissant with smoked salmon and avocado, prosciutto and Brie, or blue cheese, fig and walnuts. You may also like waffles, French toast, bacon, or eggs done any way. Anything you want, I do. Now to begin, you would like freshly squeezed orange juice, coffee, or tea?"

While she spoke, Connor pulled out a chair for me and

tucked me in before seating himself. How kind he was in front of a third party.

"Thank you, Maria," he said. "I'd love a coffee and a glass of orange juice."

"Orange juice would be wonderful," I agreed, wishing again that I was back in Adelaide. I had discovered early on that most Americans don't know how real coffee should taste, and the drip filter machine I'd spied in the kitchen had ruined any hope of Connor being different.

Maria bustled out of the room, leaving me and Connor alone. He regarded me hungrily. Probably because he couldn't eat a thing until I did.

I cleared my throat. "So, what would you like to eat first . . . schnookums?"

His lips compressed, but he passed me the muesli and yogurt. I taste tested them for harmful substances with care, ignoring his long fingers tapping out his impatience on the table.

"The more ingredients a meal has, the more complex it is to test," I explained. Maybe he'd be less impatient if he had more realistic expectations.

He grunted, which I took as an acknowledgment, and I slid the bowl his way. He grabbed my hand instead. Maria was coming back, so I left it wrapped in his.

As she served our drinks, Connor drew me closer and traced the curve of my arm with his fingers.

I told myself the goosebumps his touch elicited were from discomfort.

"Have you decided what you want?" Maria asked.

I was about to request a toasted croissant with butter to keep testing simple, but Connor jumped in first.

"Actually, Maria, this gorgeous creature of mine couldn't make up her mind"—he surveyed me fondly—"so we'll have one of each of the baguettes you mentioned, to share, and finish with the waffles."

I wasn't sure how he managed to look so smug without changing his expression, but I realized by calling him schnookums I'd started a war. Not smart when I needed the job so badly. But my less rational side couldn't resist the chance to knock a condescending person down a peg or two.

Besides I could think of worse punishments than having to eat a bunch of baguettes.

I kicked off with the coffee so I could wash the taste away afterward with orange juice. Even without spotting the machine in the kitchen, I would've known immediately that the coffee was the automatic drip variety. No crema. Bitter, dirty dishwater aroma. Resigned, I sniffed it, swished it around my mouth far longer than I wanted to, and gulped it down.

"You know, your nose wrinkles when you do that," Connor said.

"At least I didn't spit it back into the cup."

He raised an eyebrow a fraction. "Don't like coffee?"

I slid the offending mug his way. "This *isn't* coffee."

He took a long drink and set it down with an exhale of

appreciation. "Whatever you say, sweetheart. Start eating."

I didn't need to be told twice. All was wonderful until I sampled the blue cheese. It was tart and delicious, but I could also taste an astringent, woodsmoke flavor I recognized as Fenella, a potent poison with symptoms that mimic severe intoxication. I spat the morsel into a napkin and tried to recall how much you had to consume before it became dangerous.

My brain felt woozy.

"Don't eat the blue cheese," I told Connor, who'd grown a second head since I'd last looked at him. I poked at one of his noses but missed and giggled when my finger hit my leg instead. Both heads wore identical worried expressions, and it occurred to me that I was supposed to alert the Taste Society to the poison so they could send out a rescue and cleanup team if necessary. I also remembered I'd forgotten to floss last night. I activated the microphone in my ring by twisting it as they'd taught us. "Feeeeneeeeella," I crooned into it.

Maybe I'd missed my life's purpose. I could have been a country singer. I could have been a somebody.

The world spun, and a three-headed monster was standing over me. I waved at it. Then I decided to take a nap.

3

I WOKE WITH THE URGE TO VOMIT and grasped around wildly for a container. Finding none, I jumped up and raced to the nearest door, praying I would find a bathroom behind it. Instead, I saw the hallway that was as wide as my bedroom. Cursing its width with every step, I rushed across it to the next door. No toilet. Halfway to the next door, I knew I wasn't going to make it and grabbed a vase that decorated a nearby shelf.

After hurling several times, I sank down on the cool floor and rested my back against the wall. It was in this position, with the vomit-filled vase between my legs, that Connor found me.

For the first time that day, I was grateful for his acting abilities. He hid his disgust well. In fact, he almost looked happy to see me.

"I see you've acquainted yourself with my great-great-grandmother's betrothal vase."

I groaned and slumped down farther.

"It's all right. I heard she was a harpy anyway." He came over and helped me to my feet, both of us careful not to touch the vase. "Let's get you back to bed."

He half carried me to the room I'd rushed from minutes earlier. My body felt so weak, I couldn't believe I'd covered the distance alone.

"Stupidly wide hallway," I grumbled to myself.

Connor tucked me into bed. "I hate to bring this up, but in case there's a next time, the bathroom's just through there." He pointed to the only other door in the room.

I groaned again. Apparently I'd picked the wrong door as well as the wrong job.

"Get some rest. You should feel better in an hour or two."

———

THE SECOND TIME I woke, it was to the sound of my phone ringing. I answered it groggily.

"Am I speaking with Ms. Avery?"

"Uh-huh."

"Good. It's Samantha Nielson from Platypus Lending here."

Platypus Lending Inc. was the front for the loan shark. The one I owed over a hundred grand.

When I'd made a lifelong commitment to Stefan Valentino (a.k.a. Steve or Stevo), I hadn't expected it to be a year living together and the rest of my life paying for it.

When we were newlyweds, he'd convinced me to get a two-hundred-grand loan to invest in some "sure thing" stocks so we could buy a house. Yep, stupid. In my defense, he didn't tell me he was borrowing the money from a shady lending company. Plus, he'd distracted me by feeding me pasta while wearing only an apron.

The stock market crashed, Steve figured he'd pay off his half of the debt a lot quicker if we got divorced, and I couldn't afford the overhead on my newly opened coffee shop while servicing my share of the loan. Two months later, I found myself selling muffins for minimum wage, with only a battered couch, a stick blender, and an angry loan shark to call my own. I hadn't even managed to get Steve's family pasta recipe out of the whole ordeal.

"Are you aware you haven't made any compulsory payments for nine months?" the friendly voice of my not-so-friendly lending company asked.

"Did you say you were after Ms. Avery? I thought you said Ms.—"

"I know it's you, Ms. Avery. I recognize your voice from all the other times I've had to chase you up on this."

"Uh, you must be mistaken. I don't sound like myself right now because I have a cold." I wondered whether I could pull off a realistic sounding sneeze.

"Do I need to send someone to go and check this number

with your mother again? Perhaps we should tell her why we're so anxious to get in contact with you."

I grimaced. "Okay, you got me. But I can explain."

"Ms. Avery, I hope you realize that leaving the country does not exempt you from repaying your debts. We do have legal means to pursue you, even in the United States."

And not-so-legal means too. It was a good sign she hadn't mentioned those. Then again, an experienced criminal organization would be smart enough not to make illegal threats over the phone. "I know. I wasn't trying to get out of paying, I—"

"Glad to hear it, Ms. Avery."

I hauled myself into a sitting position and unclenched my teeth with difficulty. "Ms. Nielson, you will also be glad to hear that I've just completed training for a much higher paying job that will allow me to repay you instead of going backward."

With their ludicrous fifteen percent interest rate, my bakery job's minimum wage hadn't even covered the interest payments—let alone made a dent in the loan itself. My debt had climbed from $100,000 to $105,000, and Platypus Lending sent some muscle around to motivate me. So when the Taste Society invited me to apply for a classified position that paid a hundred grand a year from the day of the first assignment, it seemed like a no-brainer. Of course, at the time, I didn't know anything close to the truth about the job. Or the Taste Society. In fact, I still didn't know much about the Taste Society.

But at least I knew when my first paycheck would be. "My salary started yesterday, so I'll be able to pay back most of the outstanding payments in just two weeks."

"I'm happy you're bettering your circumstances, Ms. Avery, but we can't afford to wait around for you to sort your life out."

"It's fourteen days."

"It's nine and a half months, and you said you'll only be able to repay *most* of the outstanding amount. Can't you organize an advanced paycheck?"

"I'm afraid I can't, Ms. Nielson."

"Then I'm afraid, Ms. Avery, that late penalties will apply."

"Fine!" I shrieked. "Then I'm afraid I have to go."

"It was nice speaking with you, Ms. Avery. Have a lovely day, and don't forget to forward us your new address."

I hung up before I could say something I'd regret. While I hoped "late penalties" wasn't code for broken bones, I had a bad feeling it might be. No way was I giving them my address.

I shoved the thought down into the handy little hole inside of me to keep my other fears company and slumped back against the cushions. It was then I noticed how large the bed was. A chill crept over me. Surely I wasn't in Connor's own bed? I looked around. The room was like the rest of the house I'd seen so far: white walls, minimal but tasteful furniture, and no decoration beyond an abstract oil painting and three floating hardwood shelves that held a single ornament each. No help there. I sniffed one of the pillows. It was definitely Connor's. And my breath definitely smelt like vomit.

I hauled myself into the bathroom and spent a few moments trying to find the shower. It was only when I stumbled down a small step that I realized the shower area was one whole side of the room, with no glass or curtain to divide it. There were also no taps or a shower head that I could see, but I pushed some buttons and water began pouring out of the ceiling. I undressed and hunted around for a new toothbrush. Not finding one, I squeezed toothpaste into my mouth, stepped under the hot water, and used a finger to scrub my teeth.

I wanted to keep my head dry because I didn't have any makeup or hair products with me, but it was near impossible with the flow coming straight from the ceiling. In a matter of minutes, my hair was wet enough that it was starting to kink, even with the expensive serum. At least I managed to keep my face out of the worst of it. After washing the rest of me with whatever I found in the shower, I felt a hundred times better.

Except that I didn't have any spare underwear.

It was a tough choice between going free as an eagle, or borrowing a pair of Connor's, but I figured I'd feel marginally less uncomfortable wearing his underwear than none at all. Especially in a skirt.

Serves him right for putting me in his bedroom, I thought as I rummaged through his underthings. He must have had half a dozen guest rooms in the house he could've stashed me in.

His briefs were folded and arranged by color. Definitely a neat freak. If anyone who saw Connor's underwear drawer also saw the shopping bags still piled in the middle of my bedroom floor, they'd know immediately our pretend relationship was doomed.

Fully dressed save for my heels, which seemed like too much effort, I left the bedroom and entered the grand hallway once more. I was relieved to see someone had taken the vase away.

"Hello?" I called. "Is anyone here?"

I didn't get a response, so I wandered my way into the kitchen. I was feeling peckish, but the thought of blue cheese made my stomach churn. Training had taught me this would fade soon enough. We'd had to taste every relevant poison, by itself and in a variety of foods, to memorize the subtleties of its unique scent and flavor. We'd also had to forgo the antidote so we'd be able to recognize the distinctive symptoms. Some things can't be learned by textbook.

Some things can only be learned by subjecting yourself to eight months of stomach cramps, projectile vomiting, and diarrhea.

The average person wouldn't survive this teaching method, but all Shade trainees have the rare gene mutation PSH337PRS, which increases resistance to toxic substances.

The Taste Society didn't tell us how they got ahold of this confidential genetic information that we'd never knowingly been tested for (well, I had some idea, but mine was a unique case). Some of us had speculated about it during training and decided it probably involved underhanded dealings with pathology labs all over the world—paying them to test all blood samples for the gene mutation in addition to whatever blood work had actually been requested. That would explain the secrecy around it.

Shades were also supposed to have above-average senses of taste and smell to assist our identification abilities. I figured we must be chosen for our above-average skills in screwing up our lives as well. Desperation was at least as important as the gene mutation in this line of work.

Yet none of that had harmed my appetite. I considered rummaging through the fridge, but knowing I might be expected to test lunch soon, I decided to find Maria or Connor first.

Okay, I was also nosy.

The house was huge, so I took a strategic approach, beginning at the front door and looking in every room I came across. Each one was tastefully outfitted in Connor's uncluttered, ordered style. In fact, I didn't spot a single item out of place, and it wasn't for want of trying.

I was peering into what had to be his office, and noting with amusement that this desk, too, held only a MacBook Pro, when he came up behind me.

"Looking for something?"

I spun around, refusing to be embarrassed. "You, actually. Is it time for lunch?"

He was a lot taller when I wasn't wearing any shoes.

"Yes. We'll be eating here again."

"Have you, uh, reported the poisoning attempt?"

Taste Society policy was to have a doctor monitor any Shade exposed to a psychoactive or harmful substance, no matter how low-risk the drug, or how little they'd ingested. Just in case. I hadn't been in any danger from the Fenella I'd spat out, but I was wondering if the microphone on my ring was broken.

"Let's talk about that over lunch. There's been a change of plans." He strode away, assuming I'd follow.

I followed, but not before sneaking a last peek at the floor-to-ceiling filing cabinets in his office. I bet every one of them was locked.

"Why did you put me in your bedroom?" I asked as I trailed him down the hallway. "You have at least four other bedrooms here."

He answered without turning. "You're supposed to be my girlfriend. Try to remember that."

"While we're on the subject, when I was looking for you, I noticed every room was spotless…"

"Yes?"

"So, I was wondering . . . It's nothing to be ashamed of or anything, but I feel like I should know the truth if I'm supposed to be your girlfriend."

"Spit it out."

"Do you have obsessive compulsive disorder?"

"No." He pulled my seat out for me and tucked me in

again. "I just like order."

As an experiment, I moved one of the salt shakers on the table a smidgen to the left.

Connor looked at me, unimpressed, but made no move to correct it. "Maria will bring us hamburgers shortly."

I wondered if they'd be safe to eat this time. The Taste Society had taught us that poisonings were common practice among the elite, but I hadn't expected my first meal to be drugged, or for Connor to be so casual about it. Maybe he was used to danger. Me? Not so much. It felt different outside the classroom.

I ran through the tasting procedure in my head. I'd have to test several sections of the burger since experts could concentrate the harmful additive in just one area or ingredient of a meal. Of course, it would need to be the rare combination of almost tasteless and extremely potent to put a fatal dose in only a small section. Even then, if the client ate some and showed any symptoms, the Shade could taste the same section and identify the poison so the correct antidote could be administered immediately. All that meant that the overall risk of a fatality was low, but I had to be thorough regardless.

To distract myself, I peeked at Connor to see if he was showing any signs of strain from resisting my salt shaker trap. He was watching me with an expression I hadn't seen before.

I forgot about the salt shaker thing. This must be Connor the businessman.

"I need to level with you," he said.

For a fleeting second, I thought he was going to tell me he had security surveillance in his bedroom and knew I'd stolen his underwear.

The truth was so much worse.

He folded his hands in front of him. "I work for the Taste Society, too."

"What? What do you mean?"

"All Shade graduates are given a false assignment before being assigned to a real client. This is yours. It's a quality control measure to make sure you can survive and thrive outside the classroom. Think of it as a final practical assessment. Only graduates who perform well will continue on with the Taste Society."

My appetite vanished. The conversation with Ms. Nielson was fresh in my mind, and I had the abrupt urge to throw up again. I needed this job. I'd given up my friends, my family, and the last bit of cash I had to get here, and if the job didn't work out . . . well, I guess I wouldn't have to worry about how to get home.

For my parents' sake, I hoped transporting a body in the cargo area of a plane was cheaper than the going rate for an economy ticket.

I pushed my need for the job to the forefront of my mind and tried to keep the anger out of my voice. "How come no one warned me that after flying over here and eating poison for eight bloody months, I *still* might not get the job?"

Nope, the anger was very much in my voice. To be fair, I was recovering from being poisoned.

Connor's expression was the same now as it had been a minute ago. "Relax. I was impressed by how quickly you recognized the Fenella, and I know your grades were excellent. There's no reason you won't pass as long as you can stay in character and keep your attitude in check."

My left eyelid spasmed. This jerk, who had toyed with me the last two days, deliberately poisoned me, and probably didn't even know what a debt was, held my future in his hands.

"Attitude?" Yep, my tone hadn't lost its anger. "You're the one who treated me like I was something you'd stepped in yesterday. You're the one who chose a poison for my first test that would make me vomit my guts up even if I did recognize it straight away. And you think I'm the one with attitude?"

"It does seem that way," he said, deadpan.

I was less deadpan. "If you're from the Taste Society, why didn't you at least give me the antidote?"

He stared at me, unflinching. "Something came up. I needed time to figure out what to do with you."

I gaped at him. "You couldn't tell me to read a book? What the hell is wrong with you?"

He didn't offer any suggestions, and his expression *still* hadn't changed. Like nothing I said could touch him. Like he was waiting for me to pull myself together.

I took a few calming breaths, but it didn't help as much

as I'd hoped. "I might need to work on my attitude, but you ought to work on your problem-solving skills. Even if leaving me puking in your bedroom seemed necessary to you, it doesn't take a genius to think of giving me a bucket to be sick in or warning me to bring a change of underwear."

He took a second look at my wet hair, the clothes I'd been wearing this morning, and then down at my crotch. His pupils dilated. "Are you going commando?"

I heard a choking noise come from my throat. "That doesn't even merit a response!"

He met my eyes and smiled genuinely for the first time since we'd been introduced.

4

NOTICING HIS SMILE WAS NOT being returned, Connor snapped back into business mode. "Aren't you wondering why I'm telling you this? Most graduates never find out even after they've passed. It stops word from getting around, and I need you to keep this quiet."

No surprise there. The bloody Taste Society needed me to keep everything quiet. What else hadn't they told me?

Up until now, I hadn't cared too much about their oh-so-secretive ways. If they wanted to steeple their hands and chuckle to themselves in their dark, shadowy rooms, they were welcome to it—as long as I got my paycheck every two weeks. How bad could they be if they're saving lives?

Maybe I should've paid more attention to the speculation buzzing around the training facility.

Connor was watching me, waiting.

"Fine," I said. "I'll keep my mouth shut."

"That would be nice."

I wished I'd come up with a worse nickname than schnookums.

"Testing graduates is just a fraction of what I do for the Taste Society," he said. "My official role is Chief Investigator."

Curiosity started poking holes through my anger. "What do you investigate?"

He held my gaze. "Everything I'm about to tell you is strictly classified. If any of this gets out, I'll fail you on the spot. Understand?"

I hesitated. Not that I was planning on telling anyone, but my acting experiment with Oliver hadn't filled me with confidence in my ability to hide information. What choice did I have, though? "Understood."

"Only a few select individuals in government and law enforcement know about the underground poison scene and the Taste Society. The rest of them are as ignorant as the general public, and we like to keep it that way."

Of course you do.

"We only bring in the law if someone dies, or if we have a perp to hand over to the DA with enough evidence for a conviction. The cops and feds who know about this arrangement don't like it much, but they don't have the resources to cover the field as well as we do anyway, so they deal with it."

Of course they do. I'd had my suspicions, but now I knew I was working for an organization so powerful that even the law let them do what they wanted. I hoped I could stay on their good side.

"So, to answer your question, I investigate poisoning attempts. It's part of the service we offer our clients. Shades prevent the attempts from being successful, and investigators find out who was behind them and make sure they don't try it again. We have an extensive database of past offenders, and we're very discreet."

"Okay. So why tell me?"

"A case has come up that requires my immediate attention. There's no one else available to test you right now, so we're giving you a choice. You can continue your assessment while accompanying me on the case, or wait for another evaluator to become available."

"Do I still get paid in the meantime?"

His shoulders shifted in a Connor version of a shrug. "Probably. That's not my area of concern."

I thought about starting over with a different assessor. Maybe they'd be nicer. Maybe I'd get an easier cover than girlfriend. But could I really sit around for weeks waiting for someone else to become available, not knowing whether I'd pass or not? And if there was any chance my salary would go on hold until I began the next evaluation, I couldn't afford to wait. Literally.

"Any day now, Avery."

Yep, my next assessor was likely to be nicer. But I didn't want to sit at home with just Meow and the creepy pineapples for protection, waiting for Bruce-the-Bruiser to show up. Plus, the case could be interesting, right?

Anything would have to be better than having time to reflect on the state of my life.

"I'll do it," I said. "What's the case?"

Connor's mouth hardened again. Guess he was hoping he'd get rid of me. "A Shade was poisoned this morning. She identified the substance as the prescription sleeping drug, Ambience, before it knocked her out. She didn't think she'd had enough to overdose, but the Taste Society sent a doctor to monitor her anyway, as per protocol. Two hours into what seemed to be recuperative sleep, she spiked a fever and started convulsing. She was rushed to a Taste Society facility and put into a medically induced coma, but her condition is critical, and counteractive drugs for Ambience aren't working."

Connor's heel scraped the floor. Concern for the Shade? Or impatience at having to explain it to me?

"That means she was wrong about the substance being Ambience, or there was more than one poison. They're running tox screens, but we're operating in the dark here, and it takes between eight and ten days to test for all known harmful substances. Her doctors don't think she has that long."

I sank back against my chair. "What do you mean? Why don't they give her other antidotes?"

"She's too unstable. The wrong antidote could kill her."

"Then why doesn't another Shade taste the food or drink that made her sick?"

"Taste Society protocol. She should have tasted and recognized the substance, whatever it was. We have to act on the possibility that it's a new poison with no known antidote yet, and we can't risk another Shade to find out. Plus, if the mystery drug is slow-acting, it's possible her last meal wasn't when she was exposed to it anyway."

I stared at him. This wasn't supposed to happen. That's why we had so much training. That's why we had the gene mutation to protect us. Shade fatalities in the line of duty were supposed to be incredibly rare.

I squelched down the idea that the Taste Society might be hiding the truth about that, too. One of the rumors going around the training facility had been that the mutation is a lie, seeing as there's nothing about it on the Internet—but I'd dismissed it as idle speculation. Otherwise, what possible reason could they have for choosing me? That argument still held up in my mind. Besides, if they managed to hide the underground poison scene from the whole world, what was one little gene mutation to cover up?

No, the Shade that had ended up in the medical facility and was fighting for her life was a rare anomaly and she wasn't dead yet.

"If the doctors are right about the time she has left, her best chance is for us to identify the would-be killer and find out what they used," Connor said. "There's hope, but it's up to you and me."

I gripped the edge of my chair, hard. Moments after finding out the new job I thought I'd secured was hanging by a thread, I learned the same job could be more deadly than I'd been led to believe, and now, that someone's life, aside from my own, might be somewhat in my incompetent hands. It was too much. I looked up at Connor's serious face. "It's mostly up to you, right?"

His lips twitched. "Yes, mostly me."

Maria brought our burgers in seconds later and I wondered if she'd been listening at the door. Was she in on it? Did she know what Connor did for a living?

I tested the first burger and slid it over to Connor. Mine stayed untouched. I wasn't hungry anymore. Instead, I sipped a cup of tea and trawled through my knowledge of crime investigation. It didn't take long. Ninety percent of what I knew was gleaned from crime shows and detective novels and the other ten percent came from my dad who'd been known to skirt the edge of the law on occasion.

"Do we have any suspects?" I asked.

Connor answered between large bites of burger. "That's the joy of celebrity poisonings, there are always plenty of suspects. The challenge is whittling them down. And we're on a tight timeline." He stood up, the rest of his lunch forgotten. "Let's go talk to the intended victim, I'll brief you on the drive."

I stole a last mouthful of tea and trotted out after him, collecting my shoes along the way. My pace slowed considerably once I put my heels on, so Connor was well ahead of me when I reached the car.

It was a black SUV.

"Creative choice," I said.

"It blends in."

Once I'd parked my butt in the plush interior, I tried to concentrate on what he was saying rather than worrying about how my hair would look after it had air dried and whether my breath still stank of vomit. I'd gotten a glimpse of myself in a mirror on the way out, and it wasn't pretty.

"The Shade's client was Josh Summers. You might have heard of him, he's a—"

"Celebrity chef," I said, my vomit breath temporarily forgotten. Josh was the kind of celebrity I could get excited about. He started out flipping burgers at McDonald's and became one of the most renowned chefs in the Western world, with his own TV show and a Michelin two-star restaurant right here in LA. I didn't think McDonald's was that different from selling buns at Bakers Bliss, and Josh was forty-four, fifteen years older than me, so maybe my life could turn around yet.

Unlike most, Josh used his fame and riches to do good, too. His foundation gave underprivileged and academically challenged kids a shot at a decent career by teaching them to cook at a professional level.

"Yes. He applied for protection just over a month ago. According to his application, he was concerned about possible poisoning attempts from two sources. We'll go over them with him when we get there."

Who would want to kill a man doing so much good for underprivileged kids? Not to mention what a waste it'd be of culinary prowess. If I'd wanted him out of the way, I would've kidnapped him and forced him to be my cooking slave. If you're going to be a villain, you might as well be practical about it.

"Only two sources?" I asked. "You said there were lots of suspects."

"They're just the ones he told us about at the time of his application. There are always more to uncover if you know where to dig."

I shook my head. I'd fallen down a rabbit hole where all the things I understood about the real world didn't apply. Powerful people were running around shouting, "off with their heads," the general population carried on as if nothing was happening, and Shades, like me and the girl lying at death's door, were all that stood in the way of heads rolling.

I spent the rest of the trip shoving my fears down into their hole again.

––––––––

JOSH'S HOME turned out to be a two-story sandstone mansion in the hills of West LA. I'd never had reason to visit Pacific Palisades before, and I liked what I saw. The steep terrain and huge blocks gave it a sense of space that was missing from most of the city, and some of the views would've had me pulling out a picnic blanket under other circumstances. I could almost pretend I was back home in the Adelaide Hills, if I ignored all the mansions, that is.

I was still thinking longingly of home as we walked up to the front door. That changed as soon as Josh opened it.

It wasn't because his face was intelligent with striking green eyes that I was jolted back to the here and now. It was because that face was racked with worry. Someone had tried to murder this man and had almost killed the woman hired to protect him instead.

I had to do anything I could to keep the "almost" in that last statement.

"How is she?" were the first words out of Josh's mouth, after Connor introduced himself as an investigator for the Taste Society. He'd referred to me as his colleague, which meant I could cut the girlfriend act.

"Her condition is critical, but stabilized for now," Connor said. "To give her the best chance of survival, we need to find out what the poison was, which means we need you to cooperate fully. No lies. No secrets."

If Josh was offended at being spoken to in this manner, he didn't show it as he inclined his head.

"Of course. But let's sit down first. This is going to take a while."

He led us into a double-height living room where distressed, brown leather chairs faced a majestic two-story view over Sullivan Canyon Park. An earth-toned rug and several indoor trees made the scenery feel even closer.

"Please, have a seat," Josh said. "Now, how can I help?"

Connor didn't waste time admiring the view. "Tell us about how Dana was poisoned."

Hearing the name Dana, my eyes jerked away from the canyon and a string of dread began to wind its way around my throat. I hoped I was wrong. That it was a coincidence.

Josh closed his eyes and drew his brows together. "We were eating a late breakfast in, here I mean. I'd cooked the meal myself." His Adam's apple bobbed up and down. "We had a late night last night, so we were tired and aiming for a relaxing morning…" He trailed off, and his Adam's apple bounced again.

Connor said nothing. Easy to believe he was a master of the silent game.

"I'd made lemon-blackberry soufflés, and Dana insisted on trying them first, of course. I told her to hurry. I didn't want them to cool down too much before I could eat." His pained eyes met Connor's. "Maybe that's why she didn't taste it properly?"

I looked to see Connor's reaction. There was no sympathy on his face but no condemnation either. Or perhaps his expression was just as inscrutable to me as it often was.

"How much did she eat?" he asked, avoiding Josh's question.

"I'd guess three bites?"

"Okay. Go on."

"One minute she was sitting there smiling at me, the next she was talking into that microphone ring thing, reporting the attempt. She lay down on the floor so she didn't fall off her chair and fell asleep almost straight away. I called the emergency number the Taste Society gave me. They said they'd send a doctor over, but she'd be fine, that she just needed to sleep it off." His hands jerked at the memory. "The doctor came about ten minutes later. I helped him get her into a spare bedroom, and he told me to go on with my day."

Connor jotted a few notes in a battered notepad he pulled from his pocket. I would've expected expensive leather, but it was a spiral-bound thing you'd find at the Dollar Store.

"Then what happened?"

"I did what the doc said. Got on with my day. Your crime scene team was here by then, taking pictures, seizing the soufflés and the ingredients and everything else for testing. One guy told me they could determine whether the dose was intended to be lethal. They didn't need me, so I dropped by my restaurant to discuss tonight's menu with the other head chef. Next thing I knew, I got a call saying Dana was being rushed to a medical facility, and they were escalating the case to an attempted murder investigation."

Connor jotted a few more notes in indecipherable shorthand. "Has the Taste Society sent another Shade so you can keep eating safely?"

"Yes. Caleb. He's supposed to be my personal trainer. Not that I feel like eating."

Josh's distress was written in every line of his body—from the tension in his shoulders, to his hands' inability to stay still for more than a few seconds.

"There's nothing else you could have done," Connor told him. "She was here to protect you, and she did her job."

He paused to let his words penetrate. "If we can find who's behind this, she might even live to do it again. Tell us who could have reason to kill or incapacitate you."

Josh sighed and settled himself back in his chair, but the tension didn't ease.

"I've made a few enemies over time. The boutique organic chain, Wholesome Foods, is an obvious one. I publicly boycotted them about two months ago for their unfair practice of limiting employees to part-time schedules to avoid paying benefits. I heard they lost a lot of sales because of it."

"Are there any particular people at Wholesome Foods you've locked horns with?"

"Not exactly. I gave them a chance to start treating their employees fairly before I exposed them. I met with the head of their western branch, Maxwell Yates. I could tell he was angry about my demands, but he didn't threaten me. Outwardly, he was polite."

Connor grunted. "Anyone else?"

"No, not that I can think of."

"Has Yates or anyone at the company contacted you since?"

"Well, I'm not expecting an invitation to their Christmas party if that's what you mean," Josh said in a failed attempt at levity.

Connor stayed silent, to no one's surprise.

Josh realized Connor was still waiting for an answer. "No, they haven't."

"Who else might benefit from you having an accident?"

"Well"—Josh rubbed his forehead—"I ousted Albert Alstrom from his three-year title of California Culinary Champion this summer. He didn't threaten me either, but I've heard rumors he was furious. I know one of the judges on the panel, and she told me he was hassling them about their decision. Even accused her of rigging the competition."

He paused for a bit, pondering the dark subject of who else might want him dead.

How many people would I be able to name with a motive to kill me if I were under interrogation? Bruce-the-Bruiser immediately came to mind. And that girl I'd hit in second grade, even though she'd started it. There was one overly competitive Shade graduate who'd taken a particular dislike to me, too.

"I guess the charities in my will would benefit from my death, but I'm a regular donor, so I'm worth more to them alive in the long run."

Connor nodded as if that thought had crossed his mind as well. I, on the other hand, had never considered a charitable organization might murder for money. It was going to be a steep learning curve.

"Anyone else?"

"No, that's all I can think of." Josh's voice betrayed the first sign of irritation.

Connor just looked at him. When that didn't work, he prompted, "Nothing of a more personal nature? What about family members?"

"I don't have any family."

He said it quietly, and I felt a stab of pity for him. No matter how successful he was, or how much wealth and fame he amassed, that simple fact wouldn't change. Faced with the choice of having my family or living in a mansion like this and never worrying about money again, I wouldn't hesitate. I wouldn't swap my family for anything.

Okay, maybe I'd exchange Aunt Alice and her perfect children for some cash, but no one else.

"Ex-lovers then?" Connor asked. "Old enemies? Anyone who has a reason to harm you for something other than money?"

"No." Josh's fingers clenched involuntarily. They relaxed again so fast that if I'd blinked I would've missed it. But I didn't miss it.

My dad wasn't an accomplished man in many senses of the term, but he was good at reading people. It's what made him a great salesman and an even better poker player. I'd inherited some of his talent, though I was less confident about it after being blindsided by my ex-husband. Dad had never liked Steve.

Now I was certain Josh was hiding anger. But whether it was anger at Connor for being such a hard-ass, or anger at some personal memory of his, I wasn't sure.

"I hope I don't need to remind you that there's a woman's life at stake here," Connor said.

"I'm well aware." The words came out clipped, and guilt rolled off him in waves so big I didn't need any special talent to see it. It's not every day a man lets a woman take the bullet meant for him. And if my suspicion that there was something going on between them was correct, it would be even harder.

Connor stood up. "Okay, show me where you prepared the meal."

My fickle heart gave a little jump of excitement at the thought of seeing Josh's kitchen.

I couldn't help it.

Josh led the way, with Connor close behind. I tried not to step on his heels in my rush.

"Who buys your groceries?"

"Tahlia does. She graduated from my culinary school for inner-city kids, so she knows how to select the best ingredients and finds the extra income useful. She's loyal to me. I'm sure she had nothing to do with it."

We rounded a corner, and I stopped dead in my tracks. Pale stone countertops stretched out before us, beautifully lit by the skylights positioned above. A selection of the world's most elite appliances gleamed at me from all angles. The Synesso Hydra espresso machine alone, with its handcrafted timber handles, was worth more than all my worldly possessions. Even including the Corvette, which wasn't actually mine. It was the most orgasm-worthy object I'd laid eyes on in two years.

Connor hadn't batted an eye at the kitchen. "What did you use to make the soufflé?"

Josh recounted the list off the top of his head. "My

six-inch saucepan, stand mixer and mixing bowl, a favorite spatula, and a few ramekins, all of which your guys took for testing."

That answered my question about whether professional chefs used measuring cups and spoons. Unfortunately, it didn't give me any insight into saving my fellow Shade.

"And the ingredients?"

"Flour, butter, milk, eggs, salt, lemon zest, and fresh blackberries."

My bet was the Ambience would have been planted in the blackberries. It came in tablet and liquid form, and the liquid was blackberry flavored.

Unless Dana was mistaken in thinking it was Ambience. She could've been misdirected by the real blackberries.

"And can you tell me when you last used each of these items, or if any of them were unopened before last night?"

Josh could and did so.

Connor jotted his responses down. "Right. The culprit must have planted the poison in the past week and a half. I need the names of everyone who has a key to your house, as well as everyone who's been here in the last two weeks, to your knowledge. While you're writing them down, I'm going to check out your security system."

Josh accepted a sheet of paper and a pen.

I hovered by his elbow. I was a failed nobody, and he was wildly successful, but he was still human. A distraught human. And Connor was about as empathetic as a cactus having a bad day. "Mr. Summers? It's an honor to meet you.

I just wish it was under different circumstances…"

The pen paused, and his eyes met mine. "Thank you."

"It's not your fault, you know."

"Thank you," he said again, softer this time.

He turned back to his list, and I gave the espresso machine one last wistful glance before following after Connor.

I caught up with him a few rooms later. "What are you looking for?"

Connor eyed me, and I watched the microexpressions on his face go from surprise that I was still here, to remembered resignation that he'd have to drag this unproven Shade with a bad attitude around on this investigation. I wanted to tell him he wasn't such great company either, but I also wanted him to include me on the case and pass me on my final assessment, so I kept quiet.

I could use silence to get my way, too.

After a good fifteen seconds, he released me from his gaze. "I'm trying to see how easy it would've been for our perp to get in without an invitation. There are cameras around the grounds, but the security team hasn't uncovered anything suspicious yet, and inside there's no surveillance. If we know the level of skill needed to break-in undetected, we can narrow our suspects down to the people Josh knew were here and others with sufficient expertise."

That made a lot of sense. "And why did you introduce me as your colleague when you keep lecturing me on maintaining my girlfriend cover?"

"Why do you think?"

"Because appearing professional in front of a distressed client is more important?"

"Correct. But everywhere else on this investigation, you'll be my girlfriend."

Lucky me. "Got it."

He turned back to his inspection of possible means of entry and the exterior security system. I trailed behind him uselessly, trying not to stare at his ass.

It's not that I didn't want to help, I just knew nothing about security.

"It's difficult, but not impossible," he said at last.

At first I thought he was talking about not staring at his ass. Then I remembered *his* focus was on the security system.

"We're looking at either a hit for hire or someone who had a reason to be here. Only an expert could get in and out without being caught on video or leaving any sign of entry."

I nodded intelligently.

"Let's go see how Josh is coming along with those names."

I followed his ass back to the kitchen. I really wanted to ask about Dana's surname but thought it best to let him work free of any interruptions while we were here.

Connor took the completed list from Josh and slid it into his rumpled notepad without looking at it. "Thank you for your cooperation, Mr. Summers. Have you checked to make sure your spare keys are where they're supposed to be?"

"There's only one, and yes, it's there."

"Do you keep it inside or outside?"

"Inside. I've been famous long enough not to be a complete idiot about security."

Connor didn't bother to agree. "And have you lost any keys in the last few months?"

"No."

"Good. We may have more questions as the case progresses, but for now we'll be on our way."

Josh showed us to the door and shook my hand warmly as if I'd contributed somehow. His palm bore the calluses and scars of long hours in the kitchen, reminding me he'd reached his celebrity status through sweat and blood. It also reminded me that I was walking away from one of the most famous chefs in the world without having tried any of his cooking.

Then again, the last person to eat something he'd prepared was in a coma, so I managed to bite back my disappointment.

———

AS SOON as we were in the car, I turned to Connor. "What's Dana's last name?"

"Williams, why?"

I felt like I'd been sucker punched. "She taught me for the first month of my training."

It was bad enough imagining a Shade I'd never met fighting for her life, but this was Dana, the person I credited for getting me through those first miserable, homesick weeks of vomiting my guts up.

My class of eleven had consisted of three star-struck girls who thought hanging off a celebrity's arm would be glamorous (two of them dropped out a few weeks into the course); five internationals who wouldn't speak a word of English to me, despite having to understand it to be training with us; one bitter, scary guy who'd been chewed up and spat out by life and didn't want anything to do with anyone; and one woman my age who I might have been friends with had she not been so competitive that she'd poisoned one of my few untainted meals to make me miss an important test.

Dana was twenty-five, younger than me, but had been a Shade for years already and was the down-to-earth type of person I could relate to.

"Once you've survived eight months of being poisoned every day for training, the job itself is a cinch," she'd told me with a laugh.

I'd dreaded her being called back to the real world to take on a new client. The day she left, I found a large box of Haigh's chocolates on my bed, shipped all the way from South Australia.

I swallowed the lump in my throat. If there was even the slightest chance I could help, I had to try. Regardless of whether or not Connor wanted me to.

"Josh wasn't completely forthcoming with us," I said.

He didn't respond, so I elaborated.

"I think there was more to Josh's relationship with Dana than Shade and client and that there were other leads he didn't tell us about. Leads of a more personal nature maybe."

Connor raised an eyebrow, and for a second I thought he might be impressed with my powers of observation. Then he opened his mouth.

"Trust a woman to see romance in the air. There's no rule against it, you know." His gray eyes met mine suggestively. "You're free to play around with your clients, just so long as you don't keep doing it at the end of your assignment."

I felt *my* fingers clench—I could hardly blame Josh for getting annoyed at Connor.

"Here's a useful lesson for you, free of charge," I said. "The word 'relationship' is not a synonym for sex. I only meant that their relationship is somehow complicated. He showed more grief and guilt than I'd expect to see for someone he hasn't known long. I thought it might be relevant."

Connor said nothing.

I was learning to consider this as preferable to him contributing to the conversation.

"And for the record," I said, "the Taste Society may not have a policy against sleeping with clients, but I never mix work and play."

I didn't know if that was true or not, but I thought it best to nip that one in the bud. The only type of playing around I wanted to do with Connor involved a picture of his face and a fistful of darts.

"I'll keep that in mind," he said.

For a long moment, the sole noise was that of the engine.

"You're right, though," Connor said, "that he was holding back on us."

I didn't allow myself to show any satisfaction.

"It doesn't matter how nice you are, everyone has someone with a personal grievance against them, but he only mentioned enemies in the industry and those who'd get money from his death." His voice went low and sharp. "I'm sick of celebrities valuing their reputations over another person's life, but it's not uncommon. We'll just have to question others who know him well."

"But how do we find out who knows him well?"

Connor pulled Josh's list out of his pocket and handed it to me. "The people with a key to his house is a good place to start. Read it to me."

The list was dismally short. "It just says Tahlia and Dana. He doesn't even trust his maid enough to give her a key."

"Then let's talk to Tahlia."

5

TAHLIA LIVED in a charmingly restored Spanish-style bungalow in Mid-Wilshire. The small home was hidden by a yard overgrown with brightly flowering trees, shrubs, and a single lemon tree.

Once we'd found our way through the garden to the front door, it was opened by an African-American woman. She looked to be in her midtwenties, with enigmatic eyes, sensual lips, and flawless skin broken only by a smudge of flour on one cheek. This must be Tahlia. I didn't know why it was that everyone was so attractive in LA, but it was starting to grate. It was as if they didn't even realize the rest of America was experiencing an obesity crisis.

I caught my hand straying upward to pat at my hair and turned it into an awkward nose scratch.

Tahlia smiled at us without guile, unaware of her assets, and my annoyance lessened. The smell of brownies drifting out of her kitchen might have also played a part in that.

"Good afternoon, ma'am. I'm private investigator Connor Stiles, looking into a confidential matter for your employer, Josh Summers. Do you mind if we come inside?"

Tahlia's smile went away. Mine would have too if he'd called me ma'am. One hand fiddled with the pocket of her well-used apron, and her eyes flicked to me.

"This is my girlfriend, Isobel. She's just along for the ride." Connor shot me a sheepish glance. "It was supposed to be my day off."

She was watching us with a wary expression, so I shrugged. "I'm used to him working all the time. We try to make the most of it."

Her features scrunched in sympathy, making me warm to her even more.

"By the way, are those brownies I smell?" I was starving after skipping the burger, and they smelled amazing.

Moments later, I was munching happily on a brownie. They were the dark chocolate, gooey-in-the-middle kind, fresh out of the oven, and I was in heaven. Somewhere between my first and second one, I remembered Connor might be hungry too.

"Want some?" I asked, offering him the one I'd just bitten into—to check for poisons of course. He declined, and I went back to my munching.

The inside of the bungalow was even more charming than the outside. Afternoon sunlight streamed in through timber-framed windows and set off the warm whites and yellows that made up most of the decor, brightened by a fun combination of florals and stripes. We sat in the dining room, facing a sideboard that overflowed with fresh-picked flowers and pictures of Tahlia with her family as well as one or two of her in a kitchen with a group of other chefs. No boyfriend or husband that I could see. Probably for the best, if my experience was anything to go by.

I grabbed another brownie and tuned back in to the conversation. Connor was asking a bunch of questions about Josh. I noted how he chose his words with care to skirt around the true nature of Dana and Josh's relationship, and by extension, the existence of Shades. However, the more questions he asked, the less information Tahlia seemed to give. I got the impression she didn't like cops, and Connor reminded her entirely too much of one.

His phone rang while I was wondering how to get him out of the room. He looked at the the caller ID. "Excuse me, I have to take this."

I waited until he left before saying around my mouthful of brownie, "These are delicious." There was no need to fake my enthusiasm. They would've gone perfectly with my coffee shop's single-origin Costa Rican bean with its brown sugar and bittersweet chocolate notes.

Tahlia smiled at me, her eyes not quite meeting mine. "Thank you. I was taught by the best."

"Josh told us you graduated from his culinary school. He seems like a pretty amazing guy."

"He is," she said, now fiddling with the tablecloth. She raised her head, her beautiful features serious. "He's the best man I know."

I reached across the table and took her fiddling hand. "Tahlia, I know Connor comes across a bit strong, but he's on Josh's side. He thinks the real target might have been Josh, and if he doesn't work out who's behind the attempt, they could try again."

Her hand tensed under my palm as the implications sunk in.

"The reason Connor's asking you all these questions is that sometimes people don't mention things they think aren't important, or they plain forget. We don't know what's important yet, so we're trying to learn everything we can." That sounded plausible, right?

She gave a slight nod.

I let my hand return to my side of the table. "It seems like you're one of a select few who know Josh well. Could you just tell me about him generally? You don't have to break any confidences."

She searched my face. "I guess it can't hurt."

A fresh mouthful of chocolatey goodness gave me an excuse to stay quiet, pushing her to keep talking.

"I met Josh about six years ago when I was given the opportunity to go to his culinary school. He was always friendly when he was there, but it was only after I graduated and began buying groceries for him that I got to know him a bit more." She pushed her half-eaten brownie around her plate. "He's generous and kind, but his work is his life." She paused.

"There's nothing wrong with that," I said.

"True, but, it's not so much that he's a workaholic, it's more like he doesn't trust anyone. I've been working for him for four years, and I'd never met any of his family or friends, until Dana." She searched my face again. "Between you and me, I don't need the extra money from doing his groceries anymore, but I've told him I do so I can keep an eye on him." She shrugged. "It's silly I guess, but I get the feeling he's lonely and enjoys having me nearby."

"I don't think it's silly. I got the impression he trusts you more than most."

She released the brownie, which had done so many laps around her plate it was starting to crumble.

I racked my brain for questions that Connor would want answers to. "I'm sorry to ask, but can you think of anyone who might want to hurt him?"

"No. I mean aside from his competitors maybe."

"Anybody in particular?" She shook her head. "Or anyone else in his life?"

She pondered that for a while. "He's, um, had the occasional woman over the years, but they were always short affairs. I suppose some of them could have been married."

"Do you know any names?"

"No. Like I said, I've never met any of them except for Dana. I've just noticed some of the signs when I dropped off food."

I tried to think of another question and remembered the list Josh had given us. "Josh mentioned his maid, his gardener, and you came to his home in Pacific Palisades in the last two weeks. Have you seen anyone else? Or anything suspicious?"

"No. Sorry. There was a guy repairing the garbage disposal, but that was more like three weeks ago."

I kept the disappointment off my face, certain that Connor would've had better questions than I did. Which reminded me. "I know Connor already asked, but are you sure no one could have gotten ahold of your key somehow? Made a copy and replaced it, or just borrowed it?"

"I'm sure. I keep it on my main key ring. I'd notice if it went missing, and I live alone."

That fit with the photos I'd seen, and I didn't know what else to ask. I remembered my dad telling me open-ended questions were more effective at getting someone talking than the yes or no kind, so I gave it one last shot. "Can you think of anything else that might help? It doesn't matter how unlikely or insignificant it might seem, it's good to be aware of it just in case."

She shook her head, setting her golden earrings jangling, then froze, her eyes widening. "Oh, I almost didn't think of it, but I started doing his fan mail a few years ago, and sometimes he gets a threatening one. I always tell Josh about them, but he says it's normal to get a few crazies and not to worry about it. So I didn't, but I did put them aside. Should I grab them for you?"

"Yes, that would be great."

She looked alarmed at my enthusiasm.

"I mean, Josh is most likely right about them being harmless crazies, but just in case…"

She went to another room to fetch them and Connor reappeared.

"Get out," I hissed, "she's opening up to me."

"I know." He gave an unapologetic shrug. "I've been listening in since my phone call finished."

I glared at him.

"Wrap it up now. I don't think she's got much more to say about Josh, and you'll shatter any trust you've built if you ask questions about her. We need to keep moving." He left the room again, probably to eavesdrop behind the door.

Tahlia returned with a box chock-full of envelopes. "This is it for the actual letters. I also have a bunch of emails I could forward to you."

"Yes, please do." I gave her my email address. "You've been really helpful Tahlia, thank you. And thanks for the amazing brownies too."

She met my eyes this time. "You're welcome. I hope it helps somehow." I turned to leave, but she touched my arm. "Isobel? Do you think if you find out something important, you could let me know? I'm worried about him."

I had no idea if Connor would allow it but promised, "I will if I can." I gave her a quick, impromptu hug and followed Connor out to the car with her scent of flowers, flour, and brownies trailing after me.

HE WAS LOOKING SMUG as I placed the box of letters on the seat and climbed in after them.

"What are you so happy about?" I asked.

"Just that I've got you on this case."

He was either lying or there was a very big catch.

"Why?"

"Because I'm going to let you be the one to read through Josh's hate mail tonight." His tone was as cheerful as I'd ever heard it. "And you do look particularly good in that skirt."

I wanted to be outraged, but I was invested in the case, and the hate mail would be more entertaining than the sci-fi I'd borrowed from Oliver anyway. Plus, I *had* done my fair share of staring at his ass earlier, and the compliment was helpful for my self-esteem after all the gorgeous people we'd met today.

"You're welcome," I said.

His smug look got worse. "Also, you might want to check the mirror, you have some brownie stuck in your teeth."

So much for my self-esteem.

He pulled out from the curb while I removed the

offending bit of chocolate. It was delicious.

"You can't tell Tahlia anything by the way. She's a suspect in this investigation, along with everyone else. She might have owed someone shady a favor or been so in love with Josh that she wanted Dana dead or is lying to protect someone who had access to her key. You can't rule her out because she bakes well."

Damn. I should know better than to judge a person's character by their cooking talents—Steve cooked amazing pasta after all.

I didn't want to think about my ex-husband, so I asked, "Why didn't you question her about possible motives then?"

"Because one of the challenges of being a private investigator is that people don't have to talk to you. I can usually get inside the door using the weight of the high-profile client I'm protecting, but it doesn't mean someone won't kick me out again if I come on too strong. You have to learn when to push and when to tiptoe."

I tried and failed to imagine Connor tiptoeing, so I focused on how to catch the would-be killer in time to save Dana instead. The private investigator point was one more challenge in a long line of insurmountable hurdles. The nice thing about a bullet, or a strangulation, or almost any other type of murder you see on TV, was that you could narrow down the time of death, and therefore the window of opportunity, to a period of only a few hours. Then you could narrow the suspects down to those who didn't have alibis in that time period.

It was neat, efficient, and impossible to do in this situation where the time frame was a week and a half long. You couldn't accuse somebody just because they weren't able to prove their whereabouts for all those days. Probably one reason poison is the weapon of choice among the world's movers and shakers. I exhaled in frustration.

"What's wrong?"

"I don't see how we can catch the bad guy quickly enough when there's a ten-day window and a chance that any of our suspects could have hired someone else to do the dirty work for them. The possibilities are endless, and Dana can't wait for us to track them all down."

"Yes. That's why I'm going to try to rule out or get a lead on that last option. I have a contact who should be able to find out if any of the local criminals-for-hire were involved."

I felt a spark of hope. "That's good."

"We also now know that Dana was right about the Ambience. That's what my phone call was about. Tox screens confirmed it was in the blackberries in a large enough dose to be lethal. Ambience is a pretty painless way to kill someone as far as poisoning goes, but since it's relatively easy to come by and can be mistaken for an overdose, the perp might have used it for convenience rather than kindness. Either way, we know they used a second substance too, otherwise Dana would have responded to the Ambience antidote."

My throat felt constricted, like it was having a fat day and unwisely wearing its tightest pair of pants. We'd been taught that this was how things worked, and I'd thought I had a handle on it. Now that I was in the middle of it with someone I cared about as the victim, I was seeing it in a different light. And the light was dirty and dark and terrifying.

"If we have tox screens back on the Ambience already, how come it takes over a week to test for everything else?" I asked.

"It's complicated."

"I'll try to keep up."

Connor considered me before answering. "Because the machines can only confirm or deny the presence of chemicals or molecules you've told them to look for, and they can only look for so many at a time. A single test might take hours or even days to come back. We also don't know for sure whether the second poison was in the soufflé, or if she had a delayed response to something she ingested earlier. That means they're testing Dana's blood and urine too, but poisons change as soon as they're absorbed by the body, so they can be almost unrecognizable, and some don't show up in the blood or urine at all. That's not even the half of it, but you get the idea."

I did. And I didn't like it.

"The Taste Society has the best facilities and forensic toxicologists in the world. If we were relying on government resources, the timeline would be closer to a month, and they wouldn't agree to test for everything anyway."

It didn't matter for Dana. A day too late, rather than weeks too late, had the same fatal outcome.

I stared out at the passing scenery and saw we were no longer in a glamorous district of Los Angeles. Garbage littered the streets, and even the graffiti-decorated walls were grimier. About a third of the windows we passed were furbished with bullet holes, and another third were boarded up, probably due to more bullet holes.

It was a vivid reminder that pretty much everyone in America owns a gun, except me.

"Where are we?" I asked.

"Florence-Firestone."

I swallowed. "Isn't that a gang area?"

"Yes."

Now the bullet holes made sense.

Connor parked in front of a building that was as disreputable as the rest. He pulled a gun out of the glove compartment and tucked it in his waistband before looking at me. His no-nonsense business face had returned.

"I'm going to talk to my contact. Stay in the car. Don't get out or unlock the door for anyone. Call me immediately if you have trouble."

"Are you leaving me here for my own protection or to make sure your car's still here when you get back?"

A trace of humor appeared in his eyes. "Both."

I watched him go and then turned to survey the empty street, not liking how the hair on my neck stood up as soon as he was out of sight. It was late afternoon, and the sun was creeping down over the building behind me. I hoped we wouldn't still be here when it got dark.

Maybe I'd get a start on the hate mail to distract myself.

I pulled out the first letter and was rereading it for the third time, unable to concentrate, when a loud bang on my window made me jump. A pimply pale face loomed through the glass.

"Hey, lady, open the door. We could go for a ride." He leered at me suggestively, just in case his meaning hadn't been clear.

I thought about ringing Connor, but I wasn't certain one scrawny teenager counted as trouble. With the way his pants were hanging around his knees, I was pretty sure I'd be able to outrun him, even in heels and a fitted skirt. Not that I should need to outrun him.

I double-checked that the car was locked, pulled my bag up to my shoulder so my phone was in easy reach, and proceeded to ignore him. Picking up the letter again, I pretended to read.

"Hey, lady," the youth's voice, which had been ugly to begin with, was attaining new levels of nasty, "I told you to open the effing door!"

I snorted. This kid couldn't pull up his pants *or* cuss right.

I turned to give him some pointers, and my heart started working double time. He had a gun. The pimple-faced kid had a gun.

How can someone who can't even put on pants properly have a gun?

It was pointing at my head.

"Don't make me tell you again, bitch," he growled, knocking the gun against the glass for emphasis.

I was pretty sure this was what Connor counted as trouble, but unless he'd been holding out on me, I was also pretty sure he couldn't respond fast enough to stop the bullet.

Praying my assumption about being able to outrun the youth was true, and that my poor heart wasn't going to give out under the strain of six brownies and the aforementioned run, I lifted a trembling finger to unlock the door.

As soon as I did, the scrawny thug yanked it open and pulled me out with surprising strength. I flew out of the car, straight onto the sidewalk. Blood began oozing from my knees, and the gun nudged up against the back of my head.

"Stay down, bitch, and don't do anything stupid."

I stayed down. Was he about to blow my brains out? Beat me? Or worse? My eyes searched the ground for something to defend myself with.

Luck decided to give me a break; there was a broken screwdriver within arm's reach. Probably thrown away after a burglary somewhere. I didn't care. It was enough to do some damage if I got the chance. The gun left my head and a door slammed.

I snatched up the screwdriver shaft and spun around, keeping low against the sidewalk. The little bastard was stealing the car. I looked at the weapon in my hand, remembered the firearm in his, and decided to stay where I was.

The engine started. Having nothing better to do, I drove the screwdriver hard into the front tire wall. It didn't stop the kid from driving off, but I watched the tire begin to deflate with some satisfaction. Then, still on the ground, I pulled my phone from the bag looped around my shoulder and dialed Connor's number with shaking hands.

6

CONNOR ANSWERED QUICKLY. "Isobel? Are you okay?"

I surveyed my filthy skirt and bloodied knees. "Yes. But your car's been stolen."

"What? Stay put, I'll be right out."

True to his word, he was there in moments. He took one look at me trembling on the ground and pulled me up and into his arms. "Tell me what happened." His voice was stern, but his arms were protective around me.

"There was a kid. A pimply, scrawny kid."

"Go on." His words held a hint of amusement at the details I thought were important.

"He told me to unlock the door."

"I said to call me if there was trouble."

"He had a gun."

He rubbed my back. "Sweetie, this is America, everyone has a gun. And I work in security, remember? The glass is bulletproof, and there was a spare gun under your seat."

The adrenaline was wearing off, and the cuts on my hands and knees were starting to sting. Holding in tears, I let out a sob that was more like a hiccup. "You could have told me."

He rubbed my back some more. "Yes, you're right, I should have told you."

I was unable to do anything more than nod my head against his shoulder.

"I'm not going anywhere, but I have to make a few calls."

I nodded again, hoping he wouldn't remove his arms to do it. I wasn't sure I'd stay upright without them.

To my relief, he only moved one. "Hi. It's Agent 1493. I need an SUV delivered to East 81st Street in Florence-Firestone as soon as possible. My vehicle has just been stolen. If you have a spare retrieval team you can set on the case now, you might be able to get it back before it's chopped into pieces." The person on the other end said something I couldn't make out. "Yes, that's right. See you shortly."

"The tire's flat." I sniffled.

"What?"

"I saw he was stealing it, so I stabbed the tire with a screwdriver."

"You had a screwdriver?"

"A broken one. I found it. I thought it might slow him down."

The rubbing of my back resumed. "Good girl. That was quick thinking. I'll tell the retrieval team when they arrive."

Rub, rub, rub. It was starting to be less comforting and more irritating.

"You even saved Josh's hate mail."

I did a sob-hiccup again and pulled out of his arms, just to prove I could now stand on my own. "I did?"

He pointed at the box on the ground. It must have been in my lap when I'd been yanked out of the car.

"I mean, of course I did."

He smiled, or at least his eyes seemed to. I was getting better at reading him. "That's more like it." He studied my disheveled appearance again. "We've got a replacement car coming soon. I'll drop you home so you can get cleaned up. How does that sound?"

I stood there, swaying on my own two feet, thinking about my comfortable bed in my comfortable apartment, and realized a couple of things. One: Not falling apart in the last five minutes was an achievement for me and probably good practice for when Bruce-the-Bruiser came around. Two: Being held at gunpoint had burned through the brownies and left me starving. Connor was still looking at me, waiting for an answer.

"Does the plan involve food?" I asked.

"Sure, we can pick up some dinner on the way."

"Then it sounds good."

The replacement car was another black SUV. Connor drove in merciful silence, allowing me some space in my shell-shocked state. After a few minutes, I recalled why we'd been on that hellhole of a street in the first place.

"Did your contact have any information for us?"

Connor's eyes left the road to assess how I was doing, and my mind flashed back to standing in his arms. I shoved the pesky memory away.

"He hadn't heard anything, but he's going to ask around."

"Okay."

"But enough of the case for you tonight. What do you want for dinner?"

I didn't have to think long. I needed comfort food. "Pizza."

"Pizza it is."

His cheerful compliance aroused my suspicions. "Cheese pizza, hold the cyanide," I clarified.

He looked at me again, his expression unreadable. "That, I can't promise you."

Jerk.

———————

FIFTY MINUTES LATER, I was snuggled in my bed, freshly showered and first aided, with a half-empty pizza box, a pile of hate mail, and a note from Oliver:

Chin up, Izzy ol' girl. My manager said they're looking for waitstaff at the Fox, and I know you've got buckets of

experience with that sort of thing. Us heartbroken expats
have to stick together. Working late tonight—so don't cook.

Even though I wasn't in the predicament he thought I was in, my eyes felt wet. How could a near stranger care more about me than my own husband had? I folded the note and slid it under the lamp on my bedside table before grabbing another piece of pizza. Lying to Oliver on a constant basis was going to be tough. Something I'd chew over some other time.

Freed from cooking duties, I only had Meow left to organize dinner for. I fed her some bits of ham where she was, curled up on my pillow, promising myself I'd get up soon to feed her properly. Meow wasn't the only one I was neglecting. My poor Corvette was still at Connor's, but he'd offered to pick me up tomorrow morning, and my bed had proved too alluring for me to argue.

I had every intention of starting on the hate mail and feeding Meow, but halfway through my sixth piece of pizza, I fell asleep with the light on, the hate mail unread, the cat unfed, and the pizza box still beside me.

At six a.m., I woke up from a dream that had started out with a pimply teenager holding a gun to my head, only for him to morph into Bruce-the-Bruiser. He manhandled me into an abandoned building and tied me to a chair. As he'd leaned in to gag me, he'd smiled, revealing an assortment of gold teeth and nearly smothering me with a wave of rotten fish breath.

At least I woke up before I wet my pants.

I was desperate for the toilet, so I stumbled out of bed, barely registering that I'd been using the pizza box as a pillow. Maybe because Meow had been using mine. Hard to miss when I saw my reflection in the mirror, though. My right cheek made me look like a burn victim in a low budget horror film.

I groaned and stepped into the shower.

I WAS GIVING MEOW a second serving of breakfast to make up for last night, when I heard a knock at the door. The pizza box imprint was mostly gone from my face, so I opened it. Standing on the landing was a sweet little old lady, complete with sparkling blue eyes, rosy, lined cheeks, and snow-white hair pulled back in a bun.

Only she was wearing a modern turquoise shift dress that hung from her bony frame as it would from a model's, paired with opaque black stockings and ballet flats. She was possibly better looking than I was, and definitely better dressed.

"Can I help you?" I asked, feeling as out of my league as I had with Josh Summers.

She stuck out a slender, blue-veined hand. "I'm Etta Hamilton. I saw you moving in a few days ago and wanted to introduce myself. I live just over there in 3A."

"Ms. Hamilton—"

"Call me Etta."

"Etta, it's a pleasure to meet you. I'm Isobel Avery, but my friends call me Izzy."

"Well, I'm not sure we're friends yet, dear," she said, giving me a quick once-over before stepping past me into the apartment. "Do you have any cookies?"

I was pretty sure she was supposed to bring *me* cookies as a welcome gift, but I'd baked some when I first moved in and am hardly the type to deny an old lady food. I pulled them out and put them on a plate.

"Would you like tea, too?"

"That would be fabulous."

She settled herself into a dining chair with the grace and posture of a ballet dancer and surveyed the room as if it would spill its secrets. Maybe it would. I switched the kettle on.

"I thought from all those fancy store bags you lugged up here the other day that you'd have made it a bit nicer in here."

I shrugged. "Those were from my boyfriend." I was grateful my face was hidden from her while I sorted through the tea bags.

"Oooh. Is he the one that dropped you off last night?"

The kettle whistled. "That's the one." *But how do you know about him?* As I carried the mugs, milk, and sugar over to the table, it crossed my mind that Etta might be a Taste Society agent sent to keep an eye on me. She was cool enough to be a spy.

She'd eaten at least two cookies already. That made her seem more ordinary. Except she'd done it without smudging her lipstick.

She patted me on the shoulder before dumping a heaping spoon of sugar in her tea. "Thank you. I'm starting to think you might be my new favorite neighbor if all your cookies taste this good and you bring eye candy the likes of your boyfriend around here."

"Thank you?" I sipped my tea to hide my uncertainty.

"So, Oliver told me you're from Australia?"

"That's right."

"Ever killed a crocodile?"

"Uh, no—"

"That's a shame. I thought you might like to go gator hunting with me some time. I've got a friend down in Louisiana who needs the local population cut down."

"I've never even shot a gun."

Etta banged her mug down on the table. "Well . . . hell." Her face went slack and she stared over my shoulder with unseeing eyes. As if she were in shock.

Okay, probably not a spy.

When she didn't say anything after a few more seconds, I ventured my own question. "So, how long have you lived here?"

Her eyes snapped back into sharp focus and she picked up her mug. "Oh, ages. Long enough to know everyone else in this apartment building is about as much fun as a barrel of dead monkeys. Mr. Larson in 1A's a war veteran, so you'd think he might be interesting, but the only words I've ever heard him speak were to his hamster. Then that Flanagan couple in 2A are always too busy fighting or fornicating to be social, and don't get me started on Ms. Pleasant in 1B; I've never met a bigger sourpuss. I've thought about sending her on a hot date to try to sweeten her disposition, but by golly, I don't know anyone I dislike enough to send with her. Meanwhile, Mr. Winkle in 2B surrounds himself with fish like a crazy cat lady does cats. *He's* happy to talk, but if I have to hear about his Siamese fighting fish one more time I'm afraid I'll fall asleep standing up, and that's real dangerous at my age. I could break a hip, you know. And there are a couple of young Korean gentlemen who just moved in to 1C, but all they seem to do is smoke weed and play video games. They haven't invited me to join in either."

She chewed another mouthful of cookie. "If there's nothing on TV, what am I supposed to do all day?"

I shoved a cookie into my mouth to save me from having to answer. I'd just learned more about my neighbors in three minutes than I had in the last week, and I could already tell that Etta was going to be my favorite.

"Can I smoke in here?"

"Um . . ."

"That's all right. We'll go stand on the landing." She took a last swig of tea and headed to the door, expecting me to follow.

I brought my tea with me, a silly grin on my face because my imagination had just put Etta and Aunt Alice in a room together.

Etta lit up with efficient grace and pressed the cigarette to her lips. Her lipstick was still perfect. She didn't smell like an old lady either. She smelled like magnolia, maple, and tobacco.

"I only started smoking a year ago," she said. "Never smoked in my life before that."

"Oh? What happened a year ago?"

She eyeballed me as she took another drag. "Happened? Nothing happened, that's the problem. You get to my age and most of your friends are dead or in some old folks' home and can't tell you apart from their own children. I got friends who wore natural, undyed cotton and ate organic grass and beetles and stuff like that, and they were the first to go. Then I've got friends who smoked like a green branch in a fire and drank like prohibition was coming back, and they haven't been ill a day of their lives. I figure it's stress that'll kill you first. They've even done studies about it. So I decided, hell, if it feels good, I'm gonna do it. And smoking feels good after you get over the initial disgust." She shrugged and inhaled again. "Same as sex really."

I opened my mouth and shut it again.

She finished the cigarette and ground it out on the metal railing.

"Well, Isobel, it was nice meeting you. Hope to see more of your cookies and man candy 'round here soon." She gave me a wink, which she totally pulled off, and sauntered back toward 3A.

I was admiring her retreating figure with a mixture of astonishment and awe when my phone buzzed with a message from Connor. "Man candy should be here in about ten minutes, so keep an eye out," I called to her. Then I remembered I was still in my bathrobe and raced inside to finish getting ready.

CONNOR GOT OUT and opened the car door for me. The perfect gentleman boyfriend. He was wearing fitted navy jeans, black dress shoes, and a pale lilac long-sleeved shirt rolled up at the cuffs. The stubble from yesterday was gone. Professional but approachable, I guessed. Nobody seemed to wear suits in LA, so the one he'd worn at my interview must've been chosen to intimidate.

Watching him walk back around to the driver's side, I suspected Etta would appreciate today's ensemble—his tailored shirt hugged his body, and the jeans did wonders for his ass.

We were in a black SUV that was neither the stolen one nor the loaner that had replaced it. The interior held Connor's subtle leather and citrus scent, so I figured it was his.

"How many cars do you have?" I asked out of idle curiosity.

"Not so many that you can keep giving them away." He turned the engine over, his face its usual uninformative mask.

I thought hitting him was probably not the best way to start our day together. "I'll keep that in mind next time I'm staring down the barrel of a gun."

Neither of us spoke for a minute.

"I'm thinking of learning how to use one. A gun I mean."

"Good idea."

I snuck a peek to see if he was toying with me. He wasn't. I gulped. Mum would kill me if she ever found out. Dad would buy me a beer and ask if he could have a turn. Etta would drag me off to Louisiana.

"I'll take you to the shooting range later. But right now, we have a lead to follow up on."

"Oh?" I was just glad he hadn't asked me about my progress on the hate mail.

"A bunch of background checks came back. It seems that our ex-California Culinary Champion, Albert Alstrom, has been a suspect in two suspicious deaths but never with enough evidence to nail him. Each victim was a stumbling block to advancing his career, and his M.O. is consistent with hiring someone for the job."

"Does he happen to have a prescription for Ambience?"

"We don't know. Medical records are locked up tight, and if he's gotten away with murder twice, he wouldn't be stupid enough to use something he has a prescription for anyway. Ambience is pretty easy to acquire illicitly, so Albert could be our man, but he's not going to open up to a private investigator working for Josh Summers."

"So what do we do?"

He looked me over. I was wearing a pair of those A-line, high-waisted skirt-shorts thingies that seemed to be all the rage at the moment, in gray, paired with a coral blouse that somehow didn't clash with my hair. High-heeled sandals combined with the short hemline to give me the illusion of long legs—as long as I could stay upright in them anyway. It was the first outfit I'd grabbed in my rush to get ready, but once again, the stylist had worked her magic.

"Luckily for us, Albert has a soft spot for his female fans," Connor said.

I started to shake my head, but stopped when I thought of Dana.

Connor didn't miss my hesitation. "Neither of the suspicious deaths were violent or direct," he said. "One guy died of an alleged overdose, the other had a fatal crash under the influence, so you should be okay as long as you're careful what you eat and drink. Besides, you're not a threat to his career."

I closed my eyes for a moment. What's the worst that could happen?

"You don't have to do this if you don't want to. It's not part of your job description."

"I'll do it." My tone was firm. My stomach was squishy.

"Okay. I'll put a wire on you so I can hear what's going on, and I'll be nearby to bail you out if anything happens."

I nodded.

"What do you know about Alstrom?"

I'd seen him on TV a few times, but he'd never done anything to capture my attention beyond being another chef. "Not a whole lot."

Connor passed me a manila folder. "Well, as his new biggest fan, you'd better get reading."

7

WHILE I LOOKED over Albert's file, we ordered breakfast at a stereotypical American diner, complete with the red vinyl seats and Formica tables.

"I didn't think this would be your kind of place," I said.

"Just making sure your practical assessment covers a wide variety of food and environments. You'd be surprised how some celebrities eat." He grabbed a laminated menu, looking entirely too pleased with himself. "Besides, the coffee here is delicious, darling."

Of course I had to taste his meal first, including the coffee—which I very professionally resisted the urge to spit in—so my omelet and pancakes were cold by the time I got to them. I chowed down anyway, still reading the file. When I finished, I had a hard time believing Albert could hurt anyone.

He looked like the nerd next door. His high school photo depicted him with his light-blue eyes overpowered by a face full of mountainous angry red pimples, topped off with a bad bowl cut and braces. He must've been bullied relentlessly. His yearbook quote was *"I'll show you all,"* and he had. I couldn't help but be pleased for him.

Fourteen years later, he was renowned for his ingenuity in molecular gastronomy—a fancy style of cooking using scientific techniques. From the three or four words I understood in the section listing his scientific achievements, I gathered he'd invented some doodad that improved infusion outcomes in some applications. He'd also masterminded a wildly successful restaurant in LA, contributing to the explosion in popularity that molecular gastronomy was enjoying around here.

His success had come hand in hand with a string of hot girlfriends in the past few years. There was even one fiancée, but that had ended before the altar.

I stared at the more recent photographs of him. He was thirty-two now, over a decade younger than Josh Summers. He'd done well to win California Culinary Champion of the year so many times already. While his look had improved as his fame grew—his dark hair was stylishly tousled, his skin and teeth flawless, and his thin, angular face handsome in a tragic-artist kind of way—traces of nerd showed through in the slump of his shoulders and the self-conscious unease in his smile.

I tried to imagine being in love with him. It was one

thing to fake it with a client who knew I was faking (and I was doing a pretty poor job of that). It was quite another to do it well enough to trick the subject himself.

"Are you ready?" The question was asked without the usual condescension. That made me even more nervous.

I remembered all the poison-free takeout espressos Dana had snuck in for me when I was having a particularly rough time, and my mind flashed again to the image I'd conjured of her lying wan and alone with a dozen tubes sticking out of her.

Breakfast sat heavily in my stomach, so I lightened my tone to compensate. "Ready as I'll ever be."

"Good." We returned to the car and climbed in. "I have intel that Alstrom will be at the Santa Monica Farmers Market in about half an hour. You can run into him there and try to get a date." He handed me a ladies' watch. "This is your wire. It'll be more of a formality today than anything else. You won't be asking any leading questions, and you shouldn't get into trouble, but choose a safe word just in case."

I strapped on the watch and squelched down my disbelief at *me* wearing a wire and choosing a safe word. Considering I'd joined a secret, ancient, and powerful organization so I could play a deadly game with the rich and famous and those who wanted to kill them, the wire should've been no big deal.

Still, I was nervous. Not so much about Albert deciding I was a threat and trying to take me out. The larger risk was he'd find me unappealing amidst all the surgically enhanced, would-be actresses of LA and ignore me.

Connor pulled to a stop. "Your safe word?"

"Squishy."

His lips twitched, but I thought I'd done well. It wouldn't be too hard to avoid using in natural conversation, and I could use it to describe food, a seat, or even my stomach if the need arose.

"Alstrom should arrive in about twenty minutes. In the meantime, wander around, do some shopping, then find a place where you can observe Sal's Stall. According to our source, Alstrom stops there whenever he comes to the market."

I left Connor in the car and joined the throng of people milling around the produce stalls lining the street. Rummaging around in my bag for my sunglasses, I considered whether it was worth applying sunscreen too. Unlikely. Albert would probably walk away laughing, if he deigned to talk to me at all. I wouldn't be here long.

To prevent the exercise from being a total waste of time, I purchased ingredients for a vegetable lasagna for Oliver while I looked around. Halfway down the street, I found Sal's Stall, and after that, limited my shopping to nearby stands, resisting my urge to bargain hunt. It was a good thing Oliver had left me some cash for his share of the groceries.

I only had garlic left to buy when I spotted my target. Glancing down at my top, I undid two more buttons and rearranged things so they were more to my advantage. Then

I grabbed the nearest weird-looking vegetable and sidled up to Albert where he was inspecting a selection of black truffles. Even a quick glimpse told me the nerd vibe was stronger in person than his photo shoots portrayed. He could've been a geeky kid hunched over a magician's kit.

"Excuse me," I said, keeping my eyes on the vegetable. "Do you know what this thing is?"

The voice beside me was amused. "It's a Romanesco."

I knew that, but what man doesn't like to share his expertise? Another fun fact taught to me by my salesman father. "What do people do with it?" I asked, trying to sound confounded.

"It's generally considered similar to broccoli and cauliflower, with an earthy, nutty flavor."

I rolled the spiky green vegetable in my hands and made a show of sniffing it. "Yeah, I can see that now." I looked up at him at last. "Thank you so mu—" I widened my eyes in faux recognition. "Albert? Albert Alstrom? I don't believe it!" I lifted my sunglasses up onto my head and purred, "I am *such* a fan."

Unfortunately, I slid my sunnies too far and they started slipping backward. I caught them by slapping myself in the back of the head.

Fortunately, at that point Albert's eyes had moved down to my cleavage, so he didn't notice.

I waited until his eyes returned to my face. They were even more pale in the bright sunlight. "I can't believe it's actually you."

He gave me a goofy smile, and I relaxed a little. "And who might you be?"

"I'm Izzy. Izzy Avery. Your number one fan." I hid a cringe when I remembered Connor was listening in.

"Really?" he asked.

For a moment, I thought I saw something predatory flicker in his pale gaze, and my legs urged me to run. Instead, I pasted on a bright smile and nodded enthusiastically, wondering if I was looking into the face of a killer.

The possible killer glanced at my cleavage again. Or maybe it was at the Romanesco I was still holding in my left hand. "Are you going to try cooking that?"

I looked down at it too. "I think I will. You've inspired me."

"Glad to hear it." His goofy smile made another brief appearance, making the light coloring of his eyes appear gentle now, like a soft-blue baby blanket. "Your accent, you're not from around here are you?"

"No, I moved here a few months ago from Australia."

"Australia, hey? I've always wanted to go there."

"Really? But our nation's classic cuisine is pretty much sausage sizzles, pavlovas, and fairy bread!"

He laughed. "I don't know what any of that is, but it sounds delicious. Plus, I hear you have some of the best cattle in the world, not to mention pretty much the only source of kangaroo. Don't be so hard on your country."

"It's true. We have good coffee too, and enough cultural diversity to offer far more dining options than traditional Australian, thank goodness."

"And there's more to a country than its food."

"Are you allowed to admit that?"

He laughed again. "You must have that famous Aussie sense of humor I've heard about. How are you finding Los Angeles, anyway?"

"It's wonderful. So many attractions"—I hefted the Romanesco again—"and vegetables it turns out, that I've never seen. And where else could you run into the most amazing molecular gastronomist in the world at the local market?"

His glance this time was definitely at my cleavage. "Then perhaps I should introduce you to a few more experiences you won't get anywhere else. Would you be interested?"

I tried to squeal, I really did, but I'm more the jaw drop and drool type, so I settled for placing a hand on his arm and gazing adoringly up at him. "I can't think of anything I'd like more."

His eyes flicked toward my hand, and his smile broadened. "My schedule is full today, but what are you doing tomorrow? Lunchtime?"

"Seeing you, I hope," I said with another inward cringe at the thought of Connor hearing this drivel.

"How about I cook you a meal? At my place."

I didn't have to feign my excitement this time. I was touched by his offer. If playing the besotted fan worked this well on all celebrity chefs, I could sample the talents of every gastronomy icon in Los Angeles.

"That would be incredible!"

Albert pulled out a business card. "It isn't my private line of course," he apologized, "but if you text your address to this number, my personal assistant will have a car pick you up at eleven thirty." He gave my chest one last peek and turned back to his truffles. "I look forward to seeing you tomorrow, Izzy."

I nodded again, hoping he'd put my lack of words down to being star-struck, and stood there for an awkward moment wondering whether I was allowed to go or if I was supposed to gush over him some more. When he started talking to the booth owner about the history of the truffles, I made a judgment call and fled.

I returned to the previous stall where I'd been lurking and purchased the Romanesco. I could add it to the lasagna, and besides, it would be rude not to buy it after holding it in my sweaty hand for so long. Then I headed to the car with a bit of a spring in my step. I'd done it. I'd caught the attention of a celebrity, albeit a nerdy one, and won an invite to his home. Even more exciting, I was going to enjoy a meal personally prepared for me by a famous chef.

Pity about the potential murderer part. My spring turned into a shuffle.

When I opened the car door, Connor's eyes dropped straight to my unbuttoned shirt. "Ah. So that's how you did it."

I plonked my groceries on the floor and climbed in after them. "Shut up."

"You did well, Avery. Maybe too well."

I blushed and did the buttons back up. "What do you mean? I did exactly what you told me to do."

His eyes lingered for a moment where my cleavage had been on display before he cleared his throat and looked away. "He invited you to his house. You know what that means, right?"

"That he's going to cook for me?"

"That he's expecting sex."

I felt like an elephant sat on my chest. "Crap."

Trust me to miss the obvious implication because I was distracted by food.

Connor noticed my pale face. "It's okay. You can play the no-sex-on-the-first-date card, and in case that doesn't work, I'll give you something to slip in his drink that'll ruin any bedroom plans he might have."

I started breathing again.

"Plus, I'll be right outside, ready to rescue you if you say the safe word."

That sounded pretty safe. I was just starting to feel better when I remembered. "Dammit!"

"What?"

"I forgot the garlic."

8

CONNOR SHOOK HIS HEAD and started the car. I
didn't want to risk running into Albert again at the market,
so I resigned myself to shopping later.

"What's next?" I asked.

"Our researchers haven't dug up anything so far to impli-
cate Wholesome Foods or anyone there, and going into a
corporation of that size blind would only waste time." He
handed me the two manila folders that had been on his
lap. "For now, let's focus on the people we know were in
Josh's house."

I flicked the first one open. Juan Castillo was a fifty-
seven-year-old silver-haired emigrant from Mexico. He'd
worked for Green with Envy, a landscape maintenance
and improvement service, for the last eighteen years. He

was married with two adult children and lived in a modest home in one of the safer suburbs of East LA. The house was almost paid off, but the savings in the Castillos' joint bank account were minimal. Could Juan have been convinced to participate in a celebrity murder for the promise of a comfortable retirement or to set his kids up for an easier life than he'd had?

He didn't have a key to Josh's mansion, but Josh had written that he'd invited Juan to come in and help himself to a soda from the fridge anytime the door was unlocked. That meant he'd had ample opportunity to put Ambience in the blackberries.

I closed his folder and turned to the next one. Josh's maid was not what I expected: Colette Merle, a twenty-six-year-old Frenchwoman. The photo showed a pretty and sophisticated-looking blonde in an expensive suit. Her glowing references had been double-checked and were all authentic. She held a degree in cultural studies from a French university. Her credit rating made me envious and she had no police record. She appeared to be the perfect employee. What I couldn't figure out was why she was a maid. And why she was doing so much better at life than me.

I raised my eyes from the folders to find we were in El Sereno. Juan's home was tucked in amongst the commercial buildings on Alhambra Avenue, a block back from the railroad tracks. A van with the Green with Envy logo on it was parked out front. We got out and knocked. A freight train rumbled past, rattling the windows, before the door was opened by Juan's wife, Francisca. She was comfortably plump and wore her silver-streaked black hair in a thick braid over her left shoulder. Her eyes narrowed when she saw we were strangers, but her generous mouth and the lines around it suggested she was just as quick to smile.

"What you want?"

"I'm Connor, a private investigator looking into a matter for one of Mr. Castillo's customers, and this is my girlfriend, Isobel. We were hoping Mr. Castillo might be able to help us."

"You have proof?"

Connor handed her his PI photo ID card. She gazed at it a moment then stepped back to allow us inside. "Juan is home for lunch now. You talk to him, you see he know nothing."

The interior was colorful, cozy, and cramped. We sat down at the tiny wooden dining table where Juan was shoveling down a spicy bean concoction that made my mouth water. He was looking dapper in a mint green, open-necked shirt, with dark charcoal pants, and brown leather lace-up boots poking out from under the table. If you wanted to work on a celebrity's garden, you better look good while doing it.

"You want food?" Francisca asked.

"Thank you, but we just ate," Connor told her.

I bit my tongue to keep from calling him a liar and sat on my hands so they wouldn't gravitate to Juan's bowl during the conversation. I have a thing for authentic Mexican food.

"Mr. Castillo, do you remember working in Josh Summers's garden last Tuesday?" Connor asked.

Juan waved his spoon in the air. "Yes, of course! I go once a week. Keep it in top condition. Have you seen it? It's a beautiful garden, yes? Mr. Summers very happy." He beamed at us like he'd given us a present and was waiting for us to open it. "And I am Juan—not Mr. Castillo."

"Do you like your work, Juan?"

He nodded and swallowed another mouthful of beans. "Yes. It is good work."

"Did you see anyone when you were at Mr. Summers's house?"

He nodded again. "Mr. Summers came to talk about growing some new herbs."

"And did you see anyone else?"

"Only plants." He laughed at his own joke.

Connor didn't. "How are your daughters doing?"

Juan raised his head at the change of topic, but humor quickly returned to his eyes. "Oh they good, good girls. We very lucky aren't we, Francisca?" Francisca gave him a fond, tired smile and nodded.

"Any financial troubles?"

"No. They good girls. Very smart. Francisca teach them to be good with money. Like this, huh?" He balled his hand into a tight fist and laughed again. Another train rattled past.

"And your health, Juan?"

Juan looked at Francisca, who hissed something in Spanish.

"My health good too." He scraped the last food from his bowl and stood up. "All is good. Very good, but I must go back to work. People need beautiful gardens, yes?"

We shook hands, thanked them for their time, and followed Juan out the door. As we stepped outside, a red Toyota Corolla pulled up behind the Green with Envy van, and the driver—a middle-aged Caucasian woman in blue nursing scrubs—helped an older Latino woman out of the passenger seat.

Juan ducked his head back inside and called, "Francisca, Rosa and Caroline are here," before jogging over to help. "Caroline, you didn't have to bring her home! Francisca was coming to pick her up."

The nurse waved his protests away. "She was ready to check out just as my shift ended, and it's hardly out of my way. Besides, no one should have to spend any more time in that place than they need to, right, Rosa?"

Rosa clasped Caroline's hand and nodded. The color of her face was washed out, like fabric soaked in bleach too long, and she took each step as if it pained her. As they made their slow progress toward us, I saw what her head scarf and penciled eyebrows had hidden from a distance— the telltale hair loss of chemotherapy.

Francisca came out the front door and brushed past us, but not before muttering, "Why you still here?"

I looked to Connor, who inclined his head, and we headed for the SUV. Behind us, I could hear Francisca echoing Juan's scolding and thanks to Caroline, and asking

Rosa how she was feeling. The car door shut out the rest of their conversation.

"Well, there's a motive," Connor said, turning the key in the ignition. "Chemotherapy is expensive."

"They could have health insurance couldn't they?"

"It's possible."

I thought glumly of their cozy home, Rosa's fond smile, and Juan's easy laugh. "I like him," I told Connor.

"For the poisoner?"

"What? No, I meant he seems nice."

Connor looked at me. "Any other insights you want to share with me?"

I turned the conversation over in my mind. "Well, I don't speak Spanish, but I guess it's possible Francisca was trying to hide Rosa's health problems from us when she hurried Juan on his way." I chewed my lip. "She might have just been reminding him of the time, maybe?" I added hopefully.

Connor shook his head. "Avery, you can't rule someone out just because you like them."

"I know! But there was a clock on the wall she could've checked. The time thing is possible."

"I'll get the research team to look into Rosa's health and who's paying for it, but medical records are almost impossible to access." He shook his head. "Normally, I'd just put surveillance on them, but I don't know if it will turn up anything within our time frame."

"Is there anyone else we could ask, then? Someone who might not know to hide the payment information from us?"

"Good thinking." He called the research team on the car's Bluetooth and told them to get someone fluent in Spanish to call a few members of the Castillo family. As soon as possible. He also told them to pretend to be from a cancer charity so the Castillos would be more forthcoming about Rosa's financial situation.

"You can't pose as a cancer charity!"

"It was your idea."

"I never said to offer them false hope—"

Connor cut me off. "It's believable, and they won't be making any promises."

"That doesn't make it right." I felt sick. What had I started? And who was the man next to me that he could leverage a family's tragedy so coldly? Did the Taste Society share his attitude?

Connor didn't respond for a long minute. "Maybe you need to trust that I have ethics too."

"What the hell is that supposed to mean?"

He exhaled slowly through his nose. "It means that if Juan doesn't turn out to be involved, and they're struggling to finance Rosa's treatment, they'll receive an anonymous donation, okay? Now back off and let me try to save Dana's life. It's not your job to question how I do mine."

I shut my mouth. For a moment, I'd forgotten this was about saving Dana. Where did my morals fit into that? Did the ends justify the means when no real harm was done and a life was at stake? I didn't know. I gave up on figuring it out and watched the houses and blocks grow in size as we traveled to Colette's place in Larchmont.

———

COLETTE'S CONTEMPORARY HOME, with its white rendered facade, charcoal tiled roof, and timber French doors, wasn't a mansion, but it was easily worth seven figures. How could she afford it on a maid's wage?

My mind answered the puzzle by putting "French" and "maid" together in a new light. Did she provide services other than those I first assumed? It was with this idea in my head that I watched Colette open the door.

As per her photo in the file, her hair and makeup were flawless. Her large blue eyes and pale pink lipstick softened the coiffed perfection and lent a certain innocence to her look.

She smiled coquettishly at Connor, shattering the illusion of innocence, before turning to give me a hard once-over.

"How can I help you?" she asked in a sophisticated French accent, which made my Australian one sound rough and crude. Her come-hither gaze was back on Connor, as if I'd ceased to exist.

Connor introduced us both, name-dropping Josh Summers as usual, and she invited us inside.

As we followed her through the elegantly appointed home, Connor grabbed my hand and whispered in my ear.

"Play the jealous girlfriend, then find an excuse to leave. She might talk more if she views me as a potential conquest."

This was a good chance to prove I could act, so I wrapped myself around his arm and switched my tone to whiny. "Schnookums, why do you always have to work on our days together?"

"I'm sorry, gorgeous, but criminals don't run on schedule. And I thought we agreed that you'd stop calling me schnookums."

Our voices were pitched low, but I was certain Colette could hear us and was paying attention. The movement of her hips seemed more exaggerated than it was several steps ago. I glared at her shapely behind while plotting my next line.

She led us to a sitting room that held a cream sofa, three eclectic, yet perfectly harmonized, high-backed chairs, and a neutral-toned herringbone rug that tied them all together. Colette took the sofa, so Connor and I had to sit apart from one another.

The high-backed chairs might be pretty, but they weren't comfortable.

I looked around. There were two copper floor lamps, a copper and glass coffee table, as well as three copper vases and an ornate mirror that graced the mantel. The place was spotless too. Did she clean it herself or hire a cheaper maid to do it for her? Either way, Connor and Colette would do well together. That reminded me, I had the part of jealous girlfriend to play.

"How do you afford this on a maid's salary?" I blurted out.

Connor reached over from his chair and gave my hand a hard squeeze while sharing an apologetic glance with Colette. "Please forgive my girlfriend's tactlessness."

"Oh no, that's quite all right," Colette said, smiling at me with a few too many teeth. "Let's just say that my employers are *extremely* generous."

She angled her body so that Connor would get the best view. He admired it.

"Now, can I offer you any refreshments?"

My acting role overruled my grumbling stomach. "No, thanks," I said hastily.

Connor dragged his eyes off Colette to look at me. "Sweetheart, if you don't want anything, maybe you should go to the car and phone your friend back?"

I eyed him, and then Colette, with open suspicion.

"You know you get bored with all this work talk."

I lifted my chin and stood up. "You're right. Lily's waiting for my call." I put a possessive hand on Connor's chest and sent a nasty look to Colette. "I'll let myself out. Don't be too long, schnookums."

As I made my way back through the house, I wondered just how far Connor would go to get information. Then I wondered why I was wondering.

I didn't like this Colette woman. Or maybe I did like her, for the murder attempt.

I paused before the French doors at the entrance, spotting a key fob hanging on the tasteful coatrack. Closing my hand around the keys slowly but firmly to stop them from jingling, I hoisted them from the hook, grabbed my phone, and took a photo of each key. Just in case. Then I returned them to the coatrack and hightailed it back to the car.

9

WHEN CONNOR RETURNED, I made a point of not mentioning the pink lipstick smeared on his cheek. "How'd it go?"

"She suggested we look into Tahlia."

"What? Why?"

"According to Colette, she's pathetically infatuated with Josh Summers and was jealous of Dana."

I folded my arms and harrumphed. I suspected that in Colette's eyes, everyone was pathetic and jealous.

"Colette seems to be a more viable suspect," Connor said. "She insinuated she did more for Josh than clean. She could've been angry about being cast aside for Dana. Still, I'd say it's more likely someone offered her big bucks to do the deed, and she considered it a convenient business transaction."

"Wouldn't she worry about the risk?"

"Not if the bribe was generous enough. The only thing that woman loves more than herself is money. I'll get our research team to look into her financial history." He peered in the rearview mirror and wiped the lipstick off his face with a handkerchief he procured from his pocket.

I don't know why, but every time Connor referred to the research team, I imagined a bunch of people and computers sitting in a room with blacked out windows and harsh fluorescent lighting. In reality, the Taste Society had enough money that the office was probably the height of luxury, with floor-to-ceiling windows and a real espresso machine.

Okay. Maybe not a real espresso machine, but only because the demand wasn't there for it.

"While you were being hit on, I did some sleuthing of my own."

"Oh?"

I told him about the keys.

"Good," Connor said. "She had easy enough access without them, but if she did make copies, then someone else might have too. And it'll give us another excuse to question her if we need to."

I nodded like I'd thought of all that. "Where to next?"

"Dana's apartment."

"What? Why?"

"Shades are well positioned to notice if anyone acts suspiciously around the target. I usually question them first, but in this case, I'm hoping her apartment will give us a clue."

I gaped at him, horrified by the idea of him searching *my* apartment. *Another thing the Taste Society failed to mention about being a Shade.* "That's an invasion of privacy. What if she has personal items she doesn't want you digging through? What if she keeps a journal?"

"That would be useful."

"But it's private!"

Connor sounded bored. "Would you prefer someone read your journal to save your life or respect your privacy and let you die?"

I was learning that the more emotional a person got, the more impassive he became.

I took a deep breath and made myself consider his question seriously. When I imagined what I might have written over the last few days if I kept a personal journal—

Connor's undies are super comfortable.
I'm not giving them back.

Connor's ass is so beautiful, it deserves its own poem:
I've seen Picasso's paintings,
And Rodin's molded clay,
But when I gazed upon your buttocks,
I could not tell night from day.

—the answer was easy. "Let me die," I said.

AFTER A BRIEF STOP at an organic place for takeout to appease my stomach, we pulled up at a modest block of apartments in Koreatown.

"You're welcome to stay in the car, but I'm going in," Connor said.

I was convinced Dana would hate the idea of us looking through her things. She was a private person and had barely told me anything about her past. Again, I couldn't figure out if the ends justified the means. But what if Connor missed something and she died? Could I live with that? I got out of the car.

We made our way up to the third floor and passed a row of uniform wooden doors until we reached Dana's. Her door was painted an incongruous yellow. Connor produced a key, and I sent Dana a silent apology as we stepped inside.

The apartment was modest and impersonal, like she was just passing through. Furniture was sparse and ordinary. Photos and artwork were nonexistent. It made the yellow door even more incongruous, and I wondered if it had been painted by the previous tenant.

I couldn't bring myself to start rummaging through her stuff yet, so I decided to clear the perishables out of her refrigerator and take out her trash. That way, if she ever came home . . . I blinked back a few pesky tears. We'd make sure she came home.

There wasn't much in the fridge—skim milk, a few slices of deli turkey, lettuce, bread, and half a dozen condiments. No point having more than snack food around when you're a Shade on the job. I pulled out the perishables and put them on the counter.

I stared a long time at the garbage can. If I were a PI, I would go through it, but I wasn't a PI.

Yet what if it held a vital clue?

I blew some escaped hair out of my eyes and peered under the kitchen sink for gloves. I found a yellow rubber pair. Out of excuses, I pulled them on, grabbed an extra garbage bag, and returned to the trash can. Holding my breath as much as possible, I transferred each item from one garbage bag to the other. There were a few unrecognizable food scraps, a bunch of soggy tea bags, some soiled paper towels, and a couple of bread crusts.

Maybe someone smarter than me could divine wisdom from that, but I had nothing.

I chucked in the perishables I'd left on the counter, added the gloves for good measure, and took the garbage bag to the door to take out when we left.

Connor had searched her bedroom and was now going through the single filing cabinet. I didn't know whether to be upset or relieved that he hadn't found a journal yet.

I went back to the kitchen and started sorting through the cupboards for anything out of place. I hesitated when I came across a Royal Dansk cookie tin—not that it was out of place, but because I'm a sucker for cookies of any kind. Some kids dream of being astronauts; I wanted to marry Cookie Monster. Dana wouldn't mind if I ate just one.

Maybe I was still procrastinating, but I pried off the lid anyway. Instead of cookies, I found a newspaper clipping of a black-and-white photo of three teenagers. That was odd. I found it even more suspicious (and disappointing) that there weren't even any cookie crumbs.

I scanned the caption: *Pictured left to right: Henry Smythe, Josh Summers, and Kate Williamson.*

Sure enough, the kid in the middle was a younger version of Josh. I didn't recognize the names or faces of his companions, but that wasn't surprising, given the photo must have been taken over twenty years ago.

I brought it over to Connor.

"Add it to the pile."

I placed it on top of Dana's laptop and a bunch of official-looking statements.

The rest of our search yielded very little, but Connor was hopeful the research team would find something useful on her laptop. He'd also instructed them to track down the article the photo had been clipped from.

As we walked back to the car, the air seemed heavier than it had before. Maybe it was the garbage bag I was carrying. "Can I visit Dana?" I asked. "I know she's unconscious, but she might like company."

Connor's eyes actually showed pity. "I'm sorry, but Taste Society protocol is that no one without top security clearance can visit a poison victim. Can't risk someone finishing the job."

I nodded numbly, dumped the bag in the trashcan, and

got in the car. I wasn't mad about it, but I wasn't up to conversation either, so I stared out the window.

I was still staring unseeing out of it when Connor stopped the car and shut the engine off. I shook my head to clear it and followed him outside. It was only when he handed me some earplugs that I realized we'd entered a shooting range.

"Time for your first lesson."

He walked me through the safety rules, which pretty much amounted to keeping my finger off the trigger and pretending it could go off of its own accord at any moment. This did not fill me with confidence.

He handed me the gun. It might've been because my only previous experience with guns was with the water pistol variety, but it was larger, heavier, and uglier than I expected.

"This is a Ruger Mark II 22/45," he said, as if that would mean something to me. "It's a good weapon to learn on because it has a simple single action, low recoil, and is consistent and accurate. It also has a nice natural hold."

"That's great," I said, holding the monstrous thing awkwardly in two hands and concentrating on pointing it down and away from our toes in case it went off. "But I only understood a third of what you just said."

"That's okay. I'll run through it again as we go." He stepped up behind me and positioned my feet, arms, elbows, and hands. It occurred to me that this was the part in the movie where I'd feel his body pressing against mine and realize I was falling for him. But I was too worried about the death device in my hands to focus on his hot, hard body against mine. Mostly.

"That's it." He flicked off the safety. "Now, sight your target, squeeze the trigger gently, and be prepared for the recoil."

The gun bucked in my hand, and I squeaked and dodged when a bit of metal ejected from the top of it and flew straight at me.

Connor steadied my waving hands. "It's okay. That's supposed to happen. That's why you're wearing safety glasses. Now look at how you did."

I studied the target while Connor shifted me back into position. I'd hit the outside edge of the paper.

"Good. Now do it again."

I took a deep breath and did it again. And again. He showed me how to reload what he said was a ten-round magazine, adjusted my stance, and repeated the procedure.

Twenty-two shots in, I realized the death device was starting to feel less alien in my hands, and my focus had shifted from trying not to shoot myself in the foot, to hitting inside the black line every time. After another round, my aim had improved, and Connor was only making minor adjustments to my stance.

"Good. That's enough for today."

Seeing as both my arms were trembling, and the ground was littered with bullet casings, I agreed with him.

We left the din of the shooting range and went to get coffee. Or in my case, tea. The numb fog that had settled on me in Dana's apartment had lifted, and I thought there might be something to this gun thing. At least in a safe, controlled environment with a paper bad guy as the only victim.

I did my taste testing routine, complete with the nose wrinkle, on Connor's coffee and slid it over to him.

"Thanks for the lesson," I said.

He nodded acknowledgement and took a sip. "We've run out of people to interview today, so you might as well go home and work on the hate mail. I'm going to hand in Dana's things and look over the case files again."

AFTER A HAPPY REUNION with my Corvette, I arrived home, groceries and newly acquired garlic in hand. Oliver was on the couch with Meow, watching a sci-fi movie on his laptop. He paused it when he saw me.

"Izzy, how are you doing?"

"Good. What about you? Did Meow have any presents for you when you got home?" Aside from accepting food and cuddles, Meow's favorite pastime was hunting cockroaches. She was good at it, too. She left their crunchy carcasses as gifts by the front door for whoever came home first. Impressive, given how hard they are to kill.

"Yep! Three today, and one was as big as they come." He tickled her under the chin, proud as any father.

"I'm starting to think she's saving them up for you. I haven't found any for a few days."

He grinned. "That's my girl. She knows I appreciate them more than you do."

I piled the groceries on the counter. "Well, a dead cockroach is the best kind of cockroach, but she might be right."

Oliver's expression sobered. "I was wondering, Iz, have you thought any more about that waitressing job at the Fox?"

I rummaged in the utensil drawer for a peeler. "That was very sweet of you, but I don't need it. My new job is great. Loads more money than waitressing too."

He slid Meow off his lap and came over, bringing his familiar scent of lime and smoky rum with him. I could never figure out if it was his cologne or a side effect of bartending.

"That's good." His tone implied otherwise. "What does the job involve?"

I hesitated. "I can't say exactly, I signed a confidentiality agreement." Or took a weird, archaic oath and signed a thousand confidentiality agreements. Meow wandered over, and I picked her up for a snuggle.

"You've got to admit that it sounds shady."

Thanks to Meow's calming influence, I managed not to react to his choice of words. "I'm just working for people who value their privacy." *Not so much their Shades' privacy, though.* I stroked Meow's back. "It's nothing dodgy, I promise."

Oliver's serious mood didn't lighten. It seemed unnatural on someone so easygoing. He was eyeing my designer coral blouse and gray skirt; a big change from the jeans and T-shirts I'd worn all the times he'd seen me at the Fox.

"I don't know," he said. "New secret job. New rich boyfriend. And a new glamorous wardrobe. You don't have to tell me what you're doing, but you do need to tell me if you're not okay."

I put Meow down, kicked off the sandals that were killing my feet, and started peeling veggies. "Look, it's lovely of you to worry about me, but you have to trust me on this one." I wondered how I could convince him.

Or if not convince, distract.

"Besides," I said, "I thought you'd enjoy having a glamorous housemate. We all know how much you love that glamorous monarch of yours."

Oliver's rants about the Queen of England were legendary at the Fox. No one knew if he actually felt strongly about it or was just hamming it up for a laugh, but it was public knowledge that if you mentioned her, you'd get at least sixty seconds of entertainment.

It was like a free jukebox.

"Glamorous? The Queen? Are you messing with me?"

I smiled. "Not at all. She seems very chic."

Oliver's voice rose with indignation. "Where, in the vast vista of the universe, have you been hiding all these years? There's nothing glamorous about a little old lady parading around in a rainbow of matching outfits with matching hats, covered in corgi hair." His hands started waving about for emphasis. "Think of her poor servants who have to get all that dog hair and drool off her clothes! Think of the poor hat makers who have to design a carriage load of ridiculous hats every single year! And think of me, and all her other wretched subjects, laboring under her rule to pay for it!" His face dared me to dispute it. "Tell me, Izzy, what in all of the blue oceans, is glamorous about that?"

I smothered a laugh. "Are you still paying tax to Britain, then?"

He sent me a fiery glare and stalked back to the couch.

Distraction successful. "Dinner will be ready in an hour and a half."

He shook his head. "Sometimes I feel bad about you cooking for me all the time, but right now, I can only hope your servitude will teach you some sympathy for the poor, beleaguered citizens of England." With this lofty pronouncement, he started the movie again.

I laughed to myself. *Better* than a free jukebox.

I covered the veggies with olive oil, celery salt, and a few herbs and threw them in the oven to roast. Preparing the white sauce was next, and while I was at it, I whipped up another batch of cookies so I could leave a plate of them outside Etta Hamilton's door. The kitchen had been my domain ever since I'd joined Mum there as an eight-year-old, and I was used to multitasking from my years of making coffees, plating up meals, and serving customers.

Meow had returned to the couch with Oliver. She was happy enough to hang with me when Oliver was out, but whenever he was home she was his shadow cat. I didn't hold it against her. Loyalty was a trait I admired. One my ex had lacked.

This time, I made sure to feed her before showering and climbing into bed.

Tucked away in my room, I pulled out the box of hate mail and withdrew the first letter from its envelope. I took note of the postmark and the handwriting, just in case I could spot any patterns. The writer threatened various sexual acts, many of which I didn't think were anatomically possible. I wasn't tempted to try them to find out either. There was no mention of death, so I put it on my "unlikely" pile.

The next letter simply stated, "I'm watching you." It wasn't overtly threatening aside from the creepy stalker vibe, so it too went on the unlikely pile. The letter after that was so violent that I couldn't imagine its writer having the subtlety to poison someone.

A small mountain of letters later, my eyes were starting to blur, and I'd lost a lot of faith in the human race. I had four letters in the "worth investigating" pile.

Three were from the same person, a man who lost his job at Wholesome Foods after cost cutbacks and blamed Josh, with increasing anger, for all his unemployment woes. I didn't think it was a great lead because, outside of the secret world of the rich and powerful, poison tends to be a woman's weapon rather than a man's.

The Taste Society told us it's one of the reasons the authorities help cover it up—publicity would risk popularizing poisoning among the masses. Think of what the anonymous, indirect nature of the Internet did to bring out the ugly in some people. No one wants to shine the spotlight on an anonymous, indirect method of murder.

Besides, unless this ex-Wholesome Foods employee had really lost his mind, it would be dumb to send a whole series of signed letters threatening his intended target. I thought Connor might want to look at them anyway. Maybe the guy's wife did it, not knowing about the letters. Maybe some criminals are that stupid.

The other letter was from the mother of an underprivileged kid who'd attended Josh's culinary school and never returned home. She blamed Josh for stealing her son away and expressed a fervent wish that one day he'd understand what it felt like to have his heart ripped from his chest. I didn't think she'd have the money to hire a hitman, but she might know people who knew people who might be convinced to do it as a favor. And a mother's love is a powerful motivator.

Possibly powerful enough to commit murder.

10

NOW THAT I WAS NO LONGER trapped indoors at the Taste Society's training facility, I was starting to understand why Oliver stuck around for the weather. It was another beautiful seventy-seven-degree day, and in just eleven more I'd receive my first paycheck.

Bruce-the-Bruiser could suck it.

I was further cheered when I realized that because of my lunch date with Albert, Connor probably wouldn't even poison my breakfast today.

I headed downstairs to meet him, pleased to see Etta had taken in the plate of cookies I'd left her. Either that or Mr. Lawson had stolen them to feed to his hamster.

Ever since Etta had given me the low-down on my neighbors, I'd noticed the faint sounds of sex or shouting whenever I passed the Flanagans' door. Today they were enjoying morning makeup sex. Good for them. Trying not to think about the last time *I'd* had sex, I climbed into the car, Connor holding my door as usual.

He slipped into the driver's seat beside me, a hint of a smile on his lips. "Notice anything?"

I looked him over. He hadn't grown any less attractive overnight. If anything, his quiet kindness after Dana's apartment yesterday had made him even more appealing. Or maybe it was having sex on my mind.

Lucky my time in LA was making me immune to beautiful people. "Nope?"

He patted the steering wheel. "It's the car you gave away. Complete with a new tire."

I crossed my arms. Nope, no matter how good-looking he was, my knees were just weak from hunger. "I resent you saying I *gave* it away, like I had a choice."

"You always have a choice."

"Not when someone has a gun to your head, you don't! And I'd like to remind you I meant that literally."

"Well, technically, there was a bulletproof window between the gun and your head."

I let my face say a thousand words.

He patted the steering wheel again. "I thought you'd be happy for me."

"I'd be happier for you if you were a nicer person."

We drove in a silence for a while.

"Or maybe if you bought me breakfast."

WE STOPPED AT A LITTLE sandwich place in Culver City. The chairs were the uncomfortable metal variety that didn't encourage you to linger, but the smells coming from the kitchen made you sit your butt down without complaint.

I ordered a BLT panini with avocado and egg added. Connor ordered the breakfast burrito. While we waited for our food to arrive, I showed him the suspect letters and he updated me on the latest research findings.

"There's not a lot to report," he said. "The sick woman we saw at the Castillos' is Juan's sister. She has stage three bowel cancer and has been undergoing chemotherapy for the last two months, but the extended family claims they've all rallied together and are managing to pay for treatment."

Juan's cheerful, weathered face flitted into my mind. No one deserves that. Of course, cancer strikes regardless of wealth, gender, or race, and death brings grief indiscriminately, but having to worry about making ends meet in those circumstances seems especially cruel. "So, will they be receiving an anonymous donation?" I asked.

Connor scowled. "You're not good at minding your own business are you?"

"My own business isn't all that interesting."

Connor didn't respond right away. Maybe he was practicing deep breathing exercises. "There were no suspicious deposits in Juan's bank account either," he said at last. "On the other hand, Colette has plenty of large deposits in her account, but that's because she charges between one hundred and four hundred bucks an hour."

Good thing our food hadn't come yet, or I would've spat mine all over the table. Why the hell was I trying to become a Shade if I could make that kind of money cleaning houses?

Connor leaned back in his chair and studied me. "There's no law against exorbitant fees you know. Her clients are paying for the prestige of having a pretty, sophisticated maid instead of the more common variety."

Damn. Sophisticated, I was not. To be fair, I'd never shown any particular aptitude for housekeeping either.

"I haven't gotten to the interesting part yet."

I flapped a hand in his direction. "By all means, don't let my shock stop you."

"Josh Summers tripled Colette's wages three weeks ago."

I really hoped he wouldn't tell me how much that amounted to. The eleven days until my paycheck didn't seem as exciting anymore.

Connor was waiting. I shoved aside my jealousy and tried to make sense of Colette's raise. "So, either Josh needed a lot more cleaning done, or something strange is going on."

"Yes. But whatever the reason, it's unlikely it led to an attempt on Josh's life. Which means your new friend Albert is still our best suspect."

The waitress arrived with our breakfast, and we put the papers away to make room for it on our tiny table.

By the time I'd sampled bits of the omelet, cheese, hash browns, bacon, salsa, and avocado in Connor's meal, I'd decided LA was onto something with this breakfast burrito thing. My toasted panini was delicious too. All I needed now was a real espresso.

Instead, Connor passed me the audio transmitter watch I'd worn yesterday and a small vial of liquid. "For your date this afternoon. It's a large dose of purified ketoconazole and will prevent Mr. Alstrom from getting too excited with you if it comes to that. It's been refined to be odorless and almost tasteless, so as long as you slip it in something besides water, he shouldn't notice. It takes fifteen minutes to start working."

I tucked the vial into my bag. My breakfast wasn't sitting quite as well as it had been a minute ago.

"Ask as many questions as you can get away with, but not so many he gets suspicious. Like yesterday, I'll be listening in nearby, so you shouldn't be in any danger."

"About that," I said, strapping the watch onto my wrist. "I think we should check out the grieving mother who wrote that hate letter." It didn't matter how my breakfast was sitting. This was important.

"Maybe." His tone was noncommittal.

"Look, it might not be her, but I think it's worth talking to her to find out if it's an angle we should pursue. I even found her last known address for you." I slid the piece of paper to him. "It's near where Tahlia grew up." As much as I didn't want it to be Tahlia, when I found the link, I knew we'd have to investigate it.

Connor left the address on the table. "Then we can both go talk to her, after your date."

"Aren't you excited to drive your car now that it's back?"

"I'm not leaving you to fend for yourself."

I glared at him. "You make me sound like I'm some defenseless maiden."

"He's tied to multiple murders, Isobel."

I looked down at my lap. He was right, but Dana's vacant apartment was still haunting my thoughts. The culinary student's angry mother lived in San Diego—over two hours away—which meant it would take us the entire afternoon if I went with him.

I raised my eyes again. So far, I'd let Connor make the decisions. He was the expert after all—but that was exactly why I was taking a stand now. He was wasted sitting around protecting me when he could be chasing down leads. When Dana *needed* him to be chasing down leads. "Allegedly tied to multiple murders," I corrected. "And this is the third day Dana's been unconscious. She's running out of time."

He stared at me for a full minute.

I kept my gaze steady until he picked up the address.

"Okay," he said. "We'll do it your way."

———

CONNOR DROPPED ME back at my apartment to await my celebrity date. Unable to relax, I touched up my hair, reapplied my lipstick, and looked down at my outfit.

I was wearing a floral pink, black, and white pencil skirt with a slit up the side, and a white, stretchy scoop-neck top. I pulled the neckline down a little lower. That done, I went over to my bag and checked to make sure the vial was still safe inside. It was there, same as it had been five minutes ago.

I hadn't realized how much of my former confidence had come from knowing Connor would be nearby. I was nervous. Meow, on the other hand, seemed unfazed. I scratched her under the chin, and she donated some gray and black hairs to my skirt. At least they kind of blended in.

There was a knock on the door, and my heart fluttered in my chest until I saw it was Etta. She was wearing an elegant fitted dress this time with half-length sleeves in navy and white. The ensemble was completed by a string of pearls, wedge sandals, and a cigarette in her fingers.

"Care to keep an old lady company for a bit?"

"Did you run out of cookies already?" I asked.

She shot me a sharp look then broke into a smile. "I think I like you."

I opened the door wide. "I'll put the kettle on, then."

She ground out her cigarette and followed me in. We each ate a cookie while the kettle came to a boil. I glanced at my watch. Ten minutes until the car was due.

"You look like my husband, may he rest in peace, used to when he had to go to the dentist. What are you all anxious for? Didn't you listen to anything I said about stress being the worst thing for you?"

"I'm meeting somebody famous."

She grabbed another cookie. "Ah, dear, fame and fortune are all very well, but is he good-looking?"

"Maybe, if you like that sort of thing."

"I like all sorts of things," she said mysteriously. "But what I don't like is seeing you stressed. I thought you being from Australia and all would've meant you were of hardier stock."

I shrugged. "I think the whole dangerous animals thing is exaggerated. Sure, we have a bunch of venomous snakes and stuff, but the survival strategy is simple: Don't step on them. At least you know what's dangerous and what isn't. Here in LA, the air itself is out to kill you, and the person who smiles and compliments your necklace might be thinking of strangling you with it."

Etta chuckled. "There's some truth to that, but the survival strategy here is simple too. Carry a gun and don't be afraid to use it." She rummaged in her bag and pulled out what I thought was a Glock. "As for the air. Well, we all gotta die of something."

11

AT ELEVEN THIRTY ON THE DOT, a black limousine rolled up. It looked out of place on my street. I took a deep breath, said goodbye to Etta, and hiked down the staircase. All was quiet when I passed 2A. The Flanagans must be out.

When I reached street level, the driver emerged and introduced himself as Antonio. He helped me into the limo, and I tried not to gawk at the plush, black leather seats, huge flat-screen TV, and fully stocked bar. It was early, but I sipped on the proffered champagne anyway. I was not above a bit of liquid courage.

Thirty-five minutes later, we pulled up to an ultramodern mansion in Bel Air. A ten-foot fence and manned gate protected it from unwanted guests. I must have been wanted because the security guards waved us through.

As we drove through, I could see that the mansion was made up of two giant rectangular prisms set atop one another and cantilevered at a forty-five-degree angle. Floor-to-ceiling dark windows contrasted with the smooth white walls. Beautiful, but comfortless.

I gulped the last bit of my champagne while Antonio stopped the car and then opened my door. "This way please, Ms. Avery." He escorted me to the bright blue front door and knocked. It opened before his hand had time to fall back to his side.

Standing in the open doorway was my first real-life butler.

"Welcome, Ms. Avery." His tone was faultlessly polite, yet somehow managed to convey disdain. "Mr. Alstrom is expecting you."

I tried to hide a smile. Maybe my delight was influenced by the champagne, but he was exactly how I imagined a butler should be—from the straight-faced hauteur, down to the immaculate black morning coat and English accent.

I followed him through a foyer the size of my apartment, already regretting the height of my heels, and glanced back at the door, where I'd left freedom and Antonio behind. I was sad to leave Antonio. He seemed nice.

I fiddled with my watch to reassure myself. Never mind that Connor was an hour and a half away and this place was fortified like Aunt Alice on too much communion wine.

After a minute of following the butler, I knew there was no chance of searching the building surreptitiously. It was too big. Perhaps I could ask Albert for a tour instead and take note of the rooms he didn't show me. Or at least where his office was.

Another minute later, I scrapped that plan, too. My feet would not hold up to a tour in these heels.

It was my fourth day on the job, and I was starting to think the shoes were more likely to kill me than the poison was.

We entered a room that featured a large, galley-style kitchen, a beautiful natural-edged timber slab dining table, and a tasteful assortment of modern armchairs. Albert was lounging on one of the armchairs reading a book, in a pose strikingly similar to his image on the cover of *Food for the Soul*. He held his position until the butler announced me then raised his head, his thin, angular features arranged in feigned surprise. "Izzy, I'm so glad you came."

In most people I would find the posturing arrogant and annoying, but Albert's awkward attempt was so transparent that I found myself feeling sorry for him again. He was like an eager-to-please puppy begging to be told he was a good boy.

"Are you kidding?" I asked. "I wouldn't miss this for anything."

I made myself look him over with admiration, not that the moody, tragic-artist style he'd adopted appealed to me. I'd gone through that phase in high school and no longer mistook a man's obsession with his own greatness for actual greatness.

When my eyes returned to Albert's face, I wasn't sure if my little show had been for nothing because *his* eyes were fixed on my boobs. To be fair, I had pulled my top down with the intent of distracting him from my acting skills.

It was working.

"I hope you're hungry," he said, his gaze dropping to my crotch.

Okay, I hadn't done anything to draw his attention there. I tried to turn my gag reflex into a look of sexy anticipation. "I'm starving."

He gave me the goofy grin I remembered. "Good." He unfolded his lanky frame from the chair, pulled on an apron and headed to the kitchen, fumbling with the apron tie. The cabinets, countertops, and backsplash were all glossy black, while the appliances and weird molecular gastronomy equipment were gleaming stainless steel. It reminded me of a futuristic science lab. It suited him.

"Take a seat, enjoy the show. Your first course will be right up."

I sat down at the dining table, which was set for one. "Aren't you eating?"

"No, I'm saving my appetite." He eyed me meaningfully.

I gulped and hoped he'd interpret it as eagerness. He was very forward for a man whose bearing screamed low self-esteem. I couldn't figure him out. Maybe being in the kitchen gave him more confidence. Now that he was focused on the food instead of me, his bearing had lost the self-consciousness I'd noticed earlier.

I watched as he set up some kind of apparatus I didn't recognize with quick, precise movements. His hands were pale and slender, with long fingers a pianist would envy. Somehow, on Albert they were creepy.

I picked up the menu, wondering if he'd printed it just for me, or if he had them printed in bulk for all his lady fans. Then I started reading it and forgot my unease. I also forgot I was there for anything other than the food. It was a nine-course degustation menu:

Wild Mushroom & Truffled Herb Granita
Oyster with Sea Gel & Aromas
Seared Scallops with Lemon Air & Bell Pepper & Chili Coulis
Pork Confit with Cotton Candy
Smoked Duck Breast Transparent Ravioli
Salt Grass Lamb with Chard Steam & Greens
Cinnamon Ice Cream with Yacaratia Wood, Brie & Peanut
Tuile
Tobacco Infused Chocolate Mousse
Pomegranate & Elderflower Parfait

Albert placed the first course, which looked like a small pile of snow, in front of me and contrived to brush his hand against my chest. The pawing reminded me why I was here, but anticipation still outweighed my discomfort.

"Truffle oil, my dear?"

I nodded, and he drizzled oil over the snow, which I recalled from the menu was granita, an Italian style of crushed ice, so my first impression of snow hadn't been far off.

Albert watched as I scooped up the first spoonful. Just as well tasting for dangerous ingredients looks so similar to savoring a mouthful.

I didn't have to fake my appreciation as the flavors of mushrooms, chervil, basil, and chives, delicately accentuated with truffle oil, spread across my tongue.

"Wow. This is amazing."

He smiled. "It is, isn't it?" He poured me a small glass of wine without consulting me and watched me take the next bite. The intensity of his gaze made me feel like a rat in a lab.

I sipped the wine, which was light and crisp, and chosen to complement the granita. I was worried he'd watch me eat the whole thing, but he returned to the kitchen to prepare the second course, leaving me to enjoy it alone. I had just finished when he set the next plate down in front of me.

A single oyster sat in its shell, dressed with what Albert informed me was sea gel, salicornia and tremella. Next to it sat tempura anemone and algae garnished with several oyster leaves. He poured liquid into a bowl filled with more algae, and thick white fog billowed up, bringing with it the aroma of the briny ocean. I figured that the algae must have hidden dry ice, but I was still impressed by the overall effect. The scent of the ocean brought back memories of the beach and made the food seem fresher. I took my first bite. The oyster provided a smooth background to the light crunch of the tempura. No hint of poison. Once again, I didn't have to feign my delight.

"This is incredible. I can't believe you didn't win California Culinary Champion this year instead of Josh Summers."

Albert's face, which had broken into a broad smile at my first statement, seized up like my battered stick mixer trying to beat dough. "Tell me about it." His jaw stayed clenched, and it was hard to believe this expression belonged to the same guy with the grin.

I pretended I hadn't noticed his reaction and went on. "I mean, can't those judges recognize genius when they taste it? It's so unfair!"

"Yes. It is. But it won't happen again." There was no doubt in Albert, only rage. His pale eyes looked predatory again, the angles on his face sharp.

"That's wonderful," I gushed, "but how can you be sure?"

His features transformed themselves back into his friendly grin, only now his teeth seemed a touch too perfect. He patted my arm with his long fingers, high enough up to brush against my boob, of course. "Don't worry your pretty head about it, sweet cheeks. Just relax and enjoy this experience."

Geez. Where did this guy get his lines and how could he deliver them in earnest? I smiled up at him, unsure how to continue. "Okay. Sounds good."

He patted my arm again. "Eat it while it's fresh. I'll start on your next course."

My wine had been replaced with another glass, and I realized that if I drank the paired wine for each course, I was going to get drunk. I shouldn't have had the champagne in the limo. I sipped at the delicious vintage and resolved not to finish it.

The scallops in the next course were also divine, but when I tasted the bell pepper and chili coulis, I recognized the slightly salty taste of GHB-X. It was a potent derivative of the date rape drug, GHB.

While GHB is readily available, GHB-X is hard to source, and most people don't even know it exists. It revs up your libido while wiping out your inhibitions, making you very suggestible.

Albert was studying my every move, as he had at the beginning of each course so far, so I swallowed and made another exclamation of amazement to cover for my wide eyes.

My mind raced. There was no way his average fan would notice the taste. The fact he was drugging me made him jump even higher up the suspect list, and if he was our best suspect, I couldn't blow this opportunity. My genetics were supposed to make me more resistant to drugs, so I'd have to hope I was resistant enough.

At this point, I couldn't imagine finding Albert attractive, yet alone irresistible. I decided to keep playing.

I cleared my plate, as I had every other time.

While Albert was preparing the fourth course, I whispered into my watch that I'd ingested some GHB-X but didn't need to be rescued. I knew Connor had someone stationed nearby listening to the audio and relaying any important points to him. It was time to get as much information as I could before the drug kicked in.

"So, Albert, have you gone on any glamorous trips lately?"

He answered from the kitchen without looking up from his next creation. "Nah, I've been lying low since I came back from a tour last month."

"You haven't left LA since?"

"Nope."

"Wow, then I could have run into you a whole month ago."

I saw him smile again, but he didn't look up from his work as he answered. "I suppose you could have."

It was nice I wasn't the only thing he focused a little too intensely on.

"I'm so excited to be here. I can't believe my luck."

He looked up long enough to wink at me this time. "Good to know."

"And this food is so ah-mazing! You're definitely *my* California Culinary Champion." He stiffened but stayed silent. "I'm furious about the Josh thing. What do you think of him?"

"A talentless hack. But the media loves him because of his charity work."

I nodded so fervently I got a crick in my neck. "Totally." I waited a minute, but he didn't elaborate. "Do you ever think about doing charity work?"

"I've considered it," he said, concentrating on his next creation, "but charity is stupid. This is America, and if you work hard, you succeed."

He looked up at me then, his face passionate. "No one gave me any handouts, and I'm not about to waste money on people who don't deserve it. Plus, I refuse to sell myself out for media coverage. I'm an artist. If I'm in the news, it'll be because I'm great at what I do."

I kept nodding through the pain, both physical and intellectual, until he turned back to his masterpiece. Then I rubbed my poor neck and reviewed what I'd learned.

Albert hadn't left LA recently, so if he'd hired a hit, chances were good it was local. He had little to no empathy, openly despised Josh, had no qualms about using GHB-X, and was expecting sex. Unfortunately, I was stumped about how to ask if he had any lethal drugs lying around or if he'd ever murdered anyone. The arrival of the fifth course diverted my attention.

Three courses later, with alcohol and GHB-X eroding my defenses, I noticed I was starting to like it when Albert found excuses to brush against me.

"I need to go to the bathroom!" I shouted. Albert swung around and stared at me. "Sorry. I get loud when I'm drunk."

He relaxed. "No problem, the bathroom's just through that door."

I staggered my way to it, more impaired than I'd thought. After using the toilet, I washed my hands and splashed water on my face in an attempt to clear the cobwebs from my brain. Then I remembered my makeup. Patting it dry as delicately as I could, I spoke into the watch. "I'm in trouble. Albert is starting to look *really* attractive to me. And,

I don't remember my safe word, but I think I might need an erection. I mean, an extraction. Um, so yeah. Thanks."

I wobbled my way back to my seat and felt my phone vibrate. The vibration seemed very erotic to me right then. It was a message from Connor.

Give him the ketoconazole. I'm still twenty-five minutes away.

I tried to facepalm but missed. I'd forgotten about that. And how was I supposed to dose Albert when he wasn't eating anything? Hazily recalling seeing him with his own wine glass, I retrieved the vial from my bag and sidled my way over to the kitchen. "How's it going, honey?" I said, leaning on the counter to give him a good view down my top.

He gawked appreciatively. "Last course, sweet thing. Then it's my turn."

My stomach did a little flip of excitement. He smiled at me, and I watched, mesmerized, as his long fingers wrapped around the curve of the wine glass and lifted it to his lips. It made me imagine those fingers wrapped around my curves.

He put the glass down and turned back to the other counter where he was working. There was something important about the wine that I had to remember. I shifted my stance to see what he was doing better and almost dropped the vial. That's right, the vial. With extreme caution, I untwisted the cap and emptied the contents into his glass.

Albert turned back, and I jumped, startled, but couldn't figure out why. "Almost done," he said, taking another sip of his wine. "Why don't you go sit at the table."

I followed his suggestion.

Albert brought the final course over and pulled up a chair to watch me eat. I had to force myself to focus on the food because his intense stare turned my insides to mush.

"What do you think?" he asked.

"You're amazing."

He grinned, and my stomach did another flip. How had I ever thought of his smile as goofy? "You're not bad yourself," he said.

I beamed back at him. "Really?"

He came over to me, pulled me to my feet, and kissed me hard on the mouth. "Really." His erection pressed against my abdomen. "Why don't you come over to the couch where it's more comfortable?"

I tottered after him. He lay down on a plush sofa, and I went to join him but he stopped me. "How about you undress for me?"

I regained my feet and started fumbling with my top, trying to get it off. It got stuck halfway over my head, and in the close confines of the fabric, I could hear myself breathing hard with excitement. When I finally wrestled free of the stretchy material, I saw Albert was undressing too.

He'd unbuttoned his shirt to reveal the expanse of his thin, pale chest, lightly dusted with brown hair around his nipples and beneath his belly button. It made me think of a bony, badly plucked chicken breast.

I wanted to marinate him and eat it all up.

My eyes traveled down the trail of hair to his straining erection.

With poultry on the brain, it looked like a fat chicken neck.

"That's good," he said, his eyes glued to my chest. "Now the skirt."

There were a button and a zipper I had to fight this time. After a few minutes, I succeeded in getting it off and turned back to Albert with a triumphant smile. But he wasn't looking at me. He was looking at his wilting manhood.

"What's wrong?" I asked, feeling bereft.

His eyes dilated as he took in my heels and mismatched lingerie. His little friend, however, gave no response. He got off the couch and grabbed me, hands roving over my breasts and tongue ravaging my mouth. I wanted him so badly I gasped, but he pushed me away, his face red.

Someone knocked on the door.

"Sir?" The voice was muffled, but I vaguely recognized it as belonging to the butler. "I'm terribly sorry to intrude, but a gentleman is at the gate claiming your guest is his girlfriend and is threatening to call the police."

Albert's face went even redder. "He can't do anything if she's here of her own free will. You want to be here, don't you, Izzy?"

I felt lost and confused and sad. "I do?"

Albert looked down at his still flaccid penis and let out a few choice cuss words. "Get dressed and go."

Tears spilled down my cheeks, but I started fumbling once more with my clothes.

"Oh, for heaven's sake. George, come in and assist her will you?"

The butler entered the room and showed no interest in my mismatched lingerie. He helped me back into my outfit. "This way, Ms. Avery."

I followed him for an impossibly long time, until at last we made it to the front door. A security man took me from the door to the property gate and shut it behind me.

Connor and a man I didn't recognize were waiting there. Both of them were so astoundingly sexy that I would have taken my clothes off again if it wasn't so hard to do.

Connor hugged me to him. "You're okay now, Isobel. You're safe." I noted his lack of erection with disappointment. "Levi will get the drugs out of your system."

He handed me over to most-attractive-man-on-the-earth number two.

"You're safe, hon," said most-attractive-man-on-the-earth number two. "I'll have you feeling better in no time." He held a cup to my mouth. "Now, just drink this for me, that's right. Good."

The world spun, and I had the sensation of being carried in someone's arms before everything went black.

12

I WOKE UP TO the face of an angel. A Hispanic angel with warm brown eyes and eyelashes long enough to make a girl green with envy and hot with lust. Then I realized it was the same angel who had promised to get the drugs out of my system. "It's not working."

"What?"

"The detox. You're still ridiculously good-looking."

His lips quirked upward. "In that case, maybe we should go out some time because you're drug free."

Oh boy. "Are you sure?"

His answering grin was so beautiful it hurt my eyes. "Do you want to have outrageous sex right here and now?"

My cheeks flamed. "No." Never mind that part of me was imagining running my fingers through his tousled black hair as his soft lips and stubbled jaw lit a burning trail down my neck and kept on going.

His smile didn't falter. "Then I'm sure. I've got to go, but think about that date, beautiful."

He tucked a business card into my hand and let himself out. He walked with a limp. I listened to the sound of his uneven but energetic footsteps fade away and tried to ignore the lingering feel of his touch on my skin. Both real and imagined. I was in enough trouble without getting involved with a man who had a smile that good. I looked at the card. Nope, I was not going to call Dr. Levi Eduardo Reyes. Or his dimples.

I hauled myself into a sitting position and realized I was in Connor's bed again. Thinking of the devil summoned him into the room.

His expression was hard. Even compared to normal. "This is exactly why I didn't want to leave you alone with that bastard."

"Nice to see you too."

A vein in his neck bulged. I'd never noticed it before.

"Do you know how much worse it could have been if I was another half an hour away? From now on, you'll do as I say. No arguments."

As he spoke, memories of my solo investigation came trickling in, like ice water spilling down my back. I shivered and felt my face grow hot at the same time. "Did you at least find out anything worthwhile from the mother?"

"She died two years ago." He strode out of the room and shut the door louder than necessary.

I dragged myself out of bed, stumbled into the shower, and stood under the stream of hot water until my fingers started to wrinkle. I didn't try to keep my face or hair dry this time. Or to process what had happened. Instead, I focused on the water that ran in soothing rivulets down my body and then on the business of drying myself. Dried and naked, I realized I didn't have a change of underwear. Again. I rummaged through Connor's and vowed to put a spare pair in my handbag when I got home.

Leaving my hair wet and my face makeup free, I searched for Connor and found him in his office.

Hoping to lighten his mood, I stood in the doorway and saluted. "Reporting for duty, sir."

His expression informed me I wasn't funny.

I dropped my hand. "What's next?"

"I received a message from my street contact. He dug around on my behalf and said there are whispers of a local hit out on Josh Summers. But he doesn't have any more details."

"Where does that leave us?"

"Without more information, it just corroborates the theory that someone in addition to Tahlia, Colette, and Juan had opportunity to plant the poison. Which means Albert and everyone else Josh ever slighted are still on the table."

"Oh." That was less helpful than I'd hoped.

"With Albert's stunt this afternoon, we can assume he has a contact high up in the illicit drugs and poisons scene.

Only a small group of people know about GHB-X, and even fewer can get their hands on it. Albert's casual use of it suggests he has a steady supply."

"And no qualms about drugging people."

The memories I'd been suppressing reared up again, and I shuddered despite my best efforts to clamp down on it. Connor's expression was already hard and unforgiving, but at this, his gray eyes turned hostile. For the first time, I glimpsed someone I should be scared of.

He took a few controlled breaths, and his eyes returned to their usual unreadable wall of cinder-block gray. "The research team found nothing of use on Dana's laptop. She's one of those rare people who delete their emails. Her browser history didn't contain anything suspicious, and her files were mostly work or tax related. No photos either, just a collection of pirated and purchased music. She doesn't even have a Facebook account."

I nodded. "I'm not surprised. She's a private person. She barely said anything about her past in all the time we spent together, and I knew she wasn't on Facebook. Once she saw me checking it and told me that most of the people on there are self-absorbed asses using it to validate their own importance."

The corners of Connor's mouth tilted upward a tiny bit. "Is that why you use it?"

"Of course."

He handed me a piece of paper. "Remember that newspaper clipping you found? This is the article it came from."

The article told the tragic story of a car accident that left the driver, Henry Smythe, dead at just seventeen years old. Henry, the boy pictured on the left, wasn't wearing his seat belt, so when the car smashed into a tree, he'd flown through the windshield and broken his neck, dying on impact. The two passengers, Josh Summers and his girl-friend, Kate Williamson, had both been wearing seat belts and escaped with only minor injuries. The article went on to say that the police were still waiting on results to find out whether Henry had been under the influence of alcohol or drugs, but that he was an honor roll student with no prior accidents or run-ins with the law. It was noted that Henry and Josh had been best friends since elementary school, but Josh had not been available for comment.

I mulled it over but couldn't make the pieces fit together. "Why would Dana have this?"

Connor shrugged. "The only reasons for someone unconnected to a tragedy to have clippings of it are black-mail or research. So, you tell me."

"Is it possible she was wrapped up in something she shouldn't have been?"

"Yes, but there was nothing on her laptop to lead us to it, so your guess is as good as mine."

"We could ask Josh about it."

"It can't hurt. From what we know right now, it doesn't make any sense, and I don't like pieces of information not making sense. We should compare his keys with the pho-tos you took of Colette's at some point and also ask him why he tripled her wages, so I'll see if he's available." He sent a text message.

"You have Josh's private number?"

"For emergencies, yes, but I texted his new Shade." Connor's phone vibrated. "They're home. Let's go."

I remembered my hair and makeup. "Um . . ."

Connor looked me over. "You have five minutes."

"What about your reputation?"

He eyed the dark window. "We'll hope he's using mood lighting."

13

ARMED ONLY WITH MASCARA and lip gloss, I found myself once again a passenger in Connor's car driving to see Josh Summers. After being poisoned, again. Wearing Connor's underwear, again. At least he hadn't noticed this time. I let my hair fall to cover my face and pretended to be enthralled by something on my phone.

Josh met us at the door in a casual outfit of T-shirt, shorts, and suede moccasins. He mustn't have been expecting guests this evening. He led us back to the same sitting room with its brown leather chairs and now darkened view out the double-height window. We were in luck with the mood lighting—several floor lamps filled the room with a soft glow and cast warm reflections on the glass.

Josh offered us refreshments. Connor declined for both of us, not caring that I would've killed for a coffee from the Synesso Hydra.

"We'll try not to take up too much of your time. First of all, would you mind if we take a look at your house key?"

Josh retrieved his key chain, and we flipped through the images on my phone. One of them was a match.

"Are you sure you never gave Colette a copy?" Connor asked Josh.

"Of course I'm sure."

"Any idea how one ended up on her key ring then?"

Josh's jaw tightened. "No. But I'll be sure to ask her about it."

"Please don't address it with her until we've finalized the investigation. Just in case."

"Fine."

Connor handed the keys back. "Thank you. Have you ever slept with Colette?"

Josh gripped the keys hard enough to turn his fingers white. "What does that have to do with anything?"

"That's a yes, then. What about with Dana?"

"No! And how is this helping her?"

Connor leaned forward. "I don't tell you how to cook, Mr. Summers, so please don't tell me which questions need asking."

Josh stood up and ran his fingers through his hair in agitation.

"You said you wanted to help Dana," Connor reminded him. "No lies, no secrets."

Josh's hand dropped to his side, and he lowered himself back into the chair. Even the blond hair that his fingers had drawn into a peak flopped over. "You're right."

"What was Dana like toward you? Was she distant, polite, a huge fan?"

"She was nice, but definitely not star-struck. She didn't even laugh at most of my jokes."

This made me smile. Dana was a hard nut to crack.

"Did she seem interested in your past?"

Josh gave him an odd look. "She did ask a couple of questions over the month we spent together, but she didn't push for answers. Why?"

"Are you being blackmailed, Mr. Summers?"

Josh went a shade lighter, and he hesitated too long before answering. "Where is this coming from?"

"I have no interest in uncovering your secrets. I'm trying to save Dana's life."

There was a long silence as each man tried to outwait the other.

Connor won. Of course.

"Fine," Josh said. "Colette came on to me a few weeks ago, just after I supposedly started dating Dana. We slept together, as you figured out already. Colette told me to triple her pay or she'd tell. Dana wouldn't have cared, obviously, but I couldn't let Colette know that, so I went along with it." He shrugged. "It pissed me off to give money to her rather than to people in need, but it's not like I couldn't afford it."

So *that's* how Colette earned so much. I'd bet my last four bucks that Josh wasn't the first client she'd seduced and blackmailed. It was a stroke of genius to make it appear as a wage increase so it could be explained to significant others and the IRS.

Connor's face showed no surprise. He probably had it figured out from the get-go. Nice of him to enlighten me.

"Any other blackmail you want to tell us about?" he asked.

Josh stared him down. "I already answered your question. If you don't have anything further—"

Connor pulled out a copy of the newspaper clipping we'd found in Dana's apartment and handed it to Josh. "Does this mean anything to you?"

Josh's hand shook as he held it. He looked like he was going to be sick. "Henry. My good friend. He died in a car accident over twenty-five years ago. This is the picture they used in one of the news articles on it."

"Any idea why Dana would have that in her apartment?"

Josh stared at the picture for a long moment before answering. "No." He shook his head, as if to clear it. "It's public knowledge, but I'd hate for the media to get hold of it and dredge it all up again."

"Why?"

He didn't look up, his eyes snared by the paper in his hands. "It was a senseless accident that never should have happened. No one can do anything to fix it. A media storm will just be painful for everyone who knew him." He handed the paper back to Connor. "If that will be all?"

His escort to the door was a little less good-natured than his welcome had been.

———

WE PULLED AWAY and turned toward Connor's place in Beverly Hills. "Were you watching him when I asked about blackmail?" Connor asked.

"Yes, it shook him up pretty bad. Maybe more than the whole Colette thing warranted."

Connor nodded. "That was my impression, too. You're not bad at reading people. Mostly."

"Mostly?"

"You didn't read your ex-husband well."

I bristled. "You read my file?"

"Of course." He leveled his gaze at me, daring me to object.

I stifled my gut reaction. I should've known.

When I refused to take the bait, he continued. "He seemed very upset about a death that happened twenty-six years ago."

Glad we were no longer talking about my ex, I thought about it. "If they were best friends his entire childhood, it makes sense it left a lasting wound. He seems to hold everyone at arm's length these days. Maybe that's why."

"It's possible. Too bad it doesn't help us with the case."

The case. I had no idea how we'd get to the bottom of it, and Dana's numbered days were running out fast. "Why do you think Colette made a copy of the key?"

"Spite? I suspect it irked her that Tahlia was trusted with one and she wasn't."

Damn. That sounded plausible and didn't make it any more likely that Colette was the person who planted the Ambience. So much for my sleuthing.

We drove in silence a while. "Why did you turn down refreshments for both of us anyway? I'm starving."

Connor shook his head, still unable to believe he'd been saddled with me. "I wanted his Shade out of the room in case having him there would make Josh less talkative. If he ate, Caleb would've had to join us."

"Right. Of course."

"What do you want to eat?"

"Everything."

"You realize that means an awful lot of taste testing?"

"On second thought, maybe Maria can make us something for dinner. And dessert."

———

OLIVER WAS HOME when I got back around ten o'clock and came out of his bedroom to greet me. Meow stayed in bed.

"You've scored an admirer, I see," he said.

"I have?"

He gestured to the dining table, which was overflowing with flowers. "I hope this doesn't mean you'll be leaving me to cook for myself."

Red roses. Baby's breath. Entirely unoriginal but expensive. I walked over and searched for a note amidst the blooms, my pulse thrumming in my ears. Who would send these? I used to love flowers, but now I associated them with Steve, who'd bought them for me on every occasion and divorced me at the first inconvenience. What good are pretty things without kept promises?

Oliver was watching me search, and there were so many of the damn things to dig through that after a whole minute I still hadn't found the card. I'd pricked myself twice though. "Did you find the lasagna?" I asked.

"Yes. I ate it."

"All of it?"

"It didn't have any meat in it, so I needed extra to fill me up. It was delicious while it lasted."

My hand brushed cardboard. The note.

Can't stop thinking about you. Call me. A.

Albert's personal number was included.

The thudding in my ears grew louder. Was he serious? Did he think I found him so irresistible I wouldn't notice he'd drugged me? And if he believed that, why did he feel the need in the first place? I took a few deep breaths.

If he was really insecure, the drug would help his confidence, and if I was really his number one fan, I might not have noticed its effects, or at least put them down to the wine. Except he hadn't been able to get it up.

"Izzy?" Oliver tapped my arm. "Don't swoon on me now girl, I'm starving and have to go to work soon."

Glad to be distracted, I considered my fast and simple recipes. "How do cheesy scones sound?"

"Superb."

At least he was easy to please. I got the ingredients out and started the oven preheating. When I turned around, Oliver was fingering the note that had come with the flowers. "So, who's responsible for ruining our perfectly good dining table, anyway? Look, you can't even see the Ninja Turtle stickers anymore!"

"Connor, of course. Who else? And they're beautiful." My lying skills were improving.

"Then why is it signed *A*?"

I made a show of sighing. "It stands for a nickname, okay? A private one."

"Oooh, let me guess. Aardvark? Angel-berries? Archetypal-God-of-Arousal?"

"Ugh. Stop or you can cook your own dinner." In truth, I'd have hugged him for his ridiculous suggestions if it wouldn't have made him suspicious. Imagining Connor going by Angel-berries dispelled the power of my bad memories, like flicking a light switch on the monsters under the bed.

I grabbed the cheese and started grating, holding back a smile.

"You're no fun at all, Adorabubbles," Oliver said, coming over to pinch some cheese.

I swatted at his hand. "You know having your own personal chef is a bit like being the Queen, right?"

He snickered. "Yeah, only I never waste it by ordering jam sandwiches with the crusts removed. And if I did order jam sandwiches, I would damn well eat the crusts too."

"You're the picture of frugality."

"*And* I don't wear silly hats."

AFTER FULFILLING my housemate duties, I sat down on my bed to tackle another mountain of hate mail. Meow migrated to my pillow to keep me company as soon as Oliver left for work. I thanked her with some neck scratches before concentrating on the task at hand.

Connor had warned me not to bring anything to his attention unless it was a much stronger lead than what I'd come up with so far. Except if it related to blackmail.

"Most murderers have better things to do than write us handy dandy letters that lead us to them," he'd said. "That's why I gave the job to you."

I huffed again in remembrance. One minute Connor showed empathy and concern for me and others, the next he went back to being an arrogant ass. An arrogant ass with a particularly nice ass, but he didn't have Levi's dimples. *Oh dear.*

My phone buzzed with a text.

Did you like the flowers? Because I like you. A.

The bad memories crept back. I stared at the message longer than it warranted, unable to process it with my tired eyes and more tired brain. It was midnight. That meant four thirty p.m. in Australia. The perfect time to ring my best friend.

I couldn't face going to sleep thinking about Albert, Steve, or Dana on her deathbed.

"Hey, doofus," Lily greeted me. "How're you doing?"

We've been best friends since third grade, when Sophia Yale, the most popular girl in class, blew a giant wad of pink bubblegum into Lily's hair and I cut it out for her using blunt plastic art scissors. Her mother burst into tears when she saw my handiwork, but we were inseparable from that moment on.

"Oh, you know, I'm over eight thousand miles away from my dear ex-husband, and no one has asked me for a sticky bun in months. So, unbelievably marvelous," I lied. "What about you?"

"Let's see. Four hangovers. Three sexual encounters. Two pairs of new shoes. And zero ex-husbands and hundred-grand debts. So, I guess that would make me unbelievably more marvelous than you."

"Gee, I don't know how I'd cope without your support," I said, feeling better already. "How many men made up the three sexual encounters?"

"Depends how you define *men*. Two were sexually inappropriate comments from my malodorous coworker—you guessed it, Chad—and one was with myself."

I snorted. "That's my girl. How's work aside from the malodorous Chad?"

"The usual. It's a toss-up whether I'm selling the products or my soul faster."

She worked as a copywriter for an advertising agency, and she was excellent at it. Probably why she'd been so successful at talking me into so many things. When we were thirteen, she had me convinced for an entire month that unicorns were real and lived in Africa with the zebras.

"And the children's books?" I asked.

"Gah. Don't even get me started. I can't believe how hard they are to write."

"It might help if you liked children."

"Nobody *likes* children. Parents just have instinctive urges that mimic liking them, and they chalk it up to love."

"So, you've become less cynical since we chatted last?" I asked.

"Absolutely."

"And how's the family?" We both knew who I meant. When we were growing up, her parents had worked long hours and taken business trips every other weekend, which meant she'd spent so much time at my house that she became an honorary family member. To this day, she was closer to my family than her own.

"Mum's doing well. It's hard to miss you too badly when she has me."

"Good. And Dad?"

"On another trip. So I've been making sure to pay extra visits to Mum."

"Thank you." I was grateful they had each other for company. A teeny bit jealous too.

"I guess I should confess that her cooking is also a strong motivator," Lily said.

My mouth watered at the memory of Mum's roast lamb on the Weber and mulberry pie. "I can't judge you for that. Is Dad on a sales or poker trip?"

"Does he even differentiate anymore?"

"Good point." I caught a yawn in the palm of my hand. "I better go, but tell Mum I miss her and will ring soon. And maybe you can use Chad as inspiration for a character in one of your stories? The smelly kid? Without the sexual harassment, of course."

"Sure. Everyone wants to read about the smelly kid. But you can't go yet, you haven't told me anything about your new job."

"Then I've told you almost everything I'm allowed to."

She exhaled noisily. "I'm not a fan of this classified rubbish. When we're old and gray and about to cark it in a nursing home, you're going to tell me everything."

"Consider it a deal."

If I lived that long anyway.

14

SEVEN HOURS LATER, I was sitting outside my apartment cradling a cup of tea. The building didn't have any balconies. It wouldn't have suited the cement box look the builder must have been going for. But I'd dragged a chair out onto the external stair landing, added the obligatory potted plant (a cactus that needed zero maintenance), and called it close enough.

I watched the passing traffic with bleary eyes and counted up how many days it would be before I caught up with my loan payments so I could justify buying a coffee machine. I missed good coffee. I needed good coffee. There were a few shops popping up in LA that served it thanks to the large emigrant population from Europe and other civilized places that knew what real coffee was. As a student, I'd managed to visit one such place often enough to survive. As a Shade at the mercy of Connor's poor taste in coffee, I was thinking of poisoning him myself.

The answer was sixty-six days. Eighty if I wanted to pay rent in the meantime.

So, I could eschew logic, buy a coffee machine now, and take an extra two weeks to pay off my overdue payments, or I could kick my coffee habit. I wasn't sure which was more likely to be the death of me.

To put off the decision, I searched for decent local coffee shops on my smartphone. Maybe I'd catch a break and find one not too far off the route to Connor's.

Footsteps coming up the stairs interrupted my focus. A huge mountain of a man reached the landing and headed straight for me. He looked like the Hulk, only he was tan instead of green, and he was wearing a shirt.

All of a sudden I understood why balconies were better than stair landings. Balconies were private. I'd gotten out of bed, pulled on some sweats, made a cup of tea, and come right out here, which meant my hair had to be sticking up in all directions in its best electrocuted zombie impersonation. I patted it down as well as I could before he reached me.

"If you're looking for Oliver, I'm afraid he's still in bed. He worked late last night."

"That's okay, I was looking for you," the Hulk said with a big smile.

I patted my hair some more—nobody was ever that happy to see me. "What can I do for you, Mr.—?"

"Black. I'm here on behalf of Platypus Lending."

I forgot about my hair and focused on the long, jagged scar down his left cheek.

On the one hand, it made him look even more menacing. On the other, it gave me some hope because it meant he must have screwed up at least once.

"Your first name doesn't happen to be Bruce does it?" I asked.

Mr. Black looked confused.

"Uh, never mind. The point is you seem like a nice guy." My voice was squeakier than I'd hoped. "Have you ever been married?"

"Yep. Still am. Our ten-year anniversary's coming up actually." His manner was relaxed, as if he had all the time in the world. Like Aunt Alice when she'd caught me feeding my peanut-butter-smeared homework to the dog.

"Wow. That's great." I'd been hoping he might have some sympathy for a fellow divorced person. Instead, I'd made myself jealous.

"I wasn't that fortunate, Mr. Black." My dad once told me that people feel important hearing their own name, and you can use it to influence them. I needed any advantage I could get. "You see, my husband took out a big loan, and then dumped half of it on me in the divorce."

Mr. Black shifted his stance, and I silently thanked the builder for making the staircase out of cement. Anything else might have collapsed. "Sorry to hear that, ma'am. But I don't make the rules. I just follow orders. And my orders are I gotta make you pay."

I swallowed hard and measured the distance between my chair and my apartment door. It wasn't much. Actually, I was afraid there wasn't enough room to open the door without shifting the chair first. Mr. Black must have seen me looking because he moved to block the door. That left a me-sized gap between his right shoulder and the railing. I darted through it and took off running.

My bare feet slapped the concrete, making it hard to hear if he was in pursuit. When I reached the foot of the stairs, I risked a backward glance and saw he was only one flight behind me. I broke into a cold sweat and sprinted down the sidewalk, cursing myself for leaving the apartment without my keys as I raced past my Corvette. At least I had my phone. I held it out in front of me and dialed Connor without slowing down, narrowly missing a palm tree. It took forever to start ringing.

"Isobel? Are you at the gym?" Connor asked.

"The Hulk," I gasped between breaths. "Chasing me."

Something in my tone must have convinced him this wasn't a prank call. "I'm on my way. Where are you?"

"Running. Rose Avenue."

"Keep me on the line. I'll be there in fifteen minutes."

I clutched the phone in my hand and ran. As I swung a hard right up Kelton Avenue, I saw Mr. Black was closing in. He had a lot more weight to carry, but most of it was muscle. Muscle hired to break me.

Sheer terror gave me an extra burst of speed, and I darted up a short side street and sprinted left at the end, praying

I could get out of sight before he saw which way I'd gone. I looked back as I veered left again. He'd paused at the end of the short side street and was scanning the area for my escape route.

Our eyes met.

I ran on. I ran until I forgot how to breathe. My heart was pounding. My head was spinning. My feet were smarting. Even my boobs were aching from all the bra-free bouncing, and there wasn't that much of them to bounce. I knew I couldn't keep going much longer.

My phone showed the call length was at thirteen minutes and thirty-seven seconds. Connor would be here soon. I risked another peek over my shoulder. The sidewalk was empty. No sign of Mr. Black. Had he given up the chase and decided to get me later? Or had he doubled back and was now driving one of the cars on the road?

The thought made my heart beat even faster. If heartbeats were horses, I'd have a winner. As it was, I'd probably have a heart attack.

I bolted past a thick privacy hedge. A second later, I reversed my tracks and dove behind it. Then I put my head between my knees and tried to gasp quietly.

The hedge was so thick I couldn't see anything through it. Fingers walked up and down my spine as I tried to convince myself I'd hear him coming. Hell. He was so big I'd *feel* him coming. A soft voice made me jump violently enough that I hurt my ass when I landed back on it.

The voice was Connor's. I raised my phone to my ear.

"Isobel, I'm on Rose Avenue. Where are you?"

All my instincts told me to stay quiet. What if Mr. Black was still after me on foot and in earshot?

"Isobel?"

The apprehension in his voice compelled me to answer. "I'm hiding behind a hedge." I'd tried to stick close to Rose Avenue after telling Connor that's where I was, but I'd changed directions and routes so many times since that I was as confused as I'd wanted Mr. Black to be.

"Is anyone nearby? I need to know what street you're on so I can find you."

I put a hand to my sweaty forehead and breathed in and out for a few beats before forcing my shaking legs back under me. "I'll try to see." Heart thundering, I peeked past the hedge. "Queensland Street." I looked at the building behind me. "Number ten thousand, nine hundred and nineteen."

"I'll be right there."

I sank down to the cool soil. Long seconds ticked by. I told myself even if Mr. Black did find me now, Connor would arrive in time to stop him from breaking too many of my bones.

A car rolled to a stop in front of the hedge. I got into a squat, ready to run.

"Isobel?"

Connor. A wave of relief almost sent me back to the ground.

"I'm here."

He circled the hedge as I pushed myself to my feet. He didn't hesitate. Even when he took in my ensemble of over-sized Mumford & Sons T-shirt (which I'd stolen from my ex and used as a nightie), gray sweats, bare, blackened feet, aforementioned electrocuted zombie hairdo, and sweaty, red face. He strode over and pulled me into his arms.

We stayed like that for a while. "Are you all right?" he asked.

I was all right as long as he hadn't noticed that my nipples were starting to get hard through the inadequate two layers of cotton between us. I drew back and crossed my arms over my chest. "I am now. Thanks for coming."

He dropped his gaze deliberately to my crossed arms and smiled. A real smile. "My pleasure."

I was abruptly glad he didn't smile more often. It lit up his whole face and made my brain short-circuit, leaving my body all too ready to pursue its own agenda.

It was lucky for my willpower that he broke the mood by walking toward the car. I was envisioning a hot—or cold—shower, when I realized I'd left the apartment door unlocked. My breath hitched. "Shit."

Connor scanned the area around us, his hand gravitating to his gun. "What's wrong?"

"Oliver and Meow might be in trouble."

"Who?"

I yanked the car door open and clambered in. "Drive to my building. I'll explain on the way."

He slipped into his seat and started driving.

"Start from the beginning."

I took a deep breath and began talking.

ALL APPEARED NORMAL as we reached my street. It was eight o'clock, so the neighborhood was mostly awake, and I thought that boded well for Oliver and Meow. Connor parked illegally out front and raced up the stairs, hand hovering over his holster. I was close behind, despite my protesting feet. He opened the door, but had to move the chair before he could slip inside. That boded well too.

The apartment was as I'd left it, including the flowers still covering the dining table. Connor raised an eyebrow at this but didn't comment. I pointed to Oliver's bedroom door and gave the universal gesture to be quiet. It was ajar, as he always left it, so Meow could come and go as she pleased. Connor pushed it open farther with a creak, and I winced, even knowing Oliver was a heavy sleeper. He'd probably even sleep through the screams and crunches of his housemate's fingers being broken one by one.

I peeked in. Meow was sleeping in the middle of the bed, while Oliver curled around her, fighting a losing battle between not disturbing her highness and keeping enough of his body in bed to stop from falling out of it. Smiling so wide my cheeks hurt, I retreated and pulled the door back to its Meow-friendly position behind me.

Connor checked out the rest of the apartment. It didn't take long. "All clear," he said. "I'll wait while you get ready."

Forty minutes later, I was showered and made up to the stylist's standards once more, except for the flats I wore in concession to my blistered feet. They felt a lot worse now the adrenaline had worn off.

I limped out to the open plan living area and stopped short. Connor was lounging on the sofa with Meow purring on his lap. Earlier I'd had too much on my mind to be struck by how odd it was to have the man of the custom-tailored clothes, expensive mansion, and impeccable taste (excluding coffee of course) in my humble apartment. Or to realize that the man I considered dangerous and unsympathetic was the first person I'd called when I was scared and vulnerable. I was suddenly conscious of both, as well as the warm feeling I got from seeing him curled up with Meow.

I shoved the thoughts and feelings aside. "I believe we have work to do."

15

CONNOR INSISTED I LEAVE my Corvette and catch a ride with him. I was learning to pick my battles, so a few minutes later we were cruising down Palms Boulevard in his SUV.

"How much do you need?" he asked.

I knew exactly what he was referring to. Nine months of fifteen percent, interest-only payments on my $105,000 debt came to: "Eleven thousand, eight hundred and twelve dollars."

"Okay. So have the Taste Society advance you two months' pay."

Two months' pay would cover the last nine months as well as the next two and rent. Or the last nine months and a coffee machine. My shoulders slumped. "I can't. I already submitted an application for an advance, and it was rejected."

His hands tightened around the steering wheel. "I'll talk to the higher-ups for you."

"You think you have enough sway to convince them?" I shook my head.

"I might."

"Forget it. I don't want you calling in any favors for me."

"Consider it the company protecting their investment. They've just spent eight months training you and months before that identifying and screening you. Not to mention I've had to put up with you for four days. It's wasteful for everyone if you get taken out of action."

"While that's heartwarming, I'm not accepting a handout from them before I've even secured the job."

"It's not a handout. It's a loan."

"That's how I got into this mess in the first place," I pointed out.

"Oh, for goodness' sake." I hoped the steering wheel wouldn't turn to mush in his hands. It would make driving difficult. "What do you want me to do, then? Leave it be and wonder if you're being brutalized every minute I'm not with you?"

"No. Give me something to defend myself with."

At least he didn't laugh.

"You think you can defend yourself against the Hulk?"

"Isn't there some move you can teach me? Some vulnerable spot I can whack to knock him off his feet?"

"Sure. But it would take months of training for you to pull it off consistently. And even then he might disable you before you get a chance, or you might panic in the heat of the moment."

I huffed. "There's got to be something."

"There is. Pepper spray. Then you run like hell again and call me."

I thought about it for a minute. "I can work with that."

"And you have to promise me that as soon as you pass this assessment and secure the job, you'll take that advance payment."

"Okay," I agreed. I had no desire to play the high stakes version of hide-and-seek with Mr. Black for two months. I just didn't want to take out a second loan from a second dangerous organization that I had no way of repaying. Easier to dodge one debt collector than two.

We stopped at a traffic light. "Give me your phone," Connor said.

"Why?" I asked as I handed it over.

He ignored me and started tapping on the screen.

"What are you doing?"

He held the phone out to me. "Type in your password."

"Not until you tell me what you're doing."

A muscle in his jaw twitched. "I'm installing an app that will allow me to access the phone's GPS signal, so if this happens again, which it probably will thanks to your pigheadedness, I can find you. Okay?"

I typed in my password. He tapped the screen a few

more times and handed it back to me as the light turned green.

"So, can we go to Blu Jam Café?" I asked.

"Why?"

"I need coffee."

"There's coffee at my place."

"Doesn't count."

He exhaled through his nose but changed lanes. "Okay, but only because you got chased by the Hulk this morning."

I SIPPED MY ESPRESSO and closed my eyes in bliss. Ah, the joy of the properly sourced, roasted, aged, and extracted coffee. When I opened them, I saw Connor grimacing over the long black I'd made him order.

"You know your nose wrinkles when you do that?" I asked, even though it didn't.

"You call *this* good coffee? It's like the 190-proof vodka of the caffeine world."

"I know it's stronger than what you're used to, but can't you appreciate the flavor? It's rich and smooth and creamy with layers of caramel and floral notes . . ."

He tried another sip and grimaced again. "I'll stick with my automatic drip thanks."

"Sure. I can understand that. Who wouldn't prefer acrid, coffee-flavored dishwater?"

"Shut up and drink."

It was an easy order to obey. I was polishing off Connor's coffee too, when my phone vibrated with an incoming text message.

I don't appreciate being ignored. A.

That didn't sound good. I hadn't been able to face replying the night before and Mr. Black had diverted my attention this morning, but I suspected Albert was not the kind of problem that would go away if I ignored it long enough.

"What's wrong?" Connor asked.

He seemed to ask me that a lot.

I was careful to make my expression blank before answering. "Mr. Alstrom seems to be under the impression that I'd like to repeat yesterday's experience."

Connor grabbed the phone from me and read the message. "How long have you been ignoring him?"

"There were flowers waiting for me when I got home last night, along with a note to call him. I'm not sure when they arrived. He texted me late last night too."

Connor's phone rang. "Excuse me."

I savored the last mouthfuls of coffee while he answered it.

His face went from rock hard to tempered steel hard before he hung up. "Apparently, we aren't the only ones having coffee out and about today. That was Josh's new Shade. Someone just tried to kill Josh again."

Oh, what a fun morning this is turning out to be. "Are they both okay?"

"Yes, they're fine. Caleb smelled the potassium cyanide

before tasting it. He only called because of its impact on our investigation."

It was good Caleb had identified it by the faint, bitter almond scent alone. Potassium cyanide is one of the most toxic poisons in existence, so while it has a sharp, acidic taste and sets your tongue on fire, it's easy for an unsuspecting person to consume a lethal dose before it hits their taste buds in full force. Especially in a strong flavored, acidic liquid, like coffee.

"What does it mean for the investigation?"

"That's what we have to find out."

We crawled through traffic to the scene of the crime, Morning Glory. It was a ritzy place in Holmby Hills that offered coffee of both the drip and semi-decent espresso variety. Connor was delighted and ordered a drip coffee to spite me.

I thought about having the quinoa salad to balance out my splurges over the last few days, but two double shot espressos were making me jittery after my recent drought, so I ordered a donut to soak up some of the caffeine. Connor leaned back in his seat with his coffee-flavored swamp water and surveyed the room.

Josh had ordered a macchiato when he was here, so I inhaled my donut and watched the guy making the coffees behind the counter. I tried not to think of my own days behind the espresso machine. No one had ever held a gun to my head, poisoned me, or threatened to break my bones. Not even once.

I pushed my mind back to the task at hand. When the barista finished making a coffee, he'd pop it up on the counter so the waitress manning the tables could deliver it as fast as possible. It wouldn't be too hard for anyone to walk by and sprinkle something in it while it was on the counter or even as the waitress bustled past. The trickiest bit would be making sure you spiked the right cup. That suggested the culprit had been close enough to hear Josh's order and keep an eye on the coffees being served.

"Wouldn't Josh have spotted Albert, Juan, or Colette if they were in here long enough to drug his coffee?" I asked.

"Yes. Tahlia too. Unless they were disguised."

"Disguised how?"

"Heavy stage makeup, wigs, burkas, headscarves, prosthetics, you name it. It's all easy enough to get hold of in LA."

I wished I'd ordered another donut. "How do you ever solve anything?"

"The window of opportunity this time is small. We can check the alibis of all our main suspects."

"Then why don't you look happier?"

"Do I ever look happy?"

The only times I could recall involved me missing items of clothing. I didn't want to bring those times up, so I said, "Good point."

Connor drained the last of his coffee and set the mug down on the table. "The problem is, I don't think we're going to get anywhere with the alibi route. If Colette, Tahlia, or Juan did it the first time, they were hired by someone else because of their ability to access the house. That someone else wouldn't have hired them to do it here. Likewise, if Albert hired a pro for the first attempt, he's not stupid enough to risk doing it himself for the second. You get the idea."

"So we need to find the hitman?"

"Yes."

"Who's your top suspect?"

"Someone with money and motive. Alstrom maybe, or someone who had a lot to lose from the Wholesome Foods boycott."

I mulled this over. "Do we have any leads on suspects at Wholesome Foods?"

"Nothing good. We identified the top ten biggest losers from the boycott and ran background checks on them. None of them have any criminal history on record. Our team is now tackling the problem in reverse—finding stakeholders with criminal records and seeing if they had significant losses." He stared into his cup as if it might hold the answers. "It's an imprecise way of generating leads, but we don't have time for anything better."

"So we go after Albert's hitman," I said.

"Forget it. We're not using you as bait again."

"I was thinking we'd use you as bait."

He jerked his head up and looked at me. "I'm listening."

I was in the middle of outlining my plan when my phone went off. Again. Only a few people had my new number, and as it was around two-thirty in the morning over in Australia, I had a bad feeling about who it was from.

If flowers don't get your attention, maybe you're the bad boy type. I've been a bad boy. You might want to check on your cat. A.

I leaped out of my chair and ran out the door. Where the hell did I park my car? Connor appeared at my elbow.

"What's wrong?"

Again with that damn question. I shoved the phone at him, my throat too constricted to form words. He strode to his SUV, pulling me with him when I didn't follow immediately.

"Get in."

The minutes passed in a blur of nausea and fear. Connor parked illegally in front of my apartment for the second time that day, and I was off and running before he'd killed the engine. He caught up at the top of the stairs, where I was trying to insert my key into the lock with shaking hands. He tried the handle, and it opened.

It should've been locked. Oliver's car was gone, which meant so was he.

"Meow?" I shouted as if expecting an answer. I found her in the kitchen. She walked toward me on wobbly legs, and I knelt down and wrapped her in my arms. On the floor was a pile of puke and a half-eaten bowl of canned cat food. Still holding Meow close, I sniffed the cat food. Minced cod, laced with some kind of poison. My favorite.

Connor was asking me for the vet's number, but I tuned him out. The vet might not figure it out in time. I scooped up some of the gelatinous, fishy goo on one finger and popped it into my mouth. It took me a moment to get the dry heaving under control and sort through the gut-churning assortment of flavors. I spat it back in the bowl. "Ethylene glycol." I spat again. "The vet's details are on the fridge. Let's go!"

We sped to Overland Veterinary Clinic and handed her over. After our hurried explanation, they took her into another room, where I knew they'd do everything they could to minimize her absorption of the poison. The receptionist cleared her throat. "Ms. . . . ?"

"Ms. Avery. I'm the owner's roommate."

"Can you tell me how she found the ethylene glycol?"

My mind was blank. How was I supposed to explain this?

"Was it brake fluid?" she asked. "Or antifreeze?"

Connor stepped forward. "We found her licking at Ms. Avery's hand lotion and she vomited shortly afterward. Ethylene glycol was listed as an ingredient. The name rang a bell, so we looked it up and saw we needed to get her to you as soon as possible."

"Well done. Because you caught it so early, she shouldn't sustain any kidney damage. We'll monitor her here for a day or two anyway, just to make sure everything's working as it should be."

I nodded in relief. "Thank you so much."

"Now who will be paying for this?"

I pushed my last credit card statement featuring lots of big red letters from my mind and rummaged through my bag. Connor beat me to it. She processed the payment and promised to call me as soon as Meow was out of immediate treatment.

I would've sat in the waiting room all day if Connor hadn't herded me out the door.

The sunshine seemed harsh. I hauled myself into the SUV and shut my eyes to help hold back tears. We stopped a few minutes later. "Where are we?"

"Come with me." He led me to a bench overlooking a small garden. "You did well. Meow is going to be fine, thanks to you."

I did a sob-hiccup. "You mean she almost died thanks to me."

He gently grasped my chin and forced me to look at him. "This is not your fault. I'd give you the day off if I could, but I need you somewhere I can protect you."

I wiped the tears off my cheeks. "I thought I'm supposed to be protecting you."

"Isobel." His voice was soft, pleading, and a little exasperated. "I'm trying to help here."

I gave myself a mental shake. I was no good to anyone like this.

"Then you don't know me very well," I said, gesturing at the garden. "Comfort food beats nature hands down."

He grabbed my hand and pulled me to my feet. "What kind of comfort food?"

I thought about it. "A McDonald's chocolate sundae?"

He patted me on the arm as we headed for the car. "Nice to have you back."

On the drive there, I realized I needed to call Oliver and let him know about Meow. I'd have to tell him the same story Connor had given the vet. I rubbed my eyes. It seemed wrong to lie about anything important, but how could I explain the truth? Oliver didn't pick up, so I left a message on his voice mail. Then I told myself sternly there was nothing else I could do for Meow and steered my thoughts toward ice cream and murderers.

By the end of my sundae, Connor had given my plan the go-ahead. I texted Albert.

So sorry I didn't reply sooner! My boyfriend, Connor Stiles, is super jealous and trying to stop me from having any contact with you . . . He's in the bathroom now. Would love to see you again but can't unless I can figure out how to get rid of him :(. Want to break up but scared he'll get violent.

My phone buzzed with a returning message quicker than I thought possible. I'd always imagined being the object of a man's obsession would be fun. But then I'd never imagined the man as an insecure, drug-wielding lunatic, or becoming the object of his obsession because of a limp dick.

I showed the message to Connor.

I might be able to help. Is there any time coming up when he won't be with you?

"Tell him I'm meeting someone tomorrow at eleven a.m. at Grizzle and Girdles," Connor said. "The owner's a friend of mine, and it should be pretty quiet that time of day."

We were betting that Albert's suspicious history of poisoned competitors, combined with his obsession with me and obvious impatience, would lead him to use a hitman he was already in contact with. A hitman who might have been at Morning Glory earlier today.

I passed the information along. Albert replied with:

See you tomorrow, sweet cheeks.

I repressed a shudder and looked back at Connor. "What's next?"

"Next we get you pepper spray." His eyes flicked toward my phone. "And maybe a Taser."

16

A-1 SELF-DEFENSE was filled wall-to-wall with "safety" paraphernalia, almost all of it illegal in Australia. Brass knuckles: illegal. Stun guns: illegal. Automatic rifles: illegal. The safety goggles would have been okay, though.

Connor led me over to the pepper spray display, where I admired the bewildering array of small canisters ranging from Barbie-pink lipsticks to stylish patent leather carry cases. Connor selected a utilitarian black one. "We'll take two of these." The range of stun guns was impressive too, but Connor didn't bother to scan them. "And a TASER C2 with three spare cartridges."

"Of course, sir. What color would you like?" He gestured to the six display models.

Connor looked at me. "Well?"

I thought about the bad guy's reaction if I pulled out a pink weapon. "I'll take the silver." As a bonus, it'd match my Corvette.

If Connor hadn't been standing beside me I might've been tempted by the yellow.

He once again handed over his credit card before I could dig mine out. As soon as we left the store, I turned on him. "You can't pay for all this stuff."

"I didn't. The company did. I'm authorized to purchase any necessary safety gear for our Shades."

"What about Meow?"

"You know medical costs incurred in the line of duty are covered. That includes the veterinary variety."

I opened my mouth and shut it again. "Are you sure?"

Connor just looked at me.

"Okay. Well. Thanks."

"Let's teach you how to use your new toys."

Twenty minutes later, I was standing in Connor's backyard with my newly activated TASER C2 and SABRE Red pepper spray canisters, facing a cardboard cutout of Spider-Man. Because everyone has one of those lying around. Connor picked up the pepper spray. "This stuff has a range of up to ten feet. Aim for the face, but move your hand back and forth while spraying to get better coverage. You want to go ear to ear. If your attacker is wearing glasses, try to get some above the frames so it still goes in his eyes. Having said that, sometimes just a bit of this stuff on one cheek can bring the bad guy down." He handed a canister to me.

I took it from him like it was a saucepan spitting hot oil. "How does it do that exactly?"

"It sets their faces on fire, causes temporary blindness by forcing their eyes closed, and makes them cough uncontrollably."

I held the canister farther away from my body. "I see."

"Don't use it indoors unless you have no other choice, and beware of the wind. This one has a pretty powerful stream, so it's not going to reverse direction and come back in your face, but you can still get some blowback."

I licked a finger and held it in the air to see if there was any breeze.

"Don't lick your fingers or touch your face during or after handling one of those things. Wash your hands with hot water and dishwashing liquid first. Then wash them again. And get rid of the canister, even if it's only partially empty."

I waited for my tongue to explode. Nothing. Thank goodness. "Uh-huh. Good tip."

He showed me how to arm the pepper spray by sliding the tab across with my thumb and gestured to Spider-Man. "Now stand ten feet away, and give it a shot."

"What's that in meters again?"

"Stop stalling."

I paced it out and faced my target. "Is it too windy?"

Connor might have rolled his eyes, but I was looking at Spider-Man so I couldn't be sure.

"Do it, Avery."

I pushed the tab over and pressed down firmly the way he'd demonstrated. A stream of spray shot out and coated

Spider-Man's face. It felt anticlimactic after all that build-up. Not that I'd expected Spider-Man to fall to the ground coughing and screaming or anything.

"Is that it?" I asked.

"That's it," Connor said. "It's just important you're familiar with it. You don't want to be working out how hard you need to press it when the Hulk is closing in." He took the canister from me and replaced it with the unused one. "Keep this on your person at all times until Alstrom and Black have been taken care of. It's not going to do you any good if you can't get to it."

"I'll keep it on my keys."

"That wouldn't have helped you this morning. Think again."

"In my pocket?"

"Good."

"What if my outfit doesn't have pockets?"

"Choose a different outfit. Wear it around your neck. I don't care, just have it with you." He stared at me until I conceded.

"Yessir." I looked down at my current outfit. No pockets. I considered tucking it in the waistband of my undies, but I didn't fancy hiking the dress up to my ears to get to the pepper spray. Not that it wouldn't be a good distraction technique. I settled on tucking it down my cleavage, which was adequate for the purpose thanks to my push-up bra.

Connor stepped close and tugged at the top of my dress to inspect the canister's location. My skin turned hot under his touch. I panicked, thinking he had pepper spray on his fingers. Then I realized the warmth was pleasant.

"Happy?" I asked, pulling away.

His eyes glinted with amusement or appreciation. As was so often the case, I couldn't tell.

"For now." He picked up the Taser.

"Uh-uh. That thing is *not* gonna fit on my person."

"You can carry it in your handbag. As long as you take your handbag with you anytime you aren't with me."

I blew out a sigh but nodded. Staying safe was turning out to be a pain in the ass. If I had to lug around this much stuff for the sake of being prepared, I might as well become a mother, or a Girl Scout.

"The Taser has a few advantages over a gun." Connor said. "First of all, it doesn't look dangerous, so it's unlikely to escalate an attack the way a gun might."

Damn. Should've gone with the pink one after all.

"Secondly, because it's a nonlethal weapon, it should reduce your instinctive reluctance to use it. Remember, a few seconds of indecision can cost you your life."

I tucked that fun fact away for something to worry over some night when I couldn't sleep.

"At the same time, its neuromuscular incapacitation method causes the person to lose all muscular control, which is better than a bullet, because a person with a gunshot wound can still shoot you back." His eyes met mine deliberately. "Last but not least, it's harder to shoot yourself. And even if you do, you won't die."

I nodded. "All good points. You should sell these things."

"It's also less messy than pepper spray. You can use it inside and in the wind without risk to yourself."

"Maybe I should carry *that* around in my cleavage then."

Connor eyed my neckline dubiously.

I huffed because he was right. My cleavage was not going to conceal the Taser.

Connor showed me how to load and unload cartridges, operate the safety, and aim using the laser sight. "Aim for the upper torso or thigh. If you hit your target, it will zap them for thirty seconds unless you use the safety to stop it. Drop the Taser, and use the time to get your ass out of there. If you miss and don't have time to load a second cartridge, you can use it like a stun gun by pushing it firmly against your assailant. Aim for the neck, upper chest, thigh or groin. It'll hurt like hell but won't incapacitate your bad guy. It might just piss him off."

"So don't miss?"

"That would be your best option. The laser sight will help and shows where the top probe will hit. If you have a choice, wait until you're about seven feet away. That'll make the probes about a foot apart. The weapon has a top range of fifteen feet, but the farther away you are, the farther apart the probes will be, and so the more likely one will miss. On the other hand, if you shoot when you're too close and the probes land less than four inches apart, it won't work properly."

"Oh great, now the pepper spray is starting to sound better."

"If only one probe hits, you can complete the circuit by using it as a stun gun on a second point, but of course you can't hold it and get away at the same time. You also have to be wary of very thick or loose clothing."

"Am I going to be quizzed on this?" I asked.

"I suppose you could call it a quiz when Mr. Black comes after you again."

I gulped. "Point taken. Um. So what else?"

He gestured to Spider-Man. "Take a practice shot."

It was a pretty simple undertaking with a stationary target, a laser sight, and all the time in the world. I suspected it wouldn't be quite as easy in the heat of the moment. Still, I felt more confident about meeting Mr. Black again than I had a few hours ago.

"Good," Connor said. "Now I'll teach you what to do if your attacker sneaks up on you and grabs you from behind."

Oh boy. I hadn't even considered that.

A second later I found myself wrapped in Connor's arms. It had been a terrifying, exhausting day, and I hadn't been held like that in almost two years. Without thinking, I melted back into him.

"Okay," Connor said, breaking into my reverie. "Your instincts aren't bad. When someone grabs you, you want to drop your weight, but instead of leaning back, lean forward, and do it abruptly to try to break their grip."

I was glad Connor couldn't see me blush.

"Even if you can't, you've bought yourself a few extra seconds before they can lift you up, and some leverage to slam your heel into the top of their foot. Do it as hard as you can. It'll work better if you're wearing heels. That should help break his concentration and make him loosen his grip further, allowing you to get an elbow to the groin. If he's already lifted you up, you can try kicking him there instead. If you have an arm free, you can also try grabbing one of his fingers and bending it backward. As soon as his grip loosens, get out of there. You might want to pull out the pepper spray or Taser as you're running, but don't pause to use it until you're well out of his reach."

I nodded, still struggling to get back into the self-defense mindset.

"Run through the moves to see what they feel like, then I'll show you how to adjust them depending on how I grab you."

I did as I was told and tried not to think too much about the other ways I might like him to grab me.

———

MARIA MADE US an Asian beef and vegetable stir-fry for late lunch or early dinner. While she was organizing it, I checked my phone and was glad to see no new messages from Albert. I was even more glad to hear a voice mail from the vet saying that Meow was doing well and should be able to go home the next afternoon.

Connor had coffee again, and I forgot to conceal my distaste as he pushed it toward me.

"No way," he said. "You can't whine about bad coffee after I watched you eat cat food today."

I wanted to gag at the memory. "That was life and death. I'd drink it for you if it was the only way to prevent you from dying."

"Stop," he said. "You're making me feel all warm inside."

I stared at him. "Did you just make a joke?"

He raised one eyebrow. "You do realize that preventing your clients from dying is exactly why you're supposed to drink it don't you? You're lucky this assessment isn't on Shade theory."

I scowled at him, tasted the damn coffee, then turned my attention to the delicious stir-fry.

17

CONNOR HAD A LOT TO ORGANIZE for the hit-man trap and suggested I get an early night. I wasn't sure if he was looking out for me or had reached his Izzy limit for the day. He drove me home and did a walk-through of the apartment before leaving.

I locked the door behind him, then changed into more comfortable clothes, transferring the pepper spray to the right pocket of my sweats, and after a second's consideration, the Taser into the left. I even remembered to put a spare pair of undies in my handbag. Pleased with this small triumph, I limped out to the kitchen, cleaned up Meow's food bowl and puke, and started cooking.

Oliver would be home at a decent hour, and I planned to use my extra time to cook him a roast. I missed Meow weaving around my legs and making a nuisance of herself as I hobbled about the kitchen. She was always quick to notice if I was making something with meat and had me well-trained as her food dispenser.

When the roast was in the oven, I logged on to my company laptop to start going through the digital hate mail Tahlia had forwarded to me. I scrolled down to the first of them and noticed an email above it from my rat-bastard ex-husband, Steve. Oh goody. I clicked on it with dread.

The last email I'd gotten from him was a month before while I was still in training. He'd asked for my new address because Platypus Lending were threatening to break *his* legs for the missing payments if they couldn't find me. I'd replied with one word: Good.

This email, dated a week ago, informed me that due to my lack of maturity and unwillingness to *do the right thing*, he'd suggested to Platypus Lending that they get in touch with my mother.

Anger simmered hot like a pot of chili con carne. Not only had Steve seen fit to saddle me with the debt to a bone-breaking lending company in the first place, but I could thank him for my visit from Mr. Black, this morning too. For a fleeting moment, I wished he was in LA so I could practice using my new self-defense toys on him. Then I remembered it would land me in jail, unless he attacked first, and decided it was for the best that he was eight thousand miles away. And that I couldn't take my Taser or pepper spray back to Australia with me.

Since I was about to pore over hate mail to search for Dana's would-be killer, I decided not to reply to Steve. If Platypus Lending ever got to him, I didn't want to become a suspect. I deleted his email and opened the first one Tahlia had forwarded to me.

I was a quarter of the way through them when Oliver got home.

"I'm so sorry," I said as soon as he walked through the door.

"Bollocks. It's not your fault old thing. And I called the vet during my break, and they said she's doing really well."

"But still."

He patted me on the arm. "She's okay. That's what matters. Now, is that dinner that smells so good?"

I was plating up when someone knocked on the door. Oliver was slouched in front of the TV, so I went to peek out the window. The silhouette was far too slim to be Mr. Black, and far too short to be Albert. I opened the door. "Etta, we were just about to have dinner. Want to join us?"

She stepped inside, took one look at the dining table, which was still covered with flowers, and joined Oliver on the couch.

"Have you two met?" I called over the TV.

Etta elbowed Oliver. "Yes, but he's hardly ever home, and when he is, he's asleep."

Oliver elbowed her back. "If I am awake, I sometimes put up with her, but mostly just because she dresses better than the Queen."

"Darn right I do. That old bag's got nothing on me."

I brought the plates over and joined them on the couch. A cricket match was on, but only because Oliver was holding the remote above his head, out of Etta's reach.

"Tell him to be a gentleman and let a little old lady choose what to watch, won't you?"

"My TV, my satellite, my choice. Besides, if I give it to you, you'll switch it to that new disgusting medical discoveries reality show. Izzy won't be able to eat if we put that on."

Etta grabbed her plate from me and huffed. "Fine. Then at least turn it down so we can talk. It's not like anything in cricket happens too fast to watch with your eyes alone. That's why the commentators just blab on about the weather and conditions the whole time."

Oliver lowered the volume and took his plate. There was silence for a minute as we all stuffed our faces. Etta finished chewing first. "So, Izzy, who are all the flowers from? Your hot boyfriend or that mysterious famous person you were worried about?"

"Famous person?" Oliver asked. "Why didn't I hear about this famous person?"

"You once whined to me that if you had a tuppence for every time a customer said the word 'famous,' you'd be able to single-handedly bankroll Her Royal Majesty's hat collection," I said. "I figured you wouldn't want to hear about it."

"Fair point." He downed some beer. "I consider it one of life's great ironies that I escaped a continent of royal-obsessed madmen, only to end up in the one other place on earth equally obsessed with their famous figures."

Etta put her fork down for a moment to pat his cheek. "And I consider it one of life's great mysteries that you choose to stay." She turned to me, forcing Oliver to content himself with scowling at the back of her head. "So? The flowers?"

"From my boyfriend."

"And your date with Mr. Famous?"

"I never said it was a date!"

Etta smirked. "So, I guess it went well then?"

I skewered a chunk of roast potato and ate it before replying. "You could say that." *But you'd be wrong.*

"And who's that new man you had around here yesterday morning?" Etta asked, waving her fork in the air as she spoke. "The big hunky one. Is he single? Can you set me up?"

My jaw dropped. "Mr. Black? The one who looks like the Hulk, you mean?"

"That's the one."

"Sorry, he's happily married."

"Pah! All the good ones are. Still, see if he's into a little bit of hanky-panky on the side. I'm not looking for commitment."

I dropped my fork.

Oliver snorted in disgust. "You made me turn down the cricket for *this*? I'm going to my bedroom so I can watch it in peace. Thanks for the roast, Izzy."

Etta was watching me with an expression I couldn't read. I picked up my fork. Should I warn her that Mr. Black broke bones for a living?

"It's not that I don't have plenty of men to choose from," she said, before I could speak. "Only last night, I went out with Morty Howard and had some wonderful sex. It's just I like variety."

I had no idea how to respond, so I shoved more food in my mouth.

"Now, don't be like that, dear. Sex is just as good for older folk as it is for you kids. Better even, because everyone's got more experience, less inhibitions, and nobody's expecting anybody to look perfect naked. My doctor told me that as long as I can walk up a flight of stairs then I can keep having sex. That's why I chose an upstairs apartment. And let me tell you, I can walk up and down those bad boys a whole lotta times a day."

"That's great," I choked out.

"I liked your idea of turning the stair landing into a balcony, by the way. I think I might do that too. That'll show all those people paying through the nose for the fancy-pants apartments with private balconies." She smiled and cut into her remaining meat aggressively.

I opted not to point out that it would be a tripping hazard. I got away with it because we had the top apartment farthest from the stairs, but Oliver and I had to walk past Etta's door every day.

She chewed her meat thoughtfully. "And I saw you and Mr. Black went for a run yesterday. Is he your new personal trainer? And why the bare feet? Is that one of those newfangled things? Meant to make you more grounded or something? I'm not sure it's a good idea, sweetie, because when you get to my age, the last thing you wanna do is make your feet tougher. I won't go into details, but you might wanna wear a bra next time too."

She used her last piece of meat to wipe up the rest of the gravy and popped it, dripping, into her mouth. When she finished, she put her cutlery down and settled back into the couch. "Do you have any more of those cookies?"

CONNOR HAD INSTRUCTED me to get in my car fifteen minutes before his fictional eleven o'clock meeting at Grizzle and Girdles. He didn't want me alone in the apartment after the time Albert would expect my boyfriend to have been "taken care of."

I'd spent the morning reading the rest of the hate emails. The content was even worse than the letters, but sending a nasty email demonstrated less commitment than writing and posting snail mail, and I hadn't come up with any great leads.

I did not go out on the "balcony."

At ten forty-five, I dragged my aching body down to the car, eyes peeled like the Queen's grapes, hand hovering over the Taser in my handbag. Mr. Black and Albert were nowhere to be seen. I locked the doors of the Corvette as soon as I was safe inside anyway, and joined the giant conga line of traffic heading bumper-to-bumper toward Bel Air.

I couldn't go to Grizzle and Girdles until Connor texted me to say the hitman trap had been sprung, but Albert's home was in the same general direction as Sunset Boulevard. This way, if Albert had someone tailing me, it would seem as if I was hurrying back to his lair like a good little adoring fan until Connor contacted me and I turned off route.

The message came twenty-five minutes later. I swung west toward Grizzle and Girdles and felt my tension ease away.

The establishment was what it sounded like. A place for grizzled gentleman to enjoy the finest alcoholic beverages served by girls in sexy girdles, accompanying lingerie, and heels. Classier than a topless titty bar, yet catering to the same base desires. I didn't ask how Connor knew the owner so well.

When I rocked up to the address on Sunset Boulevard, Connor was waiting for me in the hedged parking lot. The retro strains of Leo Sayer's "You Make Me Feel Like Dancing" spilled out of the building behind him.

"I've got our hitman," he said.

"Are you sure? How?"

"I saw him slip something in my drink while I was feigning distraction, so my SIG and I"—he patted a holster I hadn't seen before—"persuaded him to go upstairs. Follow me."

He ushered me through the first room of the bar. The few male heads there at that hour swiveled to look at me, but turned away again after a few seconds. No girdle. No interest. Connor steered me to a small, roped-off staircase that led up two floors to a windowless attic used as a store-room. The music below us faded to nothing as we ascended.

Albert's hitman was tied to a chair amongst the stacks of dusty boxes. He looked like my old accountant—slight, balding, and boring. He was gagged, but no one would hear him if he screamed all the way up here anyway.

"What's the plan?" I asked.

Connor pulled out a syringe from his jacket and strode over to the would-be assassin, who yelled something into his gag, his eyes locked on the needle. Connor plunged it into his neck.

The muffled shout turned into a high-pitched scream.

"You've just been injected with a lethal dose of Sverinx," Connor said. "As you'd know in your line of work, that means you'll start feeling restless, and may also experience nausea, sweating, and dizziness. A few minutes after that, you'll start to have heart palpitations. A few minutes after that, you'll be dead."

I gaped at Connor in shock. His face was as cold as I'd ever seen it.

The hitman writhed in his chair, his head shaking back and forth as if he could change the truth if he struggled against it hard enough.

"Unless of course, I give you the antidote," Connor said, pulling another syringe from his jacket.

I started to breathe again.

The hitman stopped struggling.

Connor tucked the antidote out of sight again and ripped off the gag. "Tell me who hired you."

"You've got the wrong guy. I swear. I don't know anything."

"Don't waste your breath. I saw you spike my scotch." He looked at his watch. "Think fast. You only have a few minutes."

The man hesitated. "How do I know you'll give me the antidote if I talk?"

"You don't. But you can be sure I won't if you don't."

The man's face grew shiny with sweat. "Look, I want to help you, but I can't give up my client's name. I'll never work again!"

Connor shrugged and started for the stairs. "Suit yourself then."

"Wait." Connor didn't pause. "You can't do this to me. I haven't even killed anyone." Connor was halfway down the stairs and showed no signs of slowing. "I swear, last week I was a telemarketer. I thought anything would be better than that, but I'll go back to it. Please! Let me live." Connor disappeared.

I have no love for murderers, or telemarketers, but this was taking things too far. I finally picked my jaw up off the floor so I could make my mouth work. "Connor, stop." I ran after him and grabbed his arm. "He'll die!"

Connor shook me off and kept going. "I know."

I stared after him for a split second then ran back up the stairs and slapped the dying hitman on the face. "Talk, you idiot. Whatever you're protecting is no good to you dead."

The man stared at me with wide eyes. Connor was gone. I felt his pulse. It was too fast.

"Just tell me who hired you, and I'll get Connor." I found myself pleading. "I'll make sure he gives you the antidote when he's done."

The hitman's eyes darted around the room before returning to me. His face was pasty white and sweat dripped down his upper lip. A clock on the wall counted out seconds with jarring precision. We both turned to look at it. "Okay," he said, after the longest twenty-six seconds of my life. "It was the chef guy, Albert Alstrom."

I raced down the stairs to find Connor. He was exchanging appreciative looks with one of the girdle girls. I leaped in between them. "He's ready to talk."

Connor gave the girl an apologetic smile and allowed me to drag him to the foot of the stairs. He proceeded to stroll up them as if he had all the time in the world. I followed behind him biting back a scream and considered giving him a shove. I decided against it. I didn't want a needle stabbed in my neck, and I still needed him to pass me on the assessment.

Hitman looked even worse. His sparse hair hung in damp tangles, and the sweat patches under his arms had grown to the size of dinner plates.

His frenzied bloodshot eyes fixed on Connor.

"So you want to talk now, do you? What other jobs have you done for Alstrom?"

"None. I swear."

Connor headed for the stairs again.

"I mean, I haven't completed any! He hired me to kill Josh Summers, but my attempt failed."

Connor paused. "Tell me about your attempt."

"It was at Morning Glory. Yesterday. I put cyanide in his coffee, but he didn't drink it."

"And before that?"

Hitman's face went blank. "What?"

"Your attempt before the coffee shop. Tell me about it."

"There was no other attempt. I only got hired a few days ago, so I've been following him around, trying to find a good opportunity."

"I don't believe you."

Hitman's face went a shade whiter, and tears joined the sweat beading on his face. "I swear, it's the truth." A snot bubble emerged from his left nostril. "Please, you have to give me the antidote. My heart is going crazy."

Connor shrugged and rocked back on his heels, his face an expression of icy calm. "Then I guess you know how your victims feel."

Hitman shook his head. "No! Please. This is my first week on the job. I haven't ever killed anyone."

Connor leaned in close. "I have. So you better tell the damn truth."

Hitman started sobbing. "I am. Please."

"Why the hell would Alstrom hire you if this is your first week on the job?"

"I told you." He gasped. "I was a telemarketer. I know how to talk shit to make a sale."

"I think you're talking shit now."

"No!"

"Then who got past high security and poisoned Josh in his own home? Who used multiple poisons to make sure the job got done right?"

"I swear I don't know anything about it. That's out of my league."

"Whose league is it in?"

Hitman froze mid-sob. "Stalenburg," he whispered.

Connor seemed to recognize the name. "What do you know about Stalenburg?"

"Nothing! Stalenburg is smoke. No one's ever seen him. You only see his work. And only when it's too late."

Connor's phone rang. The conversation was short and terse and his face grew even colder. He turned back to the hitman. "If you live, I suggest you get a new profession." He depressed the second needle into his neck and started for the stairs. "Maybe this time you should choose one people won't want to kill you for."

The hitman slumped in his chair, sobbing quietly to himself. There was nothing I could do for him except maybe call an ambulance. Best to do that once we were well and truly gone. I ran after Connor.

18

I MANAGED TO BITE MY TONGUE down two flights of stairs, past the pretty girls begirded by girdles, and all the way to my car. A public scene was a bad idea.

"Give me your keys," Connor said.

I handed them over numbly.

As soon as we were both in our seats with the doors shut, I turned on him. "How could you?"

Connor started the Corvette and regarded me tiredly. "How could I what?"

"Poison that man. You're as bad as he is."

"Oh? I gave him a choice whether to live or die. It's more than he'd give any of his victims."

"But the Taste Society exists to stop poisonings, not increase them!"

"You could argue that taking out a paid assassin would do just that," he said, driving out of the parking lot without sparing me another glance.

I huffed and puffed, unable to find words.

"Relax, Avery. I dosed him with pure caffeine. It mimics the first symptoms of Sverinx, and fear does the rest."

The world, which had turned on its head when Connor had plunged in the syringe, gradually righted itself as his words sunk in. "Oh." Then, two beats later. "Why the hell didn't you warn me? Do you know how freaked out I was?"

Connor reached over and placed his hand on my thigh, sending alarming tingles upward. I flinched.

"Your acting needs work," he said. "You're supposed to be my girlfriend, but you shy away every time I touch you. You think you could've played your good girl role as well if you'd known the truth? It was *your* panic that broke him."

As soon as he said it, I knew he was right, but it didn't make me feel any better about the whole ordeal.

"You're a jerk."

"Yes. But a jerk who's good at his job."

I stared out the window and told myself over and over that it was all okay, it was just caffeine, we hadn't killed anyone. The knots in my stomach started to ease.

"I need a coffee."

Connor turned in to a Starbucks. Maybe he felt a little bad for what he'd put me through. Or maybe he just wanted to shut me up. It was a long way from a good coffee, but it was also a long way from a drip coffee. I took a grateful sip and thought about what we'd learned. "So, Albert *is* trying to kill Josh, but is only behind the second attempt—not the first?"

"Looks that way. If Albert had access to a pro who could pull off the job at Josh's house, he wouldn't hire an amateur to pick up where the expert left off."

"Right. So there's another poisoner out there." Even worse, if Albert wasn't the key to saving Dana, I'd set a madman on my trail for nothing. And he was still free to pursue me. "Can we at least turn Albert over to the police on attempted murder?"

"No. None of the evidence we have is admissible. The best we can do is tip them off about his habit of drugging and raping his female fans and hope they send someone in undercover."

I suppressed a shudder. "Can we do that, then?"

"I already have. I did it the same day he did it to you. But the LAPD has limited resources. It'll take them a while."

I forced myself to nod. "Okay."

"In the meantime, stay as far from him as possible. Text him expressing your disappointment it won't work out because your jealous boyfriend is still around. Make it sound like you've given up, but keep him thinking you're on his side so his focus stays on me."

"I can't do that. What if he sends a pro to eliminate you next time?"

"You can, and you will."

I chewed my lip. I hated the idea of Albert coming after

me again, but he wasn't trying to *kill* me. It seemed wrong to send him Connor's way to save my own ass.

"I'm far better equipped to deal with anything he's got up his sleeve than you are," Connor pointed out.

"Except for poison. You know—his weapon of choice for ridding himself of competitors?"

Connor was unmoved. "I'm not backing down on this. You can do it, or you can fail."

"You love to throw that threat around don't you?"

"It's not a threat, it's a warning. Shades need to follow orders."

I couldn't afford to fail. I shot a glare at Connor and picked up the phone. Before sending the message, I promised myself I'd taste all his food—even his coffees—without complaint, until Albert was in prison. I thought about sampling all of Meow's food too, but drew the line there. Oliver might get suspicious.

I hit the send button and turned back to Connor. "What do you know about this Stalenburg?"

He shook his head. "It's not her work."

"Her?"

"Since I started this job fourteen years ago, there have been three lethal poisonings of targets protected by Shades in LA. They were all whispered to be Stalenburg's work. The investigations turned up nothing actionable, but there were a few details that led me to believe the legendary Stalenburg is a woman. The only thing I know for sure is that whoever it is, they don't make mistakes. Dana would be dead, and Josh too, if Stalenburg were behind it."

"Everyone makes mistakes." I just make more than most.

"Not Stalenburg."

I patted my pocket for the reassuring bulk of the pepper spray. "What do we do now?"

"We go over everything we have again. I'll drop you home to look through the hate mail while I go and see if I can get anything useful out of our researchers."

"But I've already gone through the hate mail."

"And I've already gone through the details of this case. But we're at a dead end, and Dana is almost out of time. Her doctor called when we were finishing up with our inept telemarketer. Whatever the mystery substance is, her body can't eliminate it, and soon, treating her symptoms won't be enough. Best case scenario, she's got a few days left."

My world turned upside down for the second time that day. "But we just ruled out our best lead"—my voice cracked—"and now we've got nothing."

"Not nothing." His eyes flicked my way, maybe to check I wasn't about to take off my seat belt and jump out the window. "Sometimes when you've been on a case a while, and accumulated more knowledge about the victim, suspects, and circumstances, something you've already seen or read will have new meaning."

It sounded like looking for unicorns in Africa to me, but I nodded anyway. "Okay." I didn't have any better ideas. Maybe unicorns were real—it was possible right? Scientists still discovered new species sometimes. In the blackest depths of the deepest ocean.

My mood was heading there now.

I racked my brain for something positive. "Can we pick up Meow on the way?" Having her home safe and sound might give me the wherewithal to tackle the mountain of hate again.

<hr />

BACK TO SQUARE ONE. I thunked my head on the desk before picking up the first stack of hate mail I'd already gone through.

Maybe I'd missed something. Or maybe Connor was giving me busy work so he could do the real investigating without me underfoot. At least he'd left my Corvette here. I wondered how he'd get his car from the Grizzle and Girdles parking lot.

Not the problem I was supposed to be thinking about.

But anything was better than thinking about Dana.

I cuddled Meow—who'd decided she wouldn't hold a grudge, at least while I was her only source of petting and leftover roast—and started rereading the letters.

This time I was going to cast a wider net. I put aside any that mentioned or hinted at a Wholesome Foods link and even those that suggested the writer was well-off, like the three written on expensive card stock. I was struck again by how many people actually put their names at the bottom of their hateful, threatening letters. Some even used their personal letterhead.

No wonder Connor was so dismissive of hate mail generating credible leads.

As my eyes were glazing over and my thoughts were turning to brownies, the signature on the letter in front of me caught my eye: Kate Williamson.

It took me a moment to place it—the girlfriend from the newspaper clipping. Could it be the same one? It wasn't an uncommon name, but it seemed like a big coincidence. Had I just found a unicorn?

The letter was similar to the one written by the San Diego mother I'd sent Connor to interview, accusing Josh of stealing her daughter away. It was recent, with the postmark a mere three weeks ago. I read it again and noticed she'd written *our daughter*.

According to Josh's file, he didn't have a daughter.

Could he have one he didn't know about? Or was this Kate woman as kooky as her letter sounded? She *had* referenced turkeys on three separate occasions, including my favorite:

Turkey shit is too kind a term for you.

Still, considering Josh's reaction to our blackmail questions, and the newspaper clipping with the girlfriend of the same name, it seemed worth checking out. I called Connor.

"What's wrong?" he asked automatically.

"Why do you always assume something's wrong?"

Connor let meaningful silence trickle down the line.

I huffed. "I just found out Josh might have a daughter he doesn't know about, with Kate Williamson from that newspaper article. Maybe we should take a trip to Porterville."

––––––––––

I WAS STEPPING OUT of the apartment, when I spotted Mr. Black's bulk coming up the stairs. He spotted me too. All the terror of that morning on the streets flooded back to me and froze like a cold cement block around my ankles.

He gave me a little wave.

It was enough to resuscitate my motor skills. I hauled my ass inside and locked the door behind me. My hands shook like a wet dog. Dialing Connor, I grabbed my Taser and rushed over to the nearest window.

Mr. Black was still coming. I watched his muscle-bound mass draw closer, my lungs growing smaller with each step.

I tried to see him like Etta did, hoping it would dull my panic. Once you got past the giant factor, he was pleasing to look at—oval face, well-proportioned features with a generous mouth and brown eyes that might be considered warm if he wasn't trying to kill you. The close-shaved head wasn't to my taste, but he had the skull shape and small, neatly tucked ears to pull it off. The jagged scar on his cheek gave him a dangerous edge, but one you might find attractive if hunting gators was your thing.

He was wearing a white, long-sleeved shirt today. Probably tailor-made to fit over his biceps. I felt a flash of pity for his wife, who'd have to wash all of my bloodstains out. My heart went fluttery again.

He knocked on the door, his face bland, pleasant. A neighbor dropping by to borrow a cup of rat bait. "Ms. Avery. We need to talk."

Did he expect me to open it? I judged my window to be far enough from the door that I'd have time to slam it closed if he stepped toward me. I knew its security was purely psychological anyway. Mr. Black could shatter it with his pinky.

I slid the glass open a crack, clutching the Taser in my other hand. Would it work on him? Did they make Tasers in dinosaur size? "Mr. Black," I said, "I'm sorry I had to run out on your last visit."

Mr. Black gave me a small, tolerant smile that liquefied my insides.

I gulped and tightened my grip on the Taser until it started to hurt. "What would you like to talk about?"

"Now, this isn't polite, ma'am." He ran a giant paw over the stubble on his shorn scalp. "I'd prefer to talk face-to-face."

"I'm sorry, Mr. Black. But my mother told me not to open the door for strangers."

He gave that terrifying smile again. Was he amused? Or was he trying to make me poop my pants?

"I can always break it down," he said. A simple fact. His tone was apologetic.

"If you did that, I'm afraid I'd have to taser you in self-defense, sir."

He looked over at the window. I held up the Taser. He rubbed his chin, and I noticed he was wearing a pink Disney Princess watch.

"I don't like being tasered very much."

"I wouldn't like to taser you very much either," I said sincerely. "Listen. Surely we can work something out. I need all my bones unbroken today, and it sure would be a shame to ruin that lovely watch by falling on it when you lose control of your muscles after I zap you."

He contemplated the watch. "My daughter would be upset if I broke the watch. I'm only borrowing it on account of my other one broke."

I nodded. "Yes, we don't wanna upset your daughter. Can't we strike some kind of deal?"

"Like what?"

"Well." I thought fast. "I know you're just doing your job. What were your exact instructions?"

He searched his memory, then recited the words one at a time. "Find that stupid bitch and make her pay."

My heart sped up. "Right. And did they give you a timeline?"

He shook his head. "I don't think so."

"Well, I can make up all the missed payments in just eight and a half days. You see, I've got a new job, and that's when I get my first paycheck and finish my probation period. Then they'll loan me the money for the rest." I had no idea how long my practical assessment took, or if the Taste Society would lend me the money after they'd already turned me down once, but I figured eight and a half extra days wouldn't hurt. "The truth is, even if you break all the bones in my body, I won't be able to pay any faster. So, for the sake of your daughter and her watch, how about you tell your boss you've terrified me into getting the money, but it's gonna take me nine days to come up with it."

"What about selling your car?" he asked.

Crap. I hadn't realized he'd seen me in it. "It's not mine, I promise. It's a company car."

There was more thoughtful chin rubbing as Mr. Black considered this.

"It wouldn't be lying, Mr. Black. You really have terrified me into getting the money."

The chin thing continued.

"Please. I'm just trying to get by and provide for my family, like you are."

His hand dropped to his side. "You have a family?"

What had possessed me to say that? I thought fast. "Er. Well. I have a cat. I'll show you." I ran and fetched Meow and held her up to the window, which was difficult while clutching my Taser and phone at the same time.

"Cute," Mr. Black said.

"Please?"

"What's to stop you from bolting? Then I'd get in trouble."

I chewed my lip. "How about you hold something of mine hostage until I pay?"

He seemed to like this idea. "Like that cute cat?"

Shit. "Oh, I suppose. But she's got a medical condition

and is very delicate. In fact, she just got back from the vet an hour ago. So you need to give her lots of medicine and round the clock care. Plus, she likes to poop in shoes," I lied.

He wrinkled his nose. On him it looked a bit like a fissure splitting the earth. "I wouldn't like poop in my shoes. What else do you have of value?"

I thought fast and realized I owned nothing of value. Because I was broke. "Um . . ."

"How about that car?"

"It's not mine."

"Sure. But you could loan it to a friend for a few days. They wouldn't even know."

My mind raced, but I couldn't come up with any better ideas. "Okay."

"Deal?"

"Deal," I said, before figuring out I was going to have to open the door to give him the key. I took a deep breath, hung up my phone, put the Taser in my waistband, and removed the Corvette key from my key ring. Then I stood in front of the locked door trying to grow enough balls to open it. I thought about only opening it as far as the chain would allow, or just throwing the key out the window, but I had a feeling Mr. Black would be offended if I didn't trust him to uphold his end of the deal. I didn't want to offend him. I steeled myself and swung the door wide open.

I forgot how to breathe when I saw how big he was up close. When I regained control of my bodily functions, I handed him my key. "Please look after her for me."

He took it from my hand gently. "It was a pleasure doing business with you, ma'am."

He's just a big gentle giant, I told myself. *Wouldn't hurt a Disney Princess watch.*

I gave him a smile. "Thanks for being willing to negotiate. Say hi to your daughter for me."

He returned my smile, and I concentrated on controlling my sphincter. "Will do. You have a nice day." He turned to go, but hesitated and looked back at me. "I should warn you, Ms. Avery." He fiddled with the key I'd given him. "If you don't have the money in eight and a half days, I'm going to have to break you real bad to keep my boss happy."

He waited for me to respond. Like he needed my approval.

I couldn't give it.

The moment stretched out.

I forced my head to jerk up and down. As soon as he lumbered away again, I shut and locked the door, then yielded to my quaking legs and slid down to the floor. Okay. So I just gave away a car that wasn't mine that was worth as much as my accumulated payments. To a criminal. Who said he'd give it back. Connor would understand. It wouldn't ruin my chances of passing the final evaluation and convincing the Taste Society to advance me the money. Sure it wouldn't.

I slumped down even lower against the musty green carpet. If I couldn't get the money, running home wouldn't save me now. I was a dead woman.

19

CONNOR KNOCKED on the door a few minutes later. I scraped myself off the carpet, gave my hair a quick pat, and let him in.

"Thanks for the phone call," he said. "I guess we'll be going to Porterville in my car."

I shot him a sheepish smile, grabbed Kate Williamson's letter off the counter, and patted him on the cheek like Etta had done to Oliver. "Gosh, you're good at deducing things, schnookums. You should be a detective."

Maybe I was overcompensating for the whole lying on the carpet thing.

"Call me schnookums one more time and I'll fail you."

"You're in a happy mood then, I see." I gestured to the open door and the staircase beyond. "Shall we get going?"

He led the way out, and I locked the door behind us. We had to sidestep to squeeze past the outdoor sofa that had appeared by Etta's door this afternoon. I had only myself to blame.

"You realize giving away the company car is a lot like getting a loan from the Taste Society like I suggested yesterday, right?" he asked as we headed down the stairs. "Only dumber."

Okay. I admit it. I hadn't thought it through very well. My mind had been preoccupied with the small matter of preventing my bones from being broken. "I didn't give it away. I just let him borrow it for a few days, until I can pay them."

"And if you can't pay them in time?"

"Well, the Taste Society has the Corvette insured right? I figured they'd get their money back if they claimed it was stolen. Much faster than if they gave me a loan." I'd figured no such thing but thought it was a stroke of genius to pretend I had. I peeked at Connor to see if he was impressed. He wasn't.

"Especially if I don't pass this assessment," I added.

Connor grunted and opened the car door for me.

I waited until he'd sat down too and started the engine before chancing it. "I was meaning to ask you about how long these assessments usually take."

He gave me a dirty look. And not a sexy dirty look either. "I guess yours will have to go for a maximum of eight more days."

"You're amazing. Thanks, sch—" I caught myself just in time "—sharklike one," I finished. Brilliant save.

Connor raised an eyebrow. "Sharklike one?"

"Um. Well, I mean you seem kind of cold and scary at first, but you're just misunderstood, and responsible for way less deaths than a lot of people think."

"I see," was all he said, but the comparative lightness of his tone made me pretty sure I'd distracted him from my encounter with Mr. Black.

"So, what did you do while I was digging up Josh's potential mystery child?"

"Like I told you, I wanted to review all of the case information. Having multiple people on a case is useful for covering more ground, but it means connections can get overlooked because no one's seen the complete data set. Old information can have new meaning in the light of something you've found out since, too. So I started with Dana's file and went from there. One of the researchers looked through her file for red flags at the beginning of the case, but it's a statistical improbability that a Shade would have anything to do with the poison attempt, so I hadn't read it until today. When I did, I found out that the woman in the clipping, Kate Williamson, is Dana's mother."

"You're kidding. How did we miss that?"

"Simple. Dana ran away when she was sixteen and changed her last name to Williams. She explained everything to the Taste Society when we did the background check, but nothing about it suggested her mother would try to kill her and a celebrity, so it didn't raise any flags and no one thought any more about Kate Williamson. We only found the newspaper clipping later, and a different member of the team dug up the article it came from, so the connection wasn't made."

Okay, I could understand that.

"Even when I found out, it didn't seem worth investigating because all it did was give Dana an innocent reason for having the clipping. Her birth certificate lists her father as unknown, so when I saw she'd requested to work with Josh Summers, I figured she was just curious about her mom's old boyfriend."

Shades are allowed to nominate the top three celebrities they'd like to work with, and if a job ever comes up with one of those people, that Shade gets priority placement consideration for the assignment. So it was no coincidence Josh and Dana had been working together.

"It wasn't until you called with the news that Kate Williamson might have had a child with Josh that the connection became meaningful. If Dana is Josh's daughter, that changes things. Maybe Kate felt abandoned by both of them and did it out of spite or heartbreak, or maybe someone else knew Dana was Josh's daughter and targeted her because of it. We're about to find out."

"Good."

"I also made sure Kate Williamson wasn't dead *before* we drove all the way out to talk to her."

I rolled my eyes but turned away first so he couldn't see. "That's good too."

"In the meantime, the research team is searching for connections between Wholesome Food stakeholders and people we know accessed Josh's house during the window of opportunity. My criminal contact reported one hit out on Josh Summers, not two, and I'd expect word to get around if there were two contracts out on the same target. Since we've ruled out our telemarketer hitman from being the one who planted the Ambience, somebody at Wholesome Foods bribing or blackmailing Colette, Juan, or Tahlia seems the most likely scenario. If we don't uncover any new leads on this trip, that is."

We lapsed into silence.

A lot of admiring of the scenery later, I was starting to feel bored. I looked at the clock on the dash. We'd been driving for thirty minutes and only just reached the northern outskirts of the San Fernando Valley. Two hours and ten minutes to go.

I was going to have to make conversation. "So, Connor. Do you have a real girlfriend when you're not training up new recruits?"

"Are you asking because you'd like to be one?"

"No. I'm asking to pass the time."

"Pass the time some other way then."

Ten minutes ticked by. "Are you hungry?" I asked. "Because you look kind of hungry."

"You must be mistaking me for a shark again."

"Fine. *I'm* hungry. Can we please stop at a drive-through?"

Connor exhaled slowly. "Which drive-through?"

"Anywhere will do. Whatever one we come across next."

The lucky winner was Jack in the Box. I ordered a Bacon Ranch Monster Taco with fries and a salted caramel ice cream shake. This occupied me for another fifteen minutes.

"Do you think our caffeinated hitman has escaped yet?" I asked a few minutes later.

"For someone from Australia, where everything is miles from everything else, you're not good at road trips," Connor said.

"Well, usually I listen to music."

"Fine. Turn on some music." His car stereo had Bluetooth, so after a little fiddling, I connected my phone to it and started my favorite playlist.

Two songs later, he turned it off.

"Do you feel like talking now?" I asked.

"No, you just have terrible taste in music."

"Are you kidding?" How could he not like Montaigne or Mumford & Sons? On the other hand, he liked drip coffee, so maybe I should've seen it coming. "What do you listen to, then?"

"Classical mostly."

"Seriously?" It struck me again that we would never work as a real couple. Not that I wanted to be part of a Connor couple, but if I did, we wouldn't be able to get through a single day without arguing over coffee or music. Travel would be atrocious. Sex would be sublime. Or so I imagined anyway.

"Be honest with me. What are my chances of passing and getting hired permanently?"

A line appeared in Connor's forehead. The equivalent of me thunking my head on the steering wheel.

"Now is not the best time to ask me that."

Okay. I knew I was annoying him, but I needed the answer to this one. "Please?"

Connor exhaled slowly again. "So far, your poison detection has been excellent. I can't see you failing on that account. However, your acting is inconsistent. You seem to do okay when you put your mind to it, but often you forget your cover and react instinctively, like when you flinch. Other times, your attitude gets in the way."

My hopes sank like a scrawny kid in a swimming pool. I hoped Mr. Black enjoyed the Corvette.

"It does take some Shades a while to pull their acting together. It's one of the reasons for the faux first assignment. But you've given yourself a short timeline."

I rubbed my face. "How do I get myself into these situations?"

Connor took it as a rhetorical question. Small mercies.

"I'm happy to give you some leeway, considering the unorthodox nature of this assessment," he said, "but you need to show me you can pull it together and keep it together. On some assignments, the paparazzi will be hounding you every moment of every day. The Taste Society can't afford for you to be unconvincing."

"Makes sense." I swallowed the lump in my throat. "Should I be going to acting classes or something?"

Connor glanced at me. "You could. But it's not that

you can't be convincing, you just need to focus on staying in character better. And trying not to piss off your client too much."

I swallowed again. Okay. I could do that. Right?

"Should I be in character now?" I asked. "Have I told you how beautiful you are today?"

"When you're in a private, contained area with your client, like a car, or home alone, you don't need to talk the talk. Even so, you should maintain appropriate body language. There's always a chance of a paparazzo hiding in the bushes with a telephoto lens. If there are any staff around, it's best to stay in character audibly as well, in case any of them are in the habit of eavesdropping."

Maybe this job didn't pay enough after all. Not that I had any other options if I wanted to be free of debt sometime this decade. Short of forcing my parents to sell their house, anyway.

Connor must have noticed my downcast expression. "It gets easier, Avery."

"I guess not all the clients could be as bad as you," I joked.

He patted my leg. I didn't flinch. "That's the spirit."

One pee stop and ninety minutes later, we arrived in Porterville; a dot on the map one hundred and sixty miles north of LA. Connor might have been speeding.

Porterville wasn't any more impressive in the flesh than it had been as a dot on the map. The landscape was flatter than month-old roadkill and just as dry, with the distant mountains of the Sequoia National Forest the only point of interest. Large suburban blocks holding mostly squat, characterless houses dominated the town. Landscaping was not a high priority in Porterville either, with brown lawns and chain-link fences the current vogue.

If the address we had was correct, Kate Williamson lived in a small, run-down clapboard house on the outskirts of town. It was unfenced and isolated, surrounded by dry, vacant land and a factory of some sort in the distant background.

We parked the car on the road out front.

The home's timber facade had once been painted mint green but now sat somewhere between brown and gray. A rusted gutter on the corner was attempting to jump ship in the hopes of a happier life, and her garden was a dust bowl, even less green than the paint.

As I placed my first foot in the dirt, an abrupt chorus of gobbles rang out, followed closely by the appearance of a flock of at least thirty turkeys. They ran toward us, stopped about a yard in front of us, and stalked back and forth, their feathers fluffed. I took a step back. They took a step forward. "I don't think they want us here," I whispered to Connor.

He smirked at me. "They're just turkeys." He strode ahead. The turkeys retreated, but their feathers ruffled further, and one of them gobbled in a sharper tone than before.

"I'm serious," I said, retreating another step. "We raised chickens when I was a kid, and there were some nasty roosters that would attack. I don't trust them." These turkeys were *much* bigger than those roosters.

Connor looked back at me in exasperation. As soon as his back was turned, the turkeys closed in.

"Watch out!" I yelled.

The front door of the house opened, and an older version of the woman from the newspaper clipping stepped out.

"You're not hurting my turkeys are you?" The turkeys ran over at the sound of her voice and milled around her like ducklings around their mother.

I resisted taking another step backward. "No, ma'am. We were just admiring them," I lied.

She was pretty in a middle-aged girl-next-door kind of way, but her mismatched baggy clothing and crooked haircut suggested she didn't care about that. She patted a couple of the turkeys on their bald, wrinkly heads. "Who are you and what do you want, then?"

Connor spoke up this time. "I'm a private investigator, Connor Stiles, and this is my colleague, Isobel Avery."

I guess he'd decided presenting a businesslike front to Ms. Williamson was more important than working on my acting skills.

"We'd like to speak to you about a matter concerning Josh Summers."

Her eyes narrowed at him.

"And your daughter, Dana, too," I added.

She hesitated a moment longer, still patting the turkeys absentmindedly. "My Dana did you say? Then I suppose you better come in." Now that she'd made up her mind, she gestured at us impatiently. "Come on, come in, my turkeys won't bite."

Personally, I had doubts about that, but I kept my mouth shut and caught up to Connor so I was close behind him when we waded through the gang of turkeys.

We stepped through the door, and I was exceedingly relieved when Kate left the turkeys outside. She led us through a dark, wood-paneled hallway and into a living room crammed with a sofa, two recliners, a coffee table, and four display cabinets. Miscellaneous items were scattered over every available inch of the display cabinets, from dirty dishes and newspapers, to framed photographs and turkey figurines.

"Would you like a cup of tea?" she asked. "I'd offer you a sandwich, but I fed all my bread to the turkeys. How can anyone say no to those sweet faces?"

Connor and I exchanged a look.

"A cup of tea would be lovely," I said.

She pointed to a tattered floral couch. "Sit down there, and I'll put the kettle on."

We sat. I found a turkey feather trying to stab me in the butt and placed it on the armrest. Kate returned carrying a tray with a couple of mugs, sugar packets that looked like they'd been lifted from a café, and a jug of milk.

"Now, what's this about my Dana?"

"Do you have any pictures of her?" I asked. Years of customer service had taught me people loved showing you pictures of their kids, even if they weren't on great terms with them anymore. I guess the photos reminded them of happier times.

"Of course." She got up and grabbed a picture off the nearest display cabinet. From what I could see, all the other frames held portraits of turkeys. One had a bow tie. "Here she is when she was fifteen, just a year before she left me."

Connor and I looked at it.

It was teenage Dana Williams, holding a turkey.

I suspected the turkeys might have something to do with why she didn't talk about her past. "Where did she go when she left?"

"I don't know. She ran away and didn't see fit to tell me. I hoped you might have news for me."

"Why'd she run away?" Connor asked.

"That's what I'd love to know!" Kate flapped her arms as if they were turkey wings. "She was a teenager, I guess. I thought that's all it was at the time. Thought she needed some space, so I gave it to her. I didn't like my parents none too much at that age either. But she still hasn't come home." She lowered herself back into her chair as if she felt every one of her forty-four years.

I experienced a rush of sympathy for her.

"Could she have gone to stay with her father?" Connor asked.

"Her father? Pfft. He didn't even know she existed."

"Did Dana know who her father was?"

Kate deflated again. "Well, I sure never told her. I didn't want her to get stars in her eyes and follow him. Nothing wrong with raising turkeys. But she was always asking me about him as a kid. She must've figured it out before she left, because she found my memory box and took the picture of him and me from it."

She sank deeper into her recliner. "I don't think she went straight to him. Reckon I would've heard about it from him, if nothing else. But I saw her and Josh together in some celebrity gossip magazine just recently, so she must have caught up with him at last." She snorted. "Would you believe the stupid reporter thought they were a couple? But then, he didn't even get her surname right neither."

For the first time since sitting down, she picked up her cup of tea and took a sip. "It upset me at first—that Josh was with her and I wasn't. I thought about tracking her down, but I guess I was hoping she'd come back to me of her own volition, like my turkeys do when I let them roam." Her gaze had drifted past us, as if she'd forgotten we were in the room.

Connor pulled a photocopy of the clipping out of his pocket. "Was this the photo of yours she took?"

Kate looked at it, and her eyes went misty. "Yep, that's it. It's one of the few pictures we had of us together." She started to hand it back, but hesitated. "Would you mind if I kept it?"

"Go ahead," said Connor. "Sorry to ask, but are you sure Josh Summers is Dana's father?"

"Hell yes, I'm sure. At the time I got knocked up, he was the only one I'd ever played hide the hot dog with."

I fought back a smile. "If you don't mind me saying, you don't seem to dislike Josh. Why didn't you tell him you were pregnant?"

She looked down at her hands and started picking at a bit of skin around her thumbnail. "We loved each other, but after that car crash, every time he looked at me it just made him remember how he'd killed Henry. He left a few months later, straight after graduation, and I thought it was best for him if he stayed gone."

"Yes, we wanted to talk to you about how he killed Henry," Connor said, without batting an eye.

"Oh turkey shit," Kate said, "He didn't kill no one. I just meant he felt guilty about it."

"We both know that's not true," Connor said.

I tried not to let myself give away his bluff.

Kate searched our faces. "You guys aren't reporters are you? Or cops?"

"No, ma'am," Connor said. "We work for a company that's protecting Dana and Josh."

"Don't call me ma'am. It makes me feel old."

"Yes, ma— Ms. Williamson."

"How're you protecting them, then?"

I was leaving this one to Connor.

"Josh hired us. We think someone could be trying to harm or blackmail them, and we're working to prevent it."

"So, did Josh tell you what really happened?" she asked.

I jumped in. "He finds it painful to talk about, so we wanted to ask you for the full story." I pulled her letter out of my pocket, improvising as I went along. "But he gave us this letter to help us find you."

She stared at it for a second. "Damn, I was angry when I wrote that. It was after I first saw that picture of him and Dana together in that magazine. Like I said, I couldn't figure what right he had to see our daughter when I haven't for so long. I raised her by myself you know, just her, me, and the turkeys."

"You must have done a great job too if she's so successful now," I said.

"I guess so." Her eyes went down to her lap. "It was a terrible accident. We'd been to a party and Josh was driving us home. I was in the backseat behind Henry. All of a sudden, there was something on the road, so Josh swerved and we hit a tree. Josh and me were wearing our seat belts and were just banged around a bit, but Henry wasn't. He flew straight through the windshield, busted the whole thing. Josh got out real quick to check on him, but it was too late.

"We sat outside the car in shock, waiting for the police to show up. Then I remembered reading about some guy who'd gone to prison for killing someone in a car accident. I knew Josh'd been speeding. Maybe fifteen miles an hour over the limit. Neither of us wanted him to go to prison, so we agreed to say I was in the front passenger seat, Henry was driving, and Josh was behind him—so the seat belt marks matched up, see. The whole windshield was gone, so you couldn't tell which side he went through." She looked up at us. "Henry wouldn't have minded. Josh and him were best friends, and it wouldn't make a difference to him no more."

"Have you ever told this story to anyone else?" Connor asked.

"No. I promised Josh I never would."

"Not even Dana?"

She shook her head. "Especially not Dana."

Connor stood up. "Thank you so much for your time."

"And the tea," I added.

Kate searched our faces again. "If you see Dana, could you tell her . . . tell her I miss her?"

A large part of me wanted to spill out the whole truth: that her daughter was fighting for her life, and she might never see her again. But Dana was a private person and hadn't contacted her mother in years. Who was I to overrule that decision for her? There was no way the Taste Society would let Kate see her either, and Dana was in a medically induced coma, so it's not like they'd get a chance to say goodbye.

The best outcome for everyone was to make sure Dana survived.

"I'll tell her, Ms. Williamson, if I can," I promised.

She picked up the turkey feather that I'd dug out of my backside and placed on the armrest. "Take this with you. To remind you," she said. "Dana used to love collecting their feathers. You should have seen all the necklaces she made with them."

I took the feather, and we waded back through the turkeys to the car.

20

"YOU DID WELL IN THERE, AVERY," Connor said. "Do you want to pick up something to eat for the drive home?"

I put my hand to my heart. "You're finally starting to understand me." We stopped at Panda Express, and I was glad to see they didn't offer turkey on the menu. I ordered honey sesame chicken, shanghai steak, and spring rolls with a side of mixed veggies and a soda.

"Are you sure you don't want anything?" I asked Connor as he handed me my bag of goodies.

"I'm sure."

I started on the spring rolls and took a sip of soda to wash down the salt. At first I thought the soda must be a weird Chinese version of Mountain Dew. Then I realized it was drugged. With niohydramine, which was potent enough to put a charging bull to sleep. I spat what remained of my mouthful back into the cup. "Connor! Did you drug this?"

"Damn," he said, without bothering to look at me. "I was hoping you wouldn't notice so I could enjoy the drive in peace."

I wanted to hit him, but his lecture on my attitude and acting was still fresh in my mind. Plus, I was about due for another test, especially if I wanted him to pass me in just eight more days. I returned to my food.

"Are you going to eat all of that?" he asked after a few minutes.

"What's it to you?" I made sure to keep my body language friendly. Even if he was calling me fat.

"I wouldn't mind a bite."

"I thought you weren't hungry."

"I thought you were going to fall asleep and I'd get the leftovers."

"In that case, I am definitely going to eat all of it."

Connor watched me shovel the food down my throat. "I'll tell the higher-ups you gave your car to a criminal."

I handed him the remains. At least he hadn't said *another* car to a criminal. Maybe the pimply teenager didn't count.

"So," I said, "now that I'm not going to be sleeping all the way home, why don't you try picking a topic of conversation."

"Tell me how you think the new information impacts the case."

I shifted around to give my butt, which was growing numb after sitting for so many hours, some relief.

"Well, it could explain why Josh seems a bit paranoid and doesn't have any close relationships. And why he was so uptight when we asked about blackmail. But I don't see how it's related to Dana." I thought about it some more. "Unless someone who knew Henry somehow found out that Josh was driving and wants revenge. But how?"

Connor considered this. "In a small community like the one they grew up in, it's possible somebody remembered them leaving the party and saw Josh driving, or even passed them on the road. But why wait twenty-six years to act on it?"

"Unless the person who saw Josh driving only recently mentioned it to someone who loved Henry."

"It's possible," Connor said. "We'll ask Josh about it."

"Okay." I wiggled again to make myself more comfortable. There was nothing more we could do on the case until we got back to LA, and the sky had grown dark, so there was nothing to see out the window. Even after giving Connor half my meal, my stomach was full and content. I yawned.

I found the appropriate lever and angled my backrest down as far as it'd go. "I think I'll catch a nap." I didn't need to see Connor's face to know he must be pleased. "You can even listen to classical music if you want." I was feeling generous. After all, I'd neglected to admit before that road trip rules among my family and friends stipulate the driver picks the music.

I let out a final, jaw-popping yawn and fell asleep to the strains of Vivaldi.

———

SOMEBODY GRABBED MY ARM. I yelped and lashed out. Then I woke up properly. Connor was sporting a fresh scratch across his cheek.

"Oops," I said.

He gave me a look. "You could have warned me you're dangerous to wake up."

"I didn't know I was. It must be this case making me jumpy."

"Uh-huh. The case. Nothing to do with Mr. Black."

I gave him a bright smile. "Not anymore. Not after I took care of him this afternoon."

Connor lifted his eyes skyward for a second. "Let's go and have a chat with Mr. Summers."

We made it to the doorstep before Connor's phone rang. He spoke for a minute, disconnected, and turned to me, his mouth set in a grim line. "Bad news, Isobel. Dana had a heart attack."

Shock hit me like a right hook to the gut. She couldn't die. She wasn't allowed to.

"They've stabilized her again, but the doctor says the toxin is causing progressively more damage. At the moment, they're managing her symptoms, but they won't be able to stay on top of them as she gets worse. She's heading fast toward irreversible organ damage."

I forced the words out. "How fast?"

"He said if her deterioration continues at the current rate, about sixteen hours."

My Panda Express rose to the back of my throat, and I swallowed hard to stop it splattering all over Josh's door.

Connor knocked before I had a chance to compose myself, and Josh opened the door, as usual. Privacy comes at the cost of forgoing house staff. "Come in. You said you have news? Is Dana okay?"

My stomach heaved again. No she isn't, I wanted to yell.

"Why don't we sit down," Connor suggested.

Josh led us to the living room, and we took the same seats as last time. I kept my mouth firmly shut and concentrated on keeping my meal where it belonged while Connor relayed the doctor's news. I would've liked to shut my ears as well. Hearing it again made it more real.

Josh looked like he was going be sick too.

"But that's not what we came to talk to you about," Connor said. "We visited Kate Williamson today."

Josh flinched. "What? Why?"

"Is your Shade out of earshot?"

"Yes, he's gone home for the evening. What's this about?"

"We know you were the one driving when Henry Smythe died."

I blinked, and it was like someone had grabbed the cheerful and confident celebrity that everyone knew and loved, and replaced him with a doppelgänger. His features were the same, but somehow his golden skin looked sallow, his chiseled features blurred, and his green eyes tormented. He opened his mouth, but nothing came out.

"Please be assured, Mr. Summers, this is covered by the Taste Society's confidentiality policy. We're only concerned about this to the extent it might impact your case. It's possible someone is trying to avenge Henry."

Josh gave a slow nod, and I watched as his face transformed again, this time to a shadow of its former self.

"Kate swears she hasn't told another soul about it. She only told us after we proved we were working to protect you. We're wondering if anyone could have seen you leaving the party that night and getting into the driver's seat. Or if someone might have passed you on the road and noticed you driving?"

Josh was silent for a long time. "It couldn't have been anyone passing us on the road. It was pitch-black, and they wouldn't have seen anything except headlights." More seconds ticked by. "We said our goodbyes inside, but I think Patrick . . . Patrick MacCallum it might have been, left at the same time we did. I remember because I was surprised to see him at the party. Most of the people there were in our grade, except for a few girls who were dating seniors, but he was a grade below."

"Do you remember anything else about him?"

"No. I'm not even sure that's his last name."

"Who would've been most affected by Henry's death?"

Josh crumpled in on himself as if he couldn't bear to think about it. "His family. The rest of us, we were just kids, and no one was as close to Henry as I was. He had a girl-friend, but she was dating someone else not long afterward. His family though . . ." His voice cracked. "No parent ever recovers from burying their kid. And his little sister adored him." He got to his feet. "Excuse me, please."

Connor and I waited in silence while Josh pulled himself together in the other room. He returned a few minutes later, his green eyes rimmed with red.

"Kate Williamson told us something else, Mr. Summers," Connor said.

Josh slumped on the sofa across from us, his body language conveying he was too weary to care.

"She said that Dana Williams is her daughter. And yours."

Tactful, Connor, tactful.

Josh's head jerked up, and his red eyes latched on to Connor's with scary intensity. Connor held his gaze until Josh made a choking noise and looked away.

"H-how?" he managed to get out a few moments later.

"Kate said you were the only one she'd ever slept with when she found out she was pregnant. She didn't tell you because you'd already left, and she didn't want to force you to come back after everything that happened."

Josh put his hands over his mouth, as if to stop the choking noises coming out of it. His eyes were wet again. I studied the pattern on the rug, wishing I could give him more privacy.

Minutes passed. The noises quieted, and I heard Josh take a deep breath.

"Did Dana know?" he asked.

"We believe she did," Connor said. "She requested to work with you, and we're assuming it's why she had the newspaper clipping in her apartment. She must've wanted to get to know you before deciding whether to reveal herself as your daughter."

I realized they were talking about her in the past tense. "Does," I said. "We believe she *does* know. She's still alive. We can still save her."

Both men turned to look at me, and I experienced the full weight of their combined gazes. Then Josh nodded, Connor followed suit, and the air lightened, just a fraction.

Connor rose to leave. "Sorry for the unfortunate circumstances around this news, Mr. Summers. If you believe in God, now would be the time to pray we find her poisoner."

I rose too but hesitated before turning away. "Are you okay? Is there someone we can call?"

Josh shook his head. Connor was walking out. Even so, I stepped forward and rested a hand on Josh's shoulder. "There's still time to save her," I said. "Remember that tonight." Then I hurried after Connor.

He started the car. "We'll follow this up tomorrow."

I was going to argue, but the dashboard clock said it was past midnight, and Connor looked more drained than I'd ever witnessed. If there was one thing I'd learned about him, it was that he took personal responsibility for the safety of those around him. And Dana was a long way from safe.

I was seeing the vulnerability in all the men around me tonight.

We left the silence undisturbed as he drove me home. I tried not to wonder whether my presence had hindered his work on the case. Whether Dana would've had a better chance if I'd never come to LA.

Connor pulled the car to a stop outside my apartment and left it idling as he opened my door for me. "Night, Isobel."

I kissed him on the cheek. For the paparazzi. "Good night, Connor."

IT WAS REFRESHING to walk up the stairs and squeeze past Etta's sofa without keeping an eye out for the menacing bulk of Mr. Black. But I should've been looking out for the spindly outline of Mr. Alstrom.

He reached the stair landing seconds after I did, while I was digging through my bag for keys. "I've missed you, sweet cheeks."

I stifled a shriek. "Albert? What are you doing here?"

His long fingers stroked my jawline. "It's okay. Connor left. It's just us."

This was not good news. I surreptitiously reached for my pepper spray. As much as I'd have liked to spray the bastard, it was better to stay in character if I could.

He stepped closer. "I've been thinking about you. Every minute we've been apart. I need to have you." His hand trailed down my arm, then snaked around to the small of my back.

I gripped the canister tighter and pried my tongue off from where it was stuck to the roof of my mouth. "Um. Albert. I've been thinking about you too."

He licked his lips.

"But Connor just left to get a bottle of wine. He'll be back any minute." I didn't have to fake the urgency in my voice.

Albert's eyes switched from cloudy with lust to furious in less than a second. He swore, grabbed my head with both hands, and shoved his lips against mine. "This isn't over," he vowed, before whirling around and striding down the stairs.

I stared after him and prayed he was wrong.

———

I LOCKED THE DOOR behind me with shaking hands. They really ought to make locks that are easier to use when you're panicky.

Meow stood watch as I placed my pepper spray and Taser on the bathroom sink and took a long shower to wash the Albert off of me. Then I fed her and downed a hot chocolate in the hopes of soothing my nerves before climbing into bed.

It didn't work.

I wished Oliver would come home so I wasn't alone. Even Meow had left me, choosing to stake out Oliver's bed before he could crawl into it. I got up one last time to check the lock on the front door and transfer my Taser and pepper spray to my bedside table. I'd put Kate's feather there too.

I finally made it under the sheets, but suspected I had about as much chance of falling asleep as I did of figuring out who was behind the attempted murder.

Fourteen hours. If the doctor's estimate was correct. How could I spend any of that sleeping?

A useless hour later, once I'd gone through every clue we'd uncovered and every possible scenario I could summon up with my exhausted brain, my thoughts drifted. How tragic that an accident at the age of eighteen had tormented Josh his entire life. It had taken away his best friend, built walls that kept him at arm's length from everyone else, and trapped him in constant fear that his secret might be exposed. Yes, he'd been recklessly speeding, but who hasn't done something dumb at least once? The difference was most people didn't end up paying for their moment of foolishness for the rest of their lives.

Okay, I was still paying for my own moment of foolishness in marrying Steve. Maybe that's why I could sympathize so much. But at least mine didn't end in the death of my best friend. I might have killed a tree or two with all the overdue notices, though.

I rolled over and tried to think of something else. My mind chose Kate. She was probably fast asleep, with no clue her one and only daughter was about to die. It was all so wrong. But there was nothing I could do for any of them until my brain had rested. Maybe not even then.

My brain wouldn't take the hint, and I found myself pondering Dana's choices. Why hadn't she gone back to her mum if she'd left in a teenage huff? And why hadn't she told Josh she was his daughter? She did seem to be cautious and private to the point of mild paranoia, like her dad, in retrospect. She must have wanted to get to know him before saying anything. She might have been planning to go back to her mum too but put it on the back burner in the everyday business of life. After all, she'd have assumed she had plenty of time.

A lot more than thirteen hours.

When my sheets became so entangled with my legs that I could no longer toss and turn, I pulled out the hate mail again. I made it through the remaining pile of the snail mail variety before crawling back into bed.

This time, with the Taser tucked under my pillow and my brain too tired to form coherent thoughts, I finally managed to get a few hours' sleep.

21

CONNOR ARRIVED AT SEVEN-THIRTY in the morning looking like he'd had an equally rough night. Somehow his fatigue lent an attractive, rugged air to his handsome features.

Mine made me look like someone had poured molasses down my lower eyelids and aged me ten years overnight.

I was out on the landing, Taser and pepper spray on standby, trying to use my untapped mind powers to turn my cup of tea into coffee. He came up the stairs and trailed his hand along my arm. "Your cactus is dying," he pointed out.

I stared at it in shock. How did I manage to kill a damn cactus?

"I have news," he said. "Let's go somewhere we can talk."

I was impatient and might've argued we could talk right there if Etta's curtain hadn't just twitched.

We headed out for breakfast, and Connor let me pick the place. Maria had packed him a thermos, so I was even allowed to choose an eatery that only made espresso coffees. I didn't know whether to kiss him or Maria. Maybe both. I couldn't remember the last time I needed a coffee this bad.

I chose a tiny café in Mar Vista that served crepes and good-quality espresso. Importantly, it was only a few minutes' drive from my apartment and had fast service. Efficiency was my first priority today, after caffeine.

Once we'd squeezed ourselves into the cramped al fresco area and given our orders to the pretty waitress, Connor filled me in. "I've done some research into Henry's surviving family. His mother died a year after his death. Reading between the lines, it's likely she committed suicide. That gives Henry's father or sister a pretty good motive if they found out Josh was driving. The father has been charged a bunch of times with public intoxication since then. The sister is clean. Of course, we couldn't access either of their medical records to find out if one of them has an Ambience prescription, but the sister's a nurse so she'd have more familiarity with drugs than the average person."

My double shot short black arrived, and I savored the first sip. "How do we question them without making them suspicious? Especially if they don't know what really happened."

"We don't. I'm not about to drag them through Henry's death again unless we have hard evidence suggesting they did it. I've asked the research team to prioritize searching for any links between the Smythe family and the people we know had access to Josh's home during the window of opportunity. We should hear back within the hour. In the meantime, let's have a chat with Patrick."

"What about the hitman angle?"

"I can't see them having the contacts to get a good contract killer. The initial indicators on their finances suggest they couldn't afford one either, but the team will take a closer look."

"So, how do we find Patrick?"

"Let's see if there's a Patrick MacCallum on Facebook who went to the same school."

There was, and his profile information said he worked at Angels Elementary School in Downtown LA. I had an inkling that this kind of thing was the real reason Dana wasn't on Facebook.

Our food arrived. I tasted Connor's crepes and started on mine while he called the school.

"We're in luck," he said when he hung up. "Patrick has the first period off today, so we can talk to him right away."

Connor downed his banana and honey crepe in three bites, I chugged the last bit of my coffee, and we were back in the car within two minutes. Our speed slowed considerably as we joined the traffic crawling toward Central LA. Connor weaved through the cars in an attempt to save time, but it still took us forty-five minutes to get there. It was nine o' clock.

Six and a half hours to go.

Angels Elementary consisted of a few unimaginative brick buildings and a playground, surrounded by a tall cyclone fence.

The receptionist took a break from painting her nails to direct us to MacCallum's classroom. We found the right building and headed for 6B through the muffled sounds of children being educated. Shrieks of laughter. High-pitched voices. An adult voice calling for attention. Little angels indeed.

We found 6B and knocked.

Mr. MacCallum was a startlingly tall man. Tall enough, that when he opened the door to his classroom, his nose upward was obscured by the door frame. I looked at his tie instead, seeing it was at my eye level. It featured cartoon tigers with oversized mallets chasing cheerful bunnies around a forest.

His face, when the entirety of it was revealed, was stretched thin like the rest of him, but softened by the laughter lines around his mouth and the sparkle in his brown eyes. I was amused that such a tall person would choose to work with the shortest people around. Then again, all adults seem like giants to small children, so maybe there was method to his madness.

"Mr. Stiles and Ms. Avery, I presume? Come on in."

The walls were bright with the organized clutter of children's creations, interspersed with a few educational posters about the alphabet and seasons. He gestured at the vacant, child-sized plastic chairs. "Sorry about the seating options, but please feel free to sit."

I pulled one out from behind a desk and sat on it. Connor chose to stand. Connor wasn't wearing heels.

MacCallum sat too, and waited for us to begin.

"You attended Porterville High, is that correct?" asked Connor.

MacCallum nodded. "That's right." He'd picked up a pen and was doodling absentmindedly as he answered.

"How many kids went there back then?"

"A couple hundred, I guess."

"Did you know Henry Smythe?"

The doodling paused for a second. "I knew *of* him. Everyone did after the accident. He was a grade above me, but his sister, Caroline, was in my grade."

"So, you didn't know him before he died?"

"Well, I could've picked him out of a lineup, but I'm not sure we ever spoke. Still, in a school that size, everyone pretty much knows everyone."

"Were you close to Caroline?"

"No. She was one of the popular kids. Me?" He smiled without resentment and waved the pen over his beanstalk frame. "Not so much."

"Did you see how she reacted to his death?"

"Only from afar. She was devastated by all accounts, and then her mom committed suicide a year after. Poor girl."

"Sorry to ask, but do you know how her mother did it?"

I couldn't understand why we needed to know that. From the hesitation on MacCallum's face, neither could he.

"Your information could help save someone's life."

MacCallum put down the pen. "It was an overdose, I believe."

"Of painkillers, sleeping pills, insulin, or what?"

"The rumor mill said sleeping pills. That she saved up her prescription drugs and took them all at once. I don't know if that's true."

Oh. If Henry or Caroline was the wannabe killer, that could explain the choice of Ambience. Forcing Josh to "sleep" forever might seem like justice.

"Have you seen anyone from Porterville High recently?" Connor asked.

"Are you joking?"

Connor's humorless expression must have answered him.

"We had the twenty-five-year school reunion last month. I've seen almost everyone in my graduating class recently."

"Including Caroline?"

"Yeah, we chatted for a while actually. I guess the high school cliques don't apply a quarter of a century later." He favored us with a wide smile, guileless as a child, and I smiled back.

Connor's face remained impassive.

"Tell us about that conversation."

MacCallum looked back and forth between us before shrugging. "I dunno. She seemed like a nice woman. I'm not sure she remembered who I was, but she pretended to out of kindness. We swapped the abridged versions of what we'd been doing since high school. She was amused I was still in school. Told me she was a nurse. I asked if she had kids, and she said nope, one tragic, dysfunctional family was all she could handle. I wasn't going to ask, but she went on as if I had. She was a bit drunk by that stage of the night. Said her whole family fell apart when Henry died and, despite knowing better, she used to feel like her parents must have wished it was her, since they stopped trying after that." MacCallum's eyes had wandered away while he'd been remembering, but now they flicked back to Connor, then me. "She's not in any trouble is she?"

"We hope not. Did you talk about the night of his death?"

"Yeah, a bit. I was at the same party he was, would you believe?" His cheeks gained a faint rosy tinge. "I'd, um, kind of snuck in uninvited because the girl I had a crush on was going."

"Did you see Henry there?"

He frowned. "Funny. Caroline asked me the same thing."

"And what did you tell her?"

"That it was over a quarter of a century ago. I have a vague recollection of seeing him leave and that's it."

I bit my tongue to keep it from asking outright whether he'd seen who hopped in the driver's seat. If he had, we couldn't afford to draw his attention to it.

Connor leaned forward and offered his hand. "Thank you for your time and cooperation, Mr. MacCallum. You've been very helpful."

MacCallum unfolded himself from the chair, and I had to crane my head upward to see his face. I wondered if any of the kids who sat in the front row complained of sore necks.

He shook Connor's hand. "If you say so. Good luck with whatever it is you're investigating. I hope you manage to save that life you mentioned."

I stood up to prevent my head from popping off like my old doll's did when you pushed it back too far, and MacCallum shook my hand too. As we left the classroom behind, I wondered how many times he'd smacked his head on that particular doorframe over the years. Maybe I should buy him a hard hat. If I had any money.

We were walking down the corridor when two boys, about seven years old, came out of room 5F and headed toward us. One was pale and freckled and looked worried, and the other was Latino with the kind of big brown eyes a person couldn't say no to. They stopped in front of us. "Excuse me, sir—"

I peeked at Connor. Kids don't tend to mix well with someone who *just likes order*. Connor's face was deadpan.

Of course it was.

"Do you know if Ms. Hillier is in the nurse's office?" It was the Latino doing the talking. The pale kid was looking even more worried.

"I don't know. Sorry," Connor said.

The pale kid put his hands over his mouth.

Unfortunately, it didn't stop the puke from spilling out between his fingers and onto Connor's black leather shoes.

"S—sorry!" said the poor kid, more vomit dripping from his hands onto the floor.

"Yes, sorry about that, sir," the other chimed in. There

was a sparkle of excitement in his eyes that belied his words.

Connor's face was still expressionless.

They rushed off to the nurse's office. Connor bent down and removed his shoes.

"Uh, do you want me to find a bathroom and clean them for you?"

"That won't be necessary." He strode down the corridor in his socks, carrying the shoes just far enough away to prevent any drips landing on his clothes. I hurried after him, wondering what he was planning to do. We couldn't spare the time to go back to Beverly Hills and change, but I couldn't see him interviewing anyone in just his socks, either.

We passed a garbage can as we were escaping the bounds of the cyclone fence, and Connor dropped the shoes into it without slowing down. The shoes that were probably worth more than my first paycheck.

I was too gobsmacked to say anything. Or to grab them out of the garbage to clean up and sell on eBay.

When we arrived at the SUV, he opened up the back and pulled out another pair of black leather shoes. Puke-free. It was like a bloody magic trick.

"Does this kind of thing happen often?" I asked, as he bent down to put them on.

"More often than I'd like."

We were in our seats a minute later. Connor's phone rang before he could turn the key. "Yes?" he answered. "Uh-huh . . . Right . . . Do you have a picture? Yeah, message it through. Thanks." He hung up and looked at me. "That was the research team. Remember the nurse who dropped Juan's sister home?"

"Yes."

"What was her name?"

"Caroline, I think?"

He nodded. "That's what I thought too. It turns out that Henry's sister, Caroline Smythe, works at the hospital where Juan's sister is being treated. They're sending through a recent photo of her so we can see if it's the same nurse."

His phone buzzed with a message.

It was her.

"You know what this means, right?"

I was torn. This could be the connection we needed. If Caroline had become close to the Castillo family, Juan had motive, as well as opportunity. Hell, maybe Caroline had offered to botch some paperwork at the hospital to cut down his sister's medical bills.

But I didn't want it to be Juan.

Connor didn't wait for me to answer. "I still don't want to question Caroline when we can't be sure Patrick MacCallum said anything to her. So, let's find out where Mr. Castillo is working today."

He called the Green with Envy customer service line and told them he was Mr. Josh Summers's personal assistant. Mr. Summers was most insistent that Connor meet with his gardener *at once*, or he'd be looking for a new gardening service. Connor understood Juan had other clients and so offered to meet him wherever he was for a quick chat.

A minute later, we joined the northbound traffic flowing toward the address in Eagle Rock we'd been given.

Halfway there, Connor got another call and put it on the car audio.

"Mr. Stiles?" Josh's voice came down the line. "A kid from across the street just brought me a glass bottle—could be a medicine bottle, but there's no label—with what looks like dirty water in it. He said he was searching for his ball and found the bottle in one of my bushes on the edge of the road. I thought it might be important so—"

"Tell everyone not to touch it until we've dusted for prints."

"Too late, sorry. I think the kid's mom must have wiped it clean, because it doesn't look like it's been sitting in the dirt for a week, plus the kid had his hands all over it. We didn't want to waste your time in case it really was just dirty water, so Caleb tasted it. He said it's hellbane? Said you'd know what that means."

Connor pulled an illegal U-turn. "Sit tight. We'll be right there."

When the car behind us finished honking, I turned to Connor. "Do her symptoms fit?"

He knew what I meant. "I'll call the doctor to check, but as far as I understand, yes."

Hellbane is a highly toxic plant with white, purple-veined flowers that's grown commercially for making antispasmodic drugs. It also grows wild on roadsides, disused land, and pasture throughout California and is considered a weed. A lethal infusion could be made by anyone who bothered to soak or boil the roots in water.

Was it the answer we'd been searching for?

The doctor answered on the first ring. "I was about to call you. Dana's condition is deteriorating more rapidly than anticipated. We aren't going to be able to manage her symptoms much longer."

Connor let out a few choice curse words. "How much longer?"

"Two or three hours."

Silence, broken only by the blipping of machines in the background.

"There's a chance hellbane is our mystery substance. Would that account for Dana's symptoms?" Connor asked.

"Yes. But then, so would dozens of other possibilities."

"Ready whatever you need to counteract a hellbane overdose then, but don't give it to her yet. I'll try to get confirmation first."

"Got it."

I spent the rest of the journey silently cursing every car ahead of us that slowed down for a turn or stopped too long at a traffic light.

Too long. We were taking too long.

Josh's mansion sped into view and we raced inside. The bottle was sitting on Josh's pale stone kitchen counter.

"Taste it," Connor said to me. "I want a second opinion."

I rattled around in a cutlery drawer and found a long-handled teaspoon before unscrewing the cap. I dipped the spoon in the liquid, then sniffed and tasted it gingerly, the image of Dana alone in a sterile white bed vivid in my mind from all the times it had haunted me.

The flavors of fermented pomegranate and sweet straw burst on my tongue. "It's hellbane all right." I spat the tiny trace of it into the sink and rinsed my mouth out. "What do we do now?"

Connor was staring out into the garden where the bottle must have been found, his gray eyes shadowed. "I don't know." He spoke more to himself than to me or Josh. "I don't like it. Dana should have tasted it, even with the Ambience there as well."

It was true. Hellbane's flavor was subtle but distinctive once you knew what to look for, and if she could pick out the Ambience in a blackberry dish, she should've detected the hellbane too.

"And the crime scene team did a sweep of the house and garden and didn't find the bottle."

"The team could've missed it, couldn't they?" I asked. "This place is huge, and what possible reason could the killer have for planting the bottle in the garden for us to find now?"

"To finish her off. If we give her the wrong counteracting drugs, she'll die."

We both knew that if she didn't have the gene mutation PSH337PRS, she'd be dead already.

Josh hadn't said a word since we'd arrived, but now he cut in. "But without the right antidote, she'll die anyway!"

Connor's gaze swept to him. "The killer wouldn't be able to know that for sure. We've kept her condition a secret."

"Then wouldn't they assume she's dead?" I asked. "No one's seen her since. If it was intended as a lethal dose, why would the killer suspect she's alive?"

"Remember, we told a few people that an attempt was made on her life. That says not dead."

"But why finish off Dana if Josh was the target?"

"Maybe she saw or tasted something that could lead back to the person behind it. Or maybe they think finishing off Josh's girlfriend is an easy way to hurt him, seeing as he's turning out to be hard to kill."

My eyes flicked to Josh. His face was a rigid, pale mask. He looked like I felt. The implications weren't good.

Yes, Dana could have missed the hellbane and the crime scene team could have missed the bottle in the sweep. It was possible. But it was also possible the bottle had been planted to trick us into finishing her off. If Juan was working with Caroline like we suspected, it would have been oh so easy for him to place the bottle in the garden.

I was selfishly glad the decision was Connor's. Josh and I watched him with matching apprehension.

"Mr. Summers, I'll have a team look over the last few days of your security footage for any sign that the hellbane was planted to finish Dana off."

He turned to me. "Get in the car. We have an hour left to find and interrogate our killer."

22

I THOUGHT CONNOR had been driving fast before, but now he raced down the streets like he had sirens on. Only he didn't have sirens on.

I held on and tried to connect the dots. "If you think it's unlikely Dana missed the hellbane, is it possible it got into her system another way?"

Not all poisons have to be ingested or absorbed through the membranes under the tongue or in the nasal passages where a Shade can screen them. Some can be absorbed through the skin, aerosols and gases can be inhaled, and others injected, but these methods are unpopular. Skin absorption is slow, and usually causes irritation at the site of entry, which means there's time to seek treatment and so fatalities are rare. Aerosols and gases are volatile, dangerous to the handler, and have a high risk of accidental collateral damage. Injections are fast and effective but require basic medical knowledge, and the bad guy has to get up close to the victim, which negates most of the benefits of using poison in the first place. A bullet or a knife works just as well if you don't mind the risk of being spotted in the act.

The car screeched around a corner as Connor answered. "It can be injected, but it would have had to be administered after the Ambience, otherwise Dana would've known about it and reported it. So the theory doesn't work unless Dana was the intended victim. Plus, she was monitored that whole time."

He shook his head. "If Caroline is behind this, it doesn't matter how she did it—Juan's our best chance of putting a name to the second poison in the next forty minutes. Caroline would've needed him to lace the blackberries with Ambience. If we're lucky, she told him the rest of the plan."

"Will he know what was used, even if he did it?"

"We're about to find out."

Long minutes later, we screeched to a stop at an address in Hollywood Hills—Juan's next client. The usually forty-five-minute drive had taken us thirty-five, but the Green with Envy van we were looking for wasn't there.

Connor called the dispatcher again. She called Juan's phone but got no answer and reiterated what we already knew. He'd been scheduled to leave Eagle Rock forty minutes ago. Plenty of time to have made it to Hollywood Hills, even stopping for gas. Connor asked the dispatcher if she'd told Juan he was coming. She had. He gave a curt thank-you and hung up.

"Do you think he's on the run?" I asked.

"Could be." His eyes were hard. "We'll sit here for another fifteen minutes in case he's just very late. If he's on the run, even if he's dumb enough to go home first, it will take us more time to get to El Sereno than we have left." He let out a slow breath. "Dana's condition is so critical now that even with the right antidote she might not make it. Every minute decreases her chances."

I touched his arm. "There's a good possibility it's hellbane, isn't there? Josh's place is huge. It would be easy to miss a small bottle stuck in a bush. Plus, Josh said he and Dana were recovering from a big night, and he urged her to hurry. That, combined with being distracted by the taste of the Ambience, might have been enough to make her miss the hellbane. It's rare to have more than one poison in a single meal, right?"

Connor looked out the window in the direction Juan would come, if he was coming. Minutes dragged by.

"Could we ring his wife?" I asked. "Ask her if she's seen him? Or maybe we could call Caroline and grill her without mentioning what we think her motive is?"

Connor crushed the steering wheel. "It's too late. We're out of time." He rang the doctor. "Give it to her. Let me know as soon as her condition changes, either way." When he hung up, he sagged in his seat, aging five years before my eyes. Lack of sleep hadn't ruffled him, but admitting defeat was a whole other matter.

Best to keep him occupied. "Now what?"

He stared out the windshield and didn't respond for one long, scary minute. Then he reached for the keys. "Now we find Juan."

We drove to the Castillos' home in El Sereno. If Juan was on the run, he might've contacted Francisca, and regardless of what he was up to, there was a chance he'd answer a call from her when he wasn't answering anyone else's.

Francisca wasn't happy to see us. "You think because he's Mexican he's guilty, huh? My husband is good man!"

"We're not accusing him of anything," Connor said. Yet.

"We're just trying to find him so we can ask a few more questions," I said. "Could you please try phoning him?"

She glared at both of us but grabbed her phone and dialed. It went to voice mail.

"Mrs. Castillo, could you tell us more about Juan and the nurse, Caroline Smythe's, relationship?"

Her dark eyes smoldered. "Relationship? You think my Juan is having a relationship?" Before Connor could respond, she slapped him across the face. "How dare you? Get out of my house."

Connor backed up, hands raised. "That's not what I was asking. Really, I meant no disrespect."

She wasn't having any of it. "Get out!" She included me in her fiery gaze, and I started backing up too.

Connor placed his card on a side table on the way out. "Please call me if you hear from him."

She slammed the door in our faces.

"That went well," I said.

Connor's cheek sported a rosy imprint of Francisca's wrath. He didn't say anything.

Was it possible Francisca had hurried us out on purpose, to cover for Juan somehow? His Green with Envy van wasn't in the driveway, but that didn't mean he wasn't here.

We returned to the SUV. My mind churned. What was our next step? I came up empty. Even if we found the killer and got a full confession in the next two minutes, it wouldn't make any difference to Dana. The antidote was either stopping the hellbane from doing any more damage or making it worse and guaranteeing she'd never be unhooked from life support.

Connor hadn't started the engine. He was just sitting there, smiling.

I did a double take. His smile was as wide as I'd ever witnessed.

I checked to see if I was missing any clothes. Nope, all there.

Connor held out his phone. "Read it."

It was a message from Dana's doctor.

Appears antidote is working. Pulse, blood pressure, and vitals starting to improve. Not out of danger yet, but outlook is positive.

I felt like I lost ten pounds in an instant. The waistband digging into my hips didn't corroborate this miraculous weight loss, but I looked up at Connor and grinned anyway.

He really was breathtaking when he smiled. Just as well it was a rare sight.

"You did it," I said. "You made the right call."

"No. We did it."

I realized I was still holding his hand, the one holding his phone. I let go.

He leaned in toward me, and the atmosphere of our shared relief turned steamy. I searched his gray eyes, which were warm for once, and didn't pull back. He tucked a stray tangle of hair behind my ear, his touch sending tingles rampaging all the way down my spine. I licked my lips. He drew closer, and my breath hitched. Then his lips met mine, and my head exploded.

Or it might have if he hadn't pulled away after a minute.

I stared at him, breathless and disoriented. "Why did you stop?"

His face told me nothing. "The Taste Society contract states I need your explicit agreement, remember?" He brushed my cheek. "But your acting's improving."

I shoved his hand away and tugged up my top, which had somehow slipped down past my bra when I wasn't paying attention. "I'll have to report you for breach of contract, then."

"Yes. Only we both know you want me to do it again."

He may have been right, but he wasn't giving me any clues about what *he* wanted, or his real reason for pulling back, so I finished adjusting my top and tried to look haughty. "Then, like you said, I guess my acting is improving."

Connor didn't react. The robot. He started the engine. "Are you hungry?"

"For food? Of course."

I was way too horny to be hungry, but I couldn't let him know that. Besides, by the time food was served, I was pretty sure my stomach would have reasserted itself as overlord of my bodily urges.

Sure it would have.

23

WE WENT TO an outdoor taco stand, seeing as we were in the area for it. I was a big fan. I just hoped living by all this cheap, delicious Mexican food, with its huge portions, wasn't going to turn me into a *big* fan in the literal sense.

I was licking the last of the spicy sauce from my mouth, trying not to imagine Connor doing it for me, when his phone rang once more.

"That was the dispatcher from Green with Envy," he said after disconnecting. "Juan called in to report he was running late because his client wanted to discuss his landscaping ideas. Apparently he had a lot of ideas, and Juan left his phone in the car."

"So, he's not fleeing to Mexico?"

"Doesn't seem like it. Of course, he doesn't know what we've learned."

The thing I'd learned was that Connor was a better kisser than I'd fantasized. Somehow I doubted that's what he was referring to.

"So, what do we do?" I asked, to cover my distraction.

"Well, now that Dana's been given the correct antidote and Juan isn't halfway to the border, everything is less time critical. That means we can delay confronting Juan until we have either concrete evidence or a bluff strategy to persuade him to confess. I'll head in and work with the research team, see what we can rustle up."

"Can't I come?"

"No. You don't have clearance."

"Then, what do I do?"

"Get some sleep?"

I crossed my arms and harrumphed, but, as expected, he remained unmoved. He drove me back to my apartment, and I trudged up the stairs, feeling strangely subdued considering everything.

Dana is going to live, I reminded myself. My flat mood must be the fatigue catching up with me. I carried Meow to my bed for a quick nap.

Five hours later, I woke up to Meow's purrs vibrating through my belly. I checked my phone. It was six-thirty, and Connor had sent me a message half an hour ago:

Doctor says he's seeing steady improvements in Dana's oxygenation, pH levels, renal function, and vitals. All that means she's out of danger, and he should be able to take her off the machines and wake her up tomorrow. Thought you should know. Also, still have some things to take care of here, so I'll see you for a late dinner around 8:30.

I got out of bed and danced around the room. Meow was unimpressed. I didn't care. Dana was out of danger! It was incredible news.

Incredible news that Josh deserved to know, I realized. He'd been at least as stressed as me the entire investigation and then found out she was his daughter to boot.

It was the kind of news best delivered in person. Besides, I didn't have his number. Mind made up, I fed Meow her dinner and grabbed my keys before remembering I'd given my car away.

I swore.

Google Maps said it was a nine-mile walk. Too far. I did some more Googling. I could use my last few bucks on bus fare, catch two buses, walk two miles, and take an hour and a half to get there, or I could get Etta to drive me. The problem was, I couldn't tell Etta where I was going or she'd want to come too.

What was around Josh's place aside from mansions? I racked my brain until it came to me: the canyon. I hadn't done any exercise lately, except for running away from Mr. Black, so it was a believable tale.

Etta didn't know yet how lazy I was.

Besides, strolling through beautiful scenery was the one type of exercise I could actually enjoy. To support my story, I changed into workout gear. Having a non-slob excuse to wear sweats and comfy shoes was the best part of being active anyway. I pinched Oliver's headlamp off his dresser too. It would be dark in an hour.

As a final touch, I transferred the pepper spray and Taser to my new outfit. Who knew if Albert was still stalking me? The thought made me shudder, but I was pretty confident I could take the weasel if it came to it.

I paused in front of the mirror before leaving. I looked like myself, which meant a long way from how Josh had seen me before, primped up to Connor's standards. I didn't think Josh would care once I told him the good news.

I squeezed my way past Etta's outdoor sofa and knocked on her door. She answered it with a cigarette hanging out of her mouth and another shift dress hanging from her frame, black this time. The murmur of the television spilled out behind her. From what I could see of the apartment, it was a mirror image of ours, only fifty years into the future. Her TV was a flat-screen, her carpet a plush light gray, and her kitchen a pale oak finished with white glossy counters and a kettle, knife block, and tea towel in turquoise.

"Did you bring cookies?"

I whipped them out from behind my back. "Is the ground dirt?"

She smiled and gestured beyond the stair railing to the sidewalk below. "Looks like concrete actually, but you know how to win a woman over. Even if you can't shoot a gun." She stubbed out her cigarette and took the plate.

"I have a favor to ask," I admitted. "I loaned my car to a friend and was hoping you could give me a lift."

"Well, I can't blame you for loaning your car to *that* particular friend. I'd give him any ride he wanted."

I hid a wince while she grabbed her keys from a hook by the door and a cookie from the plate.

"Where are we going?"

Three minutes later, we were in Etta's 1970s, buttercup-yellow Dodge Charger. The black leather seats were worn in a comfortable way. The rest of the interior was immaculate.

"Nice," I said.

Etta turned over the engine and let it warm up for a bit. "I know. I bought it second-hand from the original owner twenty years ago and haven't looked back." She pulled out onto the road without signaling. Or looking back. "What do you think of my new outdoor sofa?"

I couldn't complain when she was doing me a favor. "It looks comfier than the dining chair I drag in and out."

"It is. You and Oliver can use it too, if you like."

"Thank you. Maybe I will."

She used her blinker at the first turn, but not the next. That didn't make her a bad driver by LA standards. It was as if everyone was too busy rehearsing for their upcoming audition to focus on less important things like traffic laws.

"So what gave you the sudden urge to walk Sullivan Canyon Park anyway?" Etta asked.

"Too many cookies. That and Meow has decided my stomach is as comfy as my pillow when she deigns to sleep in my room."

She smirked. "I don't have that problem. Maybe you need to have sex more often."

She was probably right, but it was pretty far down on my priority list.

Etta merged onto the Santa Monica Freeway, fifteen miles under the speed limit, and the person she cut off leaned on the horn. She rolled down her window and stuck her rude finger out of it. "Damn drivers these days, always in a hurry, even though most of 'em don't want to get where they're going." She proceeded to weave through traffic like a champion pole bender. "They hate their jobs, are irked by their families, and don't like their friends. Beats me why they're rushing anywhere."

Another point to Etta.

"Now this Connor man of yours. When do I get to meet him?"

"Um—"

"And is he as good in the sack as he looks? Those tightly controlled ones are masters in the bedroom. All that self-discipline pays off, you know, and when they let themselves go, it's like shooting at a pile of dynamite."

My face turned beetroot red, remembering the kiss.

Etta flicked me a look and swerved in front of another car.

"You've got to be kidding me! You don't know, do you?"

"Can we talk about something else?"

She shook her head in utter bewilderment, like the time she'd learned I'd never held a gun. "You young people need to learn how to live. Nobody knows how long you've got left, so you better make the most of it."

It wasn't a cheerful thought, but it was one that rang truer after the events of this week. "Connor took me to a shooting range the other day," I offered.

"Fun isn't it?"

"It was, but I wouldn't like to shoot at anything alive."

"You might feel differently if you'd seen a gator take off someone's arm right in front of you."

"Geez. That happened to you?" I felt bad for presuming she hunted for the joy of it.

"No. But it's happened to some people."

Oh.

She dropped me off at the barricade on Queensferry Road that led into the canyon. It was as close as I could get with my exercise cover story.

"Will you need a lift home?" she asked.

"No, Connor's picking me up." That's what I hoped anyway. I promised her another batch of cookies soon and said goodbye.

It was just over a mile to Josh's mansion. I started walking.

Unfortunately, I hadn't considered the steep uphill factor. About halfway there, I began to think giving away my car was one of the less clever decisions of my life. Hard to know whether all the exercise I'd have to do would be more or less painful than what Mr. Black might do to me.

I reached Josh's front door as the sun was setting. As I raised my hand to knock, I belatedly wondered whether he'd be happy to see me. Who was I to him? Connor's silent shadow girl? I wasn't sure being told good news in person rather than over the phone meant as much coming from a near stranger, especially when you value privacy as much as he did.

The nine-mile journey home in the dark compelled me to knock anyway.

Josh answered, as usual. "Ms. Avery," he said, surprised.

I was surprised too, that he remembered my name. "I don't want to intrude Mr. Summers, but I have some good news and wanted to tell you in person. Is now an okay time?"

He hesitated, disconcerted by my radical change in attire perhaps, then shrugged. "Sure, come in. Can I get you something to drink?"

I knew I should say no, but I was thirsty. And hungry. "Yes, please. A glass of water would be great." I gave myself a mental pat on the back for being grown-up and digni-fied enough not to ask for an espresso. I could prioritize. In matters of life and death. Sometimes.

He left me in the same sitting room as all the other times and returned a few minutes later with water and a plate of cookies. "I'm afraid I didn't make these myself. I haven't been in the mood to cook much since I found out . . . well about Dana. But we always had a tin of these growing up, so I have a fondness for them."

I smiled. "I won't tell anyone." There was only one glass. "Aren't you having anything?"

He shrugged. "Not allowed to. I sent Caleb home for the evening."

"Oh, sorry." I was especially grateful I hadn't asked for an espresso now. I'd have offered to test it for him, but I couldn't disclose I was a Shade. Not even to a client who already knew I worked for the Taste Society in some capacity.

Josh shook his head. "It's fine. I just had dinner anyway. You said you have good news?"

Right, Izzy, get to the point.

"It's Dana. She's going to be okay. The hellbane antidote is working, and the doctor says she's out of danger."

Josh's smile lit up his whole face. "Wow. That's great! When can I see her?"

I should have realized that would be his first question. "Sorry, she's still unconscious, and I'm not sure what the protocol will be when she wakes up. You'll have to ask Connor."

The smile dimmed. But at least it was still there.

"Sorry," I said for the third time. "I'm new to the company. I was just so excited to hear the good news that I had to share it with you." I grabbed a cookie and shoved it in my mouth to stop my rambling.

Mid-mouthful, I recognized the taste. "Are these Royal Dansk cookies?"

"They are."

I smiled through the crumbs. "Like father, like daughter. Did you know Dana likes the same brand? She even kept the picture of you in one of their tins."

"Really?"

Josh seemed less amused by this revelation than I was, and I experienced a sudden prickle of doubt. What if Josh had been in Dana's kitchen and grabbed the cookie tin for the same reason I had, only to find the picture linked to his darkest secret inside? Was he paranoid enough to think she was onto him? And would he kill to protect his secret?

The cookie had turned to sawdust in my mouth, but I forced myself to swallow and tried to keep my expression neutral. Josh had the perfect opportunity to spike Dana's food with the Ambience and then give her the hellbane while she slept. That would explain why she hadn't tasted it.

But surely not. Josh was still devastated by Henry's death twenty-six years later—and that was an accident. He wouldn't kill someone in cold blood. Connor's suspiciousness of everyone and everything was rubbing off on me, and I was looking for boogeymen in every shadow. Josh was the victim here. He'd been so distraught and now so relieved. He'd probably never even been to Dana's apartment.

But maybe it wasn't a coincidence that the bottle of hellbane that allowed us to save Dana showed up the day after he learned of his relation to her. If he *had* found the picture in her cookie tin, knowing she was his daughter would've put her possession of it in a very different light.

Josh was staring at me, and I realized I still hadn't answered him.

"Really!" I said, trying to mimic my former enthusiasm. "I was the one who found it, because I'm a cookie addict too, you see." I took another cookie to demonstrate and tried to surreptitiously taste for lethal ingredients through the sawdust. Clear. I swallowed it, gulped down some more water to relieve the drought my mouth was experiencing, and leaned back.

I had to know whether my idea was as ludicrous as it seemed.

"Have you ever been to Dana's apartment?" I asked, trying to act like the kind of girl who made casual, meaningless chitchat with celebrities all the time. I hoped I was wrong. I hoped he'd say no.

"Just once. She had a wardrobe malfunction and had to get changed."

"She kept it pretty sparse, but I liked her yellow door." That would totally throw him off track.

He watched me politely.

"She was kind to me when I met her months ago," I continued. "I'm so glad she's going to be okay."

"Me too."

He started rising, my cue to leave. I jumped in as if I hadn't noticed. "Gosh, it's lucky that kid found the bottle isn't it? Which house is his? I feel like I should bake him some cookies or something."

"Very lucky. Ms. Avery, will you excuse me a moment?"

I nodded and sat on the couch wondering what else I could ask without making him suspicious. My phone buzzed. The display said it was Connor, but I'd ring him back in a minute. I had to figure this out.

My thoughts came to a screaming halt when a gun pressed against the base of my skull.

24

"SORRY ABOUT THIS, MS. AVERY," Josh said, "but I can't let you ruin everything."

My brain scrambled like a dropped egg, trying to adjust to the sudden turn of events. "Is this a joke? What are you talking about?"

"Get up." The barrel dug in to emphasize his point.

I got up.

"We're going for a drive." He steered me through the house at gunpoint and into his garage via an internal door. It was cool and dark and smelled of car wax. He flicked on the fluorescent lights and prodded me around to the back of his Porsche Boxster.

It was gleaming black. Like Death's chariot waiting to carry me to the afterlife.

I shivered.

He handed me a canister of cooking spray.

Cold-pressed virgin olive oil. I stared at it, dumbfounded. Maybe the gun—a revolver, now I could see it—aimed at my head had turned my brain to mush, but I had no clue what the oil was for.

I scoped out the size of the Porsche's trunk. It looked like a tight fit, but not enough to need oil to squeeze me into it. And if I was going to die, I wasn't about to take part in some kinky chef sex game.

"Spray it on the license plate," he said.

I shouldn't have felt relieved with the revolver still trained on my head, but I did anyway. I uncapped the canister and sprayed the plate. I thought about spraying Josh too, but the gun dissuaded me.

"Good. Now sprinkle this over top." He handed me one of those stainless steel shakers used to dust cappuccinos with chocolate powder or desserts with powdered sugar. This one was filled with powdered sugar, and as I shook it over the oiled license plate, the blue letters and numbers turned white.

Clever.

It was hard to read, like it was caked in road dust, but not so illegible we'd be pulled over by the cops.

We repeated the procedure on the front license plate. It was like a fun art project aside from the gun thing.

When I was done, he told me to put the oil and shaker down and handed me a set of keys. "You're driving."

"I can't," I lied. "I've never driven a manual."

The gun nudged my ribs this time. "You sure about that? Because I'd feel bad about having to tie you up and put you in the trunk."

I got in the driver's seat. "I'll pick it up as I go along."

He climbed in the passenger side, keeping his revolver trained on me the whole time. After buckling his seat belt (I suspected he *always* put his seat belt on), he positioned his hand to send a bullet through my gut if he pulled the trigger. "The garage door opener is on the key ring. Open it, then follow my directions. Don't draw attention to us. I've heard a bullet in the stomach is one of the most painful ways to die."

It crossed my mind that it was possibly better than what Platypus Lending had in store for me, but I put the car into gear anyway. The engine thrummed under me, and I bunny-hopped forward out of the garage, underestimating its power.

"Don't shoot. I'll get the hang of it." The next gear change was smoother.

I knew many would consider driving a Porsche Boxster a joyride, but somehow I couldn't summon much joy. I bet Josh wouldn't let me fold the convertible roof down either. He directed me right, then left, then right again.

"Where are we going?"

"I'm truly sorry about this, Ms. Avery. I hope you can understand. It's just, I don't deserve to go to jail. It was a horrible accident. Henry was my best friend since we were assigned seats next to each other in elementary school because of our last names, Smythe and Summers, you see. Living without him is punishment enough."

"Is that why you tried to kill Dana?" I asked. "To protect your secret?"

He went on as if I hadn't spoken. "It's a question of the greater good. I've worked so hard and climbed so high in order to make a difference. So Henry didn't die for nothing. The scandal would ruin me. I'm helping hundreds of kids get out of gangs and poverty and into employment with decent prospects. What are you doing in comparison? What's your life compared to all the ones I'm saving?"

He had a point. I suppose if you have to be murdered by someone, it might as well be a polite, apologetic, famous someone who's going to do more good in the world than you anyway. He could cook a lot better than me too.

"When I saw that newspaper clipping in Dana's apartment, I thought she was planning to expose me. I couldn't allow that to happen. But then I found out she's my daughter. My daughter!" He paused to blink away the moisture in his eyes. "I knew then she only had the clipping because she wanted to find me."

"But I'm the one who figured out she's your daughter. Don't you owe me something for that?"

"I'm sorry, but knowing I have family has just given me more to lose."

"Um, what if I'm another long-lost daughter of yours?" Not my finest moment.

Unsurprisingly, my words fell on deaf ears. "I hope you understand. That you can forgive me. But you gave me no choice."

I saw a new opening and pounced on it. "You do have a choice! I promise I won't tell anyone. We can all live and be happy and you can keep doing good for Henry."

"Sorry, Ms. Avery, but I don't believe you."

Guess I shouldn't have lied about my ability to drive a stick.

We drove for a few minutes in silence. My phone started buzzing again, but Josh ordered me to let it ring. I couldn't see who'd called. Not that it mattered. Even Albert or Ms. Nielson from Platypus Lending would've been a welcome intrusion right now.

I realized we were headed south. Straight toward the neighborhoods Google had told me when I was house hunting offered very low rent and very high mortality rates. I considered crashing the car. Only there was a good chance the impact would jolt Josh's finger hovering over the trigger in the exact way I was trying to avoid.

"What are you going to do to me?" My voice came out small, but I hadn't forgotten the Taser and pepper spray in my pockets. The more I knew about what he was planning, the more hope I had of using one of them without getting a fatal bullet for my troubles.

"Ever heard of Death Alley?"

I gulped. It was a two-mile stretch of road in Westmont that had earned the name after boasting more killings than pretty much anywhere else in LA. Most of them shootings.

"Some of the kids who attended my school came from Death Alley. I don't think anyone will look too closely at yet another apparent gang shooting. It's a bit unusual for it to happen to a naive tourist, but random shootings happen all the time."

My palms started to sweat, making the steering wheel slippery beneath them.

"Hard to pin a random shooting on anyone," Josh continued. "Especially in the dark."

As much as I hated to admit it, it was a good plan. I just hoped the dark would also work to my advantage when it came to using my new defense toys.

We reached a stretch of Death Alley, a.k.a. South Vermont Avenue, that was six lanes across with a wide median strip in the middle. It was a commercial district, and the few windows facing the street were barred and dim. Everyone had gone home for the day. No bored residents around to peer through the windows and jot down the number from a dirty license plate.

The occasional car passed by, but all I could see of them were the headlights. Josh directed me to pull over in the shadows of a broken street light (there were plenty to choose from) and roll down my window. Presumably to shoot me through.

"Please, don't do this." I tried one last time.

He didn't meet my eyes. His gaze was locked on my torso where the revolver was pointing. "Take off your seat belt, slowly, then get out of the car."

I followed his instructions, heart banging like a frantic woodpecker. As I got to my feet, I kept the left side of my body angled away from him and slipped that hand into my pocket. Looks like I was going to use pepper spray.

I slid the safety tab around and rested my trembling thumb on the depressor, grateful I could do it by feel after Connor's lesson.

Josh climbed over the center console into the driver's seat without dropping his gun or gaze for a second. He put his seat belt on with one hand. Ready to make a fast getaway. "Step away from the car." His voice was all the more scary for its gentleness.

I took a slow step backward, pepper spray hidden by my hand and the murky darkness, trying to work out what distance Josh wanted me at before he'd pull the trigger. Far enough to avoid blood spatter on his car. Not so far as to risk missing. My pepper spray only had ten feet. And that was a stretch. At least it wasn't windy.

Another car rolled by on the other side of the median strip. Josh had chosen well. No one could see he had a gun, and I guessed he'd wait for the road to be empty before pulling the trigger. Even if he didn't, anyone driving in this neighborhood hearing a gunshot would only put their foot down and later tell the police they thought it was a car back-firing. Curiosity would get you killed.

Pity I hadn't learned that lesson better.

I took another step backward. Only about four more steps before my pepper spray was out of range. I needed a distraction.

In my peripheral vision, I saw a car heading our way. It was in the same lane as I was, and I hadn't chosen my black sweats and gray T-shirt for night visibility. I shut it out of my mind. If it hit me, I might survive. If the gun trained on my head hit me, I was pretty sure I wouldn't.

I took another step, watching Josh's face, hoping for a moment of inattention. The oncoming car swerved to avoid me, and the driver laid on the horn. Josh's eyes flicked toward it. I leaped sideways and simultaneously blasted the pepper spray at him.

"Shit. Shit. Shit on a shitting turkey!"

Apparently I'd hit my target.

I turned and ran, feet pounding against the asphalt. I heard coughing and then a gunshot. A bullet whizzed past my ear. He shouldn't be able to open his eyes, so he must be shooting blind. I changed my trajectory. Another bullet flew past my shoulder. *How the hell is he aiming?* My heart thundered in my ears, drowning out sound. Sound. He must be following my footsteps.

I stopped in my tracks and tried to take the next step silently. Another gunshot. Pain exploded in my thigh. I cried out and doubled over. It saved my life, as another bullet flew through the space my chest had been occupying a second before. I bit down on my cheek to stop myself whimpering. My leg was on fire, but holding my weight. I had to get out of here.

Still doubled over, I limped as quickly and quietly as I could to the promise of cover on the other side of the road. By the time I reached the sidewalk, my skin was cold and clammy and I was having difficulty catching my breath. I wouldn't be able to drag myself much farther. A car approached, and I tried to flag it down, but it sped up instead.

I had to hide. I scanned the area for cover, dismayed by the featureless, barricaded shop facades stretching in both directions, broken only by stretches of tall steel fencing where the buildings were set back from the sidewalk. The owners of these establishments didn't welcome visitors outside of business hours. There was nowhere to take shelter.

A street lamp illuminated a side road about a hundred yards farther up, but it seemed impossibly far away. I searched the area again. My best bet was an A-frame sign that had been left out on the sidewalk, advertising *Bo's Barber Shop—the best straight razor shaves in South LA*. A small part of me registered amusement at narrowly escaping death then hiding behind a sign about close shaves, but the larger part of me was focused on survival. I dragged myself over to the sign, braced myself on my good leg, and swung it ninety degrees to face the other side of the street. My hands stuck as I lifted it. They were covered in blood. My blood. I slumped down behind my meager shelter and listened for Josh.

He was still coughing, and it sounded like he hadn't come any closer. Yet.

Would he hear me if I phoned for help?

I wasn't sure how many minutes were left until the pepper spray wore off, but I knew it would. Then it was just a matter of time before Josh followed the trail of blood I'd left and finished me off. I had to risk a phone call.

"Nine one one. What's your emergency?"

"I've been shot," I whispered. "And the shooter is still here."

"What's your location?"

I racked my brain for Death Alley's real name. "South Vermont Avenue, in Westmont." The sign pressed against my back. "Outside Bo's Barber Shop."

"Please stay on the line . . . An emergency team is on its way. Where have you been shot?"

"How long?" I asked.

"Excuse me?"

"How far away are they?"

"Eleven minutes, ma'am."

The coughing had quieted, and I was afraid to keep talking. I disconnected and made sure my phone was switched to silent. It vibrated almost immediately. The 911 operator calling me back. I cut it off and strained my ears for sounds from the other side of the road. Another cough, no closer than before. I allowed myself to breathe and shuffled my rear end to get more comfortable, except the movement was like pouring gasoline on the fire in my thigh.

I was glad it was too dark to see the bullet wound clearly. I had a vague idea I should do something to slow the bleeding, but I couldn't bring myself to touch it. The world spun.

I tried not to imagine Josh getting out of his car and crossing the road. *Maybe he won't see my blood in the dark.*

Maybe he'll think I'm long gone. My phone vibrated in my hand again, and I saw I had three text messages from Connor. The first had been sent twenty-five minutes before, right after Josh had forced me to ignore the call.

Why aren't you answering your phone? Between Mr. Alstrom and Mr. Black, you have me worried.

The next one had been sent ten minutes later.

Seriously, Isobel, let me know you're okay or I'm coming to check on you.

The last one, that had just arrived, read:

What the hell are you doing on Death Alley at this hour? Are you insane? I'm five minutes away.

I was confused about that one until I remembered the tracking app he'd installed on my phone. Five minutes was better than eleven. And texting didn't make any noise.

I hope you brought your gun. I'm hiding behind the sign for Bo's Barber Shop. Josh is in his Porsche across the road with a revolver and a face full of pepper spray.

I pressed send. My phone rang, Connor this time. I cut it off and sent another text.

Can't talk in case he hears me.

What the hell is going on?

I'd have to give Connor a lecture about texting while driving. Later. For now, I answered his question.

I found out he poisoned Dana and he's trying to kill me.

Be right there.

I counted down the seconds until he arrived. The coughing from across the road had stopped, but so far I hadn't heard the car door either. The unsettling image of Josh climbing out the open window dropped into my mind.

Maybe he was out of bullets. I didn't know a lot about guns, but I thought most revolvers only held five bullets at a time. I relived those nightmarish seconds in my head and counted four shots. So he probably had one left. Maybe that's why he stopped shooting, saving the last bullet for when he could make it count. Or maybe he was reloading.

A car door slammed. My heart rate accelerated. I bit the side of my cheek again. Connor would get here in time. *Don't whimper.*

I remembered my Taser and dug it out of my pocket. Josh wouldn't shoot his last bullet until he had a line of sight. Maybe at that point he'd be close enough to zap. I tried to recall Connor's lessons instead of visualizing Josh heading my way, gun in hand.

A car pulled to a stop across the street, and I heard another door slam. Connor? Two gunshots cracked in sync. A man grunted, and the faint sounds of some kind of scuffle drifted toward me. Silence. Then hurried footsteps, growing louder.

I slid the safety back on the Taser and switched off the laser sight, fearing it would give me away. Then I listened hard, trying to work out which side they would appear on. My left. I aimed the Taser accordingly, my finger poised over the button.

A shadowy figure appeared in my line of vision, and my finger jerked before my brain registered it was Connor. I wrenched my arm back trying to throw the damn thing off course. One probe hit him in the shoulder, but the other flew wide, rendering the whole thing harmless. I exhaled hard in relief and let the Taser drop.

"Ouch," Connor said, deadpan, picking the probe out of his shoulder. "What was that for?"

"I only heard gunshots. I didn't know if it was you or Josh." My voice didn't sound like mine.

He strode over and knelt at my side. "That's your first mistake. You should know by now I always win." His tone was gentle, but his eyes were hard, looking over my bloody thigh. "I'm not sure whether I'm more annoyed you tried to taser me, or more annoyed you missed."

I thumped him. Weakly. "I threw it off course when I recognized you."

"Sure you did. Did you call nine one one, too?"

I nodded. "They should be here in a few minutes. Is Josh—?"

"Dead? No. But he won't be cooking again anytime soon. I shot him in the forearm."

I'd never get to eat something he made now.

Connor took off his shirt, and I forgot about food. Then he pressed it into my wound, and I forgot about his sculpted, naked torso. "Shit. What did I ever do to you?"

"I can write you a list if you want, but right now we need to slow the bleeding."

I ran through my repertoire of cuss words in my head until the pain subsided a little. Sirens sounded in the distance. Finally.

An ugly thought popped into my mind. "I better not have to share an ambulance with Josh."

Connor looked at me, his face and chest beautiful in the soft evening light, his hands still pressed into my wound. "I'll make sure of it."

25

DR. LEVI EDUARDO REYES stood before me in all his delicious glory. His crisp white coat accentuated the warm toffee tones in his skin that no tan can replicate, and his dimples were on display once more. I suppose there has to be some perks to getting shot.

As soon as it had been established that the bullet that ripped through my thigh had hit nothing more important than a chunk of my flesh and wouldn't require surgery, I'd been transferred to a private Taste Society facility. The hole in my leg had been thoroughly cleaned (ouch), and I'd been dosed up on painkillers and antibiotics. Now, Dr. Reyes was smirking at me over the clipboard with the forms I'd been told to fill out. "Twenty-nine, huh?" he asked. "For how many years?"

"What? I really am twenty-nine."

His dimples deepened. "Uh-huh."

I felt indignation rising up inside me, but it didn't get far. My brain was already maxed out on drugs, relief, hunger, and now lust. I concentrated on not drooling.

"How are you feeling?" he asked.

"Hungry."

His grin made another appearance, and he leaned in close, filling my nose with the scent of sweet cinnamon, jalapeños, and antiseptic. "I'm a bit busy right now, but I'd be happy to take you out on that date when my shift ends."

A little bit of drool may have escaped out one corner of my mouth.

He patted me on the hand and moved to the next bed over. I lay back and listened to him flirt with that patient, too. It might have come across as slimy if she weren't a seventy-year-old woman with a witch's nose out of a children's book and a giggle as carefree as a schoolgirl's. I had no idea what role she had within the Taste Society.

The giggle was contagious, and I found myself smiling along with her as Dr. Reyes planted a kiss on her liver-spotted hand before leaving the room. Once he was gone, I had nothing to do except wonder where Connor had gotten to. He was supposed to be acting the part of my boyfriend after all. That was the only reason I wanted him at my bedside. That and somehow, in the week since we'd met, he'd become one of the few people I knew I could trust in LA.

He was definitely the one person I knew who'd be able to keep me company in a Taste Society medical facility.

Knowing him, he'd be working the case. The case always came first. Even if I'd pretty much solved it for him and gotten shot in the process. He'd taken his leave when the doctor announced I wouldn't need surgery, and I hadn't seen or heard from him since.

I had almost finished calculating the time in Australia when I dozed off.

———

"MORNING, SLEEPYHEAD."

I opened my eyes and waited for them to focus on the blurry blob before me. The blob was Connor. And he was holding a takeout cup.

I sniffed. "Is that an espresso?"

He held it out to me. "Glad to see getting shot hasn't affected your sense of smell. I thought you'd prefer it over flowers."

I hauled myself upright, trying not to envisage the state of my hair, and took the cup. "I've taught you well."

"You're not such a bad student yourself. I brought something else for you."

"Cookies?" I asked hopefully.

His face told me no, he hadn't brought cookies.

"I take back what I said about teaching you well."

Connor looked up at the ceiling for a second. "I brought your release forms. I've come to take you home."

I had cookies at home. "That would also be nice."

"Would you like to leave with crutches or a wheelchair?"

My bursting bladder made up my mind. "Crutches. I need to use the bathroom."

Connor retrieved them from where they leaned against a wall and brought them over. "Do you know how to use these things?"

I glared at him. "Of course. This isn't my first injury, you know."

Connor raised an eyebrow a fraction. "You know that's not something to be proud of, right?"

I dragged my legs over the side of the bed, wincing as my thigh started burning again, and adjusted the crutches to my height.

Connor watched as I swung my way to the bathroom. "Call out if you need any help."

Not even if I ended up on the floor with my undies around my ears would I call you for help. Especially not then.

Bladder placated, I joined Connor again. "How's Dana?"

"As good as we could hope. They brought her out of sedation a couple of hours ago, and she's alert and breathing on her own. She should make a full recovery, but it'll take a while."

The hole in my leg didn't seem so bad anymore. We exited the room and headed down the long corridor for the car.

"So, update me on the case already," I said, puffing only a little.

"Well, Josh needed surgery on his hand, so I took the liberty of gathering up as much evidence as possible before he got a chance to dispose of it. It's impossible for him to deny shooting you between the ballistics, his prints on the gun, and the gunshot residue all over his hands, so I focused on the poisoning."

"Makes sense," I said between puffs.

"I hadn't asked you what his motive was to kill Dana in the first place, but finding that hellbane bottle yesterday seemed too convenient to me. I figured he must've planted it to save her after discovering she's his daughter. I also figured he would've gotten rid of all the evidence after he poisoned her initially, which meant he would've needed to brew up a new batch of hellbane to supposedly find in the bushes. So I had our techs test everything in his kitchen. They found traces of hellbane root in his garbage disposal."

"Very clever." Sweat prickled my forehead. *Why did they make medical corridors so long anyway?* "Did you figure out why he used two poisons?"

"He's not talking yet, but my guess is he wanted to use widely available poisons to increase the number of plausible suspects. Most easy-to-source substances take longer to work, but he felt guilty about killing her and wanted to make it as painless as possible. Ambience alone might have done the trick except he knew Dana was too skilled to consume a fatal dose by mistake."

I gave in and leaned against the cool white wall for a short break. "So how did he do it?"

"Well, you already know tox screens found Ambience in the blackberry soufflés, but I had them tested for hellbane yesterday, and the results came back negative. I think he spiked the soufflés and rushed her into tasting them so she'd swallow enough Ambience to make her sleep. Then he got the hellbane into her somehow before the doctor arrived—he could've injected it, put it under her tongue, or dribbled it down her throat. In any case, the Ambience allowed her to sleep through the painful phases of the hellbane, and using the hellbane made sure we wouldn't give her the right antidote and save her."

I hadn't summoned the energy to move away from the wall yet. "So, he's pretty much an evil mastermind with empathy for his victims?"

"That's one way of putting it." The look on his face added: *if you're given to gross exaggeration.* "It would've worked too, if he'd adjusted the dose for the gene mutation. Maybe that will help you appreciate why the Taste Society keeps everyone on a need-to-know basis."

He had a point. I guess there were good reasons for secrecy. As well as corrupt, terrible ones. "So, what will happen to Josh now?"

"The police will look into his financials and prescriptions and see if they can tie him to any Ambience purchases, but the hellbane root in his kitchen, along with the shooting, should be enough to put him away."

I felt less happy about that than I'd expected. "So it was his attempt to save Dana that will land him in jail."

"No. It was his attempt to kill her that will land him in jail. Not to mention the minor detail of how he shot you."

Connor was right, and yet I felt kind of bad for Josh. After everything he'd done to protect his secret and avoid prison, fate had caught up with him. And if he hadn't worked to save Dana after learning she hadn't been trying to expose him, he might've gotten away with it.

None of it changed how much good he'd done for a lot of underprivileged kids. More good than I'd ever managed. If he hadn't shot me, I'd almost still like him.

"Have you broken the news to Dana?" I asked.

"Yes, just before I brought you coffee."

If I was this mixed up about it, I wondered how she was coping. Would she visit her dad in prison? Or never see him again? And what about her mum? I'd promised Kate I'd tell Dana she missed her.

I pushed off from the wall and propped my crutches back under my armpits. My thigh wasn't happy about it. "Wait, if you saw her just before bringing me coffee, does that mean she's here? Can I visit her?"

Connor eyed me. "Well, she might be asleep, but the emergency protocol's been lifted, so you'd be allowed to. On one condition."

"What?"

"You go there by wheelchair. She's at the other end of the clinic."

"Fine." I hoped my relief didn't show.

"I HEARD YOU TOOK a bullet for me," Dana said, her voice rough from having a tube down her throat for the past six days. She was propped up in bed, in a private room, looking awful, but alive.

"I wouldn't say that," I protested.

Her light brown hair fell loose around her shoulders, and I realized I'd never seen it down. It softened the angles of her heart-shaped face. She looked like Kate.

Her hazel eyes glinted with humor. "Good. Because I'd hate to think I'd trained you so badly you thought bullets were part of the job."

I smiled. "No, ma'am. You were an excellent teacher."

"Don't call me ma'am. I'm younger than you are."

"Yes, Ms. Williamson." I clapped a hand over my mouth. "I meant, Ms. Williams, sorry."

She fluttered a pale hand at me, causing the tube stuck into it to jump and sway. "It's fine. Everyone knows now. I might as well put it on Facebook." She gave me a small smile.

"I can do it for you if you like," I offered.

"You always were a suck-up." We were silent a moment. "In all seriousness, this whole ordeal has been a wake-up call. I don't want to end up like Josh, pushing everyone away. I don't even want to push *him* away. I think, one day, when we're both feeling better, I might be able to forgive him." She looked at me, her eyes searching.

I nodded. "I think that would be good."

Her relief was obvious.

I wished I had the feather with me. "I don't know if Connor told you, but we visited your mum during the investigation. She asked me to tell you she misses you."

A flurry of emotions crossed Dana's face, and she looked down to hide them. "I've been thinking of her too," she said at last. "She didn't deserve me leaving like that, without a word."

I rolled my wheelchair forward and clasped her hand. "I'm pretty sure she'll be able to forgive you too."

She mulled this over, then tightened her hand around mine. "Thank you."

I squeezed back. "Anytime. I'll see you around?"

"Well, only if the all-powerful Taste Society allows it."

We shared a smile, and I wheeled myself to the door.

"Oh, Izzy, one more thing."

With difficulty, I turned the wheelchair to face her again.

"If you ever make a turkey joke, I'll shoot you myself."

I gave her a salute. "Must run in the family."

26

CONNOR WHEELED ME TO HIS CAR, picking up my crutches on the way. My leg was throbbing from my earlier exertions, and I was trying hard not to think about the two flights of stairs between me and my apartment.

"So, what am I supposed to tell Oliver? And Etta? And anyone else who hears I got shot?"

"Stick with Josh's story that you were hit in a random shooting. As far as anyone needs to know, you were just in the wrong place at the wrong time."

I couldn't help but think that if I hadn't had pepper spray, or hadn't doubled over from the first bullet, everyone would've believed that. Even Connor.

"What do I tell them I was doing in Death Alley?"

"Being a dumb tourist."

I wanted to argue, but the simplest explanation was probably the best one. Neither Oliver nor Etta would have a hard time believing I'd do something that stupid.

"Speaking of, tell me how you really got shot. From the beginning."

I told him. He didn't interrupt and didn't say anything when I'd finished. The vein in his neck had reappeared, though.

"Is there any news on Albert?" I dared to ask.

"Not yet."

"Um. I might need you to get me some more pepper spray, then."

Connor popped the center console, pulled out a new canister, and handed it to me without saying a word.

"Thanks." I rolled the cylinder between my fingers. "And thank you for, well, saving me too."

Connor met my eyes for a beat. "You saved yourself, Avery. You did well."

I thought about that for a minute.

"But if—"

"If you hadn't gone to do my job without me, you wouldn't have needed saving?"

I'd planned to point out that if he hadn't come along and shot Josh, I would've died. After his last comment, I decided he didn't need the ego boost.

"I bet you were one of those bossy kids, weren't you?" I asked instead. "The one that always got to be Batman and made the other kid be Robin."

"Maybe. But I bet you were the kid that didn't get to be Batman *or* Robin because you were in the hospital. With a broken leg. Because you didn't listen when your momma said don't jump off the roof."

"It was the trampoline actually."

Connor looked smug.

———

WE PULLED UP TO MY APARTMENT. "I should warn you, there might be a few people waiting to welcome you home," Connor said. "Don't forget you're supposed to be my girlfriend."

"Gee, Connor, if you want me to kiss you, just say so."

"I want you to kiss me."

I looked at him. He looked at me.

"Very funny." I opened my own car door for once. I wasn't falling for that again. Unfortunately, getting *out* of the car proved difficult. How the hell would I get up the stairs?

"Stop flailing those crutches around. I'll carry you up."

Thank goodness. "That's real sweet of you, schnookums."

"Remember, you haven't passed your assessment yet."

I groaned. How could I forget? On the bright side, as long as Mr. Black stuck to our agreement, I had a few days left before it was his turn to try to kill me.

Connor bore me up the two flights of stairs and sideways past Etta's sofa. At the top, he wasn't panting. In fact, even with my head pressed against his chest, I couldn't pick up any elevation in his heart rate. It wasn't fair. He made it seem easier to lug me up the stairs than it was to walk up myself. I didn't know whether to nestle my head farther into his chest or hit him.

The door swung open before I could do either, and Etta was there beaming at me, Oliver a step behind her. "I'm so disappointed in you," she said. "I'd just finished telling you how bored I was, and then you went off and had an adventure without me."

"I'll get you a drink," Oliver said, with a meaningful look at the back of Etta's head. "Actually, I might get me a drink too."

Connor carried me inside and deposited me on the couch next to Meow. "I'll grab the rest of your things."

I pulled Meow onto my lap and started petting her. I'd missed the comfort of her soft, sleek fur and rumbling purrs.

Etta sat down next to us, her eyes tracking Connor as he made his exit. "My, my, he's even better up close."

"It's nice to see you too. Did you leave me any cookies?"

Her cheeks went pink. "Ah, I'll have to check."

"I think that's the first time I've ever seen you blush."

She threw me a dirty look. "I don't blush. Your pain medication must be affecting your vision."

Oliver handed me a cup of tea and sat down on the other side of me. "Would I be able to get some of that pain medication? I've had to put up with Etta all morning."

Etta switched her dirty look over to Oliver while I smiled, sipped my tea, and stroked Meow some more.

They were still glaring at each other when Connor returned with my crutches. He leaned them next to me on the couch, then stood in front of us all with his arms folded, looking uncomfortable. Meow was very comfortable and kept rubbing her cheek against my tea cup in a demand for further attention.

"I think we need ice cream," I said.

Etta rose to her feet. "Well, wouldn't you know it, I happen to have a whole freezer full of ice cream. I'll be right back. Then you can tell us all about that time you got shot."

———————

TO MY SURPRISE, Connor claimed one of the armchairs and stuck around while the rest of us exchanged news.

Etta caught me up on our neighbors' antics. One of the Korean gentlemen in 1C had a late-night visitor she thought was a call girl. Mr. Winkle had threatened to set his fighting fish on Ms. Pleasant after she complained his unit smelled fishy to the apartment management board. And Ms. Pleasant told Mr. Winkle that if he threatened her again, she'd buy a cat and let it loose in his apartment.

Oliver favored me with his latest rant about the Queen. "Did you know she refuses to wear a helmet when she rides her herd of horses? The UK spends millions of pounds on her security every year, yet she can't even concede to wear a bloody helmet. I mean, it's no worse than a bunch of her hats, but no, a helmet doesn't fit in with her sense of self, and it's not like she has to pay her own medical bills, so tallyho, cracked skull here we come!"

And I told them the edited version of how I got shot.

One gallon of ice cream later, Oliver left for work. Etta winked at me and announced that she had to go too, leaving Connor and me alone.

I gestured to the empty ice cream container. "Well, at least my stomach hurts more than my leg now."

Connor gave me one of his lip twitches that equated to a normal person's smile. "Would you like another cup of tea to settle it?"

"You know how to make a cup of tea?"

He got up and put the kettle on, not deigning to answer. "I submitted an application for your advance pay."

"But we agreed—"

"I know what we agreed."

"Does that mean you're passing me?"

"I figured it'd take a few days to go through. As long as you can keep your act together in the meantime, then yes, I'll pass you."

"Oh. Good."

"You don't sound very excited."

"Well. I did get shot. And poisoned."

He handed me a cup of tea. "Sure, but it's not the Shade profession you should be worried about—all the bad guys were in the food industry. It's your old career you need to reconsider."

I groaned. "Thanks for pointing that out."

"You're welcome. There's another thing you might want to reconsider too."

I cupped the mug in my hands and took a sip. "Oh?"

"Once you pass, you'll get a new assignment."

Wow. He really did know how to make tea. "Uh-huh."

Connor leaned in, his breath on my neck sending lightning streaking downward. "That means there are only a few days left where you're still allowed to sleep with me."

I took another sip of the tea. "I'll keep that in mind."

27

FOR THE SECOND MORNING in a row, I woke up to someone standing over me. This time, the blob wasn't Connor. Or Oliver. Or Etta. The blob was Albert.

I stifled a scream and pasted a smile on my face. Albert looked a bit taken aback too, but that was probably just his reaction to my slept-in, electrocuted zombie hairdo.

"Albert. What are you doing here?"

"I heard you got shot. I brought soup." He held out a Tupperware container. This was the goofy, awkward Albert I'd met at the market. The one I didn't think would hurt or drug anyone.

I knew better now.

"Wow. Thank you. That's very kind, but—"

"I have someone watching Connor. They'll call me if

he heads this way. Until then, I thought we might spend some time together."

"Um."

"Your housemate is out. No one will know."

I tried to find words. "It's good to see you," I lied at last, "but I can't do much, you know, after being shot and all."

He leaned forward and kissed me. I managed not to retch into his mouth.

"I think we can still have fun," he said.

I attempted another smile. "Okay. Well, let me just make myself a little more presentable"—I gestured to my zombie hairdo—"brush my hair and all that."

He looked at my hair. "Okay. But be quick. I'm an impatient man when it comes to you, sweet cheeks."

He left the room, and I grabbed my phone. It was dead. I'd forgotten to charge it last night. I plugged it in, snatched some clothes off the floor and put them on as fast as possible while racking my brain about where I'd left my pepper spray and Taser. I found them in the bag Connor had brought home for me from the medical facility. He'd even changed over the Taser cartridge.

I sent a silent thank-you his way.

"Izzy? I'm waiting."

The outfit I'd thrown on didn't have pockets. I shoved the Taser down my skirt's waistband at the small of my back and let my top hang loose over it. The new pepper spray went down my bra.

"Do you need help getting dressed?"

"No!" I yelled. "I'll be right there."

My phone was still dead.

I limped to the mirror, wrestled my zombie hair into a short ponytail, and threw on a bit of mascara. I did *not* want to be stuck with Albert in my bedroom, so I grabbed my crutches and hopped on out to the open living area.

He was sitting at the dining table. In my absence, someone, probably Etta, had gotten rid of the dying remnants of his flowers. Oliver would have left them to rot, and then I'd be in even more trouble.

There was a steaming bowl next to Albert. "Have some soup, sweet cheeks."

Starving and glad for any opportunity to stall his intended make-out session, I sat down. As I took the first sip, he began unbuttoning his shirt.

The soup was spiked.

Not just with the date rape drug, which I'd half expected; there was belladonna in it too. Just enough to cause agonizing cramps and vomiting without killing me.

I resisted the urge to spit it out and sat back in my chair, holding my stomach. "Actually, I'm not really hungry right now. It's the painkillers I'm on. They make me nauseous."

A flash of annoyance flickered across Albert's face. He laid his shirt over the chair next to him. "The soup will make you feel better," he lied.

What was his plan? I'd thought he was hell-bent on getting in my pants, but no one finds vomiting sexy. Then again, belladonna took a couple of hours to kick in. Maybe he was planning on doing the deed, *then* leaving me to puke my guts up, but why?

"I'm sorry. It was super sweet of you to bring it, and I'm sure I'll enjoy it later, but I just can't right now."

The anger flashed across his face again. "Eat it." There was a note of warning in his voice that suggested a silent *or else.*

I looked at him, eyes wide, feigning innocence. "Albert, what's gotten into you?"

"You lied to me."

"I don't—"

"Two nights ago. When I came over. I watched and waited after you forced me to leave. Connor never came back with any wine."

I thought fast. "He said he was going to, but he stood me up. I didn't know!"

He gazed at me coldly, the anger now more than just a fleeting expression. "I don't believe you." He slammed his fist against the table. "Any of you! My fiancée lied to me. You lied to me. And I don't deserve it. I deserve better!"

He lunged to his feet and pinned me to the chair with both hands.

This was not a position Connor had shown me how to get out of.

"You do deserve better," I agreed, hoping it would calm him down. But the fury in his eyes only blazed brighter.

I calculated whether I could deliver a swift kick to his balls with my good leg, but the table leg was in the way.

"I'll show you what happens to sluts like you who tease

me," he hissed. "You'll beg me to take you, and after you've experienced the ecstasy I bring, you'll suffer the agony of being left behind."

My Taser was inaccessible, pressed between my back and the chair, and there was no chance I could get to my pepper spray, flick off the safety, and aim it without Albert intervening. I looked around for a makeshift weapon.

Etta was peering through the window. Our eyes met, and hope surged within me. *This was it.*

She gave me a thumbs up and a wink.

Then she vanished.

My mouth seesawed in disbelief. My mind struggled to make sense of it.

Had she gone to get her gun? But why wink at me? This was *hardly* a winking kind of situation. Unless…

What if she thought we were doing some kind of kinky sex thing? She wouldn't have been able to see Albert's angry face from her vantage point and could've chalked up my horror to her catching us in the act.

"Help!" I shouted.

She didn't reappear.

"Etta, pl—"

Albert released his grip on one of my arms to cover my mouth. "Hush now, sweet cheeks. I won't do anything you don't deserve."

This from the guy who thought the poor and desolate deserved what life dealt them. I was not comforted.

"Promise me you'll be quiet and cooperate, or I'll have

to knock you unconscious. It won't stop me from screwing you, it'll just make it a little less fun for both of us."

I shuddered.

"Nod if you understand."

I nodded. Let him think I was cooperating until I had a chance to grab the Taser or pepper spray. With my loose-fitting top the only thing concealing them, I'd have to make my move before he made me undress.

"Now, eat your soup."

I took the spoon from him and swallowed another mouthful, moving as slowly as I thought I could get away with. He sat back down at the table. "Keep both hands where I can see them. I'd hate to have to hurt you."

Yeah, right.

I ate more soup, Albert watching my every move.

"You're quite attractive," he said, flashing his goofy grin.

This guy was unhinged.

"Pity you didn't have time to get dolled up for me. But I thought you'd like the surprise."

I grimaced at him and took another spoonful. Maybe I could make myself throw up and pretend the belladonna had started working already. I forced my poor brain to remember Albert's roving hands on my body. It made me dry-retch. No vomit.

Dammit.

Meow ran out of Oliver's bedroom and swished herself around my legs, meowing loudly. This was her way of telling me it was time for breakfast. She meowed again.

"Get that cat to shut up."

"She's only hungry. Can I feed her?"

Albert smirked at me. "Not a chance. You just concentrate on that soup, sweet cheeks."

She wound herself between my legs some more while I took another mouthful. When I didn't respond, she moved on to Albert. It was her usual strategy: go from person to person and harass them until food appeared. It's not like she'd recognize Albert as the one who'd made her sick, so why not him?

She started doing her winding routine around his legs and let out another meow. I hoped she'd give up soon, but as the local cockroaches knew, Meow was nothing if not persistent.

As I finished that thought, Albert shot to his feet. "Ouch! You little bitch."

She must have escalated to clawing his legs.

He reached down and grabbed her.

"Please don't hurt her," I pleaded.

Albert considered me. Meow purred in his hands, thinking she was about to get fed.

"It's funny how you care more for the cat's feelings than mine," he said.

My heart sunk.

"I won't hurt her. I'll just put her outside." He backed to the door, watching me the whole time, and gave me a cold smile. "I've always wondered whether cats really do always land on their feet."

I tried frantically to choose between the Taser and the pepper spray. As far as I knew, if Albert was holding Meow when I tasered him, she'd get zapped too. And that's even giving me the benefit of the doubt and assuming I could hit him with both probes and miss her. But the pepper spray had the same problem; they'd both be hit.

I wasted precious seconds in thought. I didn't know if a Taser charge would kill a cat. I was more certain she'd survive the pepper spray. I ripped it from my cleavage just as Albert was opening the door.

"Put the cat down."

Albert's eyes grew wide at the sight of the canister, or perhaps my gaping neckline, but he didn't let go of Meow.

"Ever experienced police-strength pepper spray to the face?" I asked. "I've used it before. It makes grown men cry. And cough. And go blind."

I saw Albert's eyes dart from the canister to the cat, and back again.

"It might even do permanent damage to your sense of taste or smell," I added.

"Wait." He hesitated. "I'll put the animal down if you put down the pepper spray first."

Did he think I was stupid? "At the same time, or not at all."

We stared across the ten feet that divided us. I hoped he read the anger and resolve in my eyes.

"Okay," he said, "but you have to roll the pepper spray away from you so you can't just grab it again."

"Fine."

"Fine."

We both crouched down, our eyes locked on each other. "On the count of three," I said. "Three, two, one . . . now."

I rolled the canister toward him.

He released Meow and lunged.

I snatched the Taser from my waistband and fired it.

The probes embedded themselves in his naked chest, and he collapsed to the floor, twitching. I dropped the Taser like Connor taught me, spent ten of my precious thirty seconds picking up Meow, and half limped, half hopped out the apartment over to Etta's. "Call the police," I said as soon as she opened the door to my pounding.

She took in my disheveled appearance, Meow clutched to my chest. "You're not playacting anymore, are you?"

"Never was. Call the police, *please*."

"Oh, sorry about that." She rushed to her phone, talking the whole time. "I was so glad to see you finally having a bit of fun. It never occurred to me . . . Hello? Yes, we need the police. There's an . . . intruder." She spouted off our address while I locked the door behind me. "They're on their way."

I stared out the window, waiting for Albert to run, or stumble, past. I wasn't sure how long it would take him to recover after the Taser stopped doing its thing.

"Is he still coming after you? What did you do to him?"

"Tasered him."

"Well, I can do better than that." Etta rummaged through her handbag and pulled out the Glock. "If he tries to escape before the police get here, I'll put a bullet in his butt." She headed for the door.

I grabbed her arm. "Etta, no."

She looked back at me and rolled her eyes. "Oh boy, I was sure you Australians would be made of sterner stuff. Don't worry about me, dear. I was born with a gun in my hand." She shook off my grip, opened the door, and leaned casually on the stair rail with her Glock pointing toward my apartment.

I stayed inside, my heart pounding in my ears, trying to think about how to get her back through the door. "Please come inside, Etta. The police can track him down if he goes anywhere."

"Forget about it. I'm not letting that scoundrel get away."

I thought hard. "I'll eat all your ice cream if you don't come stop me."

"You probably need it."

"If you come inside, I'll bake you some more cookies?"

She shrugged. "You'll do that anyway."

She was right.

I sighed and lowered myself on trembling legs to the floor where I could keep an eye on her. Meow stayed in my arms. I didn't want to risk her running off, and I no longer had the pepper spray or Taser to help Etta anyway. At least because Albert had taken his shirt off, I was pretty sure he didn't have a gun, and I believed Etta when she said she was a good shot.

A minute passed. Then another. I heard sirens in the distance.

Albert must've too, because a moment later, Etta put both hands on the gun. "Stop right there, asshole."

I clambered awkwardly to my feet, ready to drop Meow and intervene somehow if I had to.

Albert was swaying on the stair landing, hands in the air. He hadn't bothered to put his shirt back on, and I could see a few specks of blood where he'd pulled out the probes. I hoped it hurt.

The sirens grew louder, and a police cruiser raced down the street. "LAPD. Drop your weapons and put your hands in the air."

They must have been focused on Etta.

"Fools," she muttered. "I hardly look like the dangerous intruder I reported." But she laid down her gun and raised her arms, gaze never leaving Albert. The police rushed up the stairs and grabbed her, then Albert, then me. Somehow with a bandaged leg, torn top, and cat clutched to my chest, I must've seemed the least threatening.

My policeman agreed to escort me back to my apartment and take my statement there seeing as I had a gunshot wound and all. Hop-hobbling across the landing, Meow still in my arms, I overheard Etta tell her cop that she was a frail old lady who was too shook up to go down the stairs. I tried not to snort lest my officer decide something fishy was going on.

I recounted what had happened, glad Etta had peered through the window so she could corroborate my story. That it wasn't just my word against the celebrity's. The drugged soup would back up my version of events too, but I didn't know if I was allowed to mention it since the average person wouldn't have known. Either the policeman taking my statement was unusually good-looking, or I was starting to feel its effects.

Connor showed up just as they were leading Albert away in handcuffs.

"I asked the research team to tell me if this apartment building or someone matching your description came up on the police scanner," he said. "I knew you couldn't stay out of trouble. Are you okay?"

There was that question again. "Yes. Thanks." I sat on my hands to stop me from carrying out the fantasy I was having. "But I have had some GHB-X and belladonna."

The GHB-X must not have been in full force yet since I wasn't ripping off his clothes.

"Why didn't you call me?"

"I forgot to charge my phone last night."

"Then why didn't you call our emergency unit?"

I held up my hand, where my Taste Society ring with its hidden microphone was supposed to be. The nurses in the emergency room had taken it off, along with my nail polish and earrings, just in case I'd needed surgery. "Um, I think my ring must be at the bottom of my hospital bag. Besides, I didn't ingest that much."

"Did you have enough to get cramps and vomiting?"

"Probably."

"And did you ingest enough that you're having a hard time not kissing me right now?"

I blew out a sigh. "Yes."

"Then for goodness' sake, Isobel, you should get treatment." He pulled out his phone.

"Is the thought of kissing me that bad?"

It was the GHB-X talking.

"No." He stepped in close and brushed my cheek. "But when we do sleep together, the chemistry's going to be all natural."

I forced my hands to stay where they were. "You say that like sleeping together is a foregone conclusion."

He smiled genuinely for the fourth time since I'd known him. "It is."

28

A HALF HOUR LATER, I was putting some serious thought into lodging a complaint with the Taste Society. This was the second time this week I'd had to deal with the most-attractive-man-on-earth number one (Connor) and two (Levi) in a drug-induced state of arousal. For the sanity of their Shades, they really ought to hire *ugly* investigators and doctors.

That said, now that Dr. Levi Reyes had given me some concoctions to drink, I was beginning to feel better. Especially since he'd promised one of them would neutralize the belladonna in my system, so no cramping or vomiting to look forward to.

I thanked him, and he told me we should stop meeting like this.

Bed was calling. I swung my way toward it but came to

an abrupt halt at the doorway to my room. Gathered in a pile on the old green carpet were four dead cockroaches. Moisture pooled in my eyes. Meow *never* put the bodies anywhere but at the front door. The only explanation I could come up with was that she'd missed me.

Of all the welcomes I'd received since coming home after being shot, this was the sweetest. She followed me to bed, and we curled up together and slept.

THREE DAYS PASSED, and I still hadn't left my apartment, except to hop over to Etta's every now and then. I wasn't keen to go up and down all those stairs on crutches. Besides, I figured I'd earned some lazy days of Skype conversations with my loved ones, bad television, and eating my way through several batches of cookies.

Albert had been officially charged with breaking and entering, possession of GHB-X, and attempted rape. It wasn't murder, but it would get him off the streets for a good long while.

Josh had been officially charged with two counts of attempted homicide, and the Taste Society had pulled some serious strings to keep Dana's and my names out of public records. I suspected they used the truth of the car accident as leverage to ensure Josh's silence about the Taste Society since there was no mention of Henry in the news.

And I had officially become a Shade.

My advance pay had come through the day before, and I'd sent it straight on to Platypus Lending to pay off my overdue payments in full.

I still hadn't slept with Connor.

Etta and I were sitting on the couch watching a sappy romance and polishing off a tub of cookies 'n' cream ice cream when we heard someone knock on the door. Etta bustled over and looked through the peephole. Before turning the handle, she smoothed out her bun and pinched her cheeks.

I smirked. *Must be Connor if she's trying that hard to impress.*

Mr. Black filled the doorway.

I pulled myself upright, grabbed one crutch to lean on, and used my other hand to check my pocket for my Taser.

Etta beamed. "Why, hello. You must be Mr. Black. Izzy's told me *all* about you."

I felt a stab of guilt. Maybe I should have told her all about him. Then she might know how much danger she was in right now.

I shuffled my way toward them, the reassuring weight of the Taser bumping against my leg.

Mr. Black raised a giant hand to scratch his giant face. "Has she? Good things I hope."

"Oh, yes," said Etta. "*Very* good things."

Mr. Black and I both blushed.

"Well, er . . . I've come to return the Corvette." He held out the keys and met my eyes. "Thanks for letting me borrow her for a while."

That seemed a mild way of referring to our agreement, but I was grateful he hadn't inadvertently spilled the beans to Etta. I was even more grateful he'd returned my car. "No problem."

"I've given her a wash for you, and I changed the oil too since it was looking a little darker than I'd like."

Huh? Etta's presence forced me to play it cool. "Wow. Thank you."

She waved an arm at the kitchen. "Would you like to come in for a cup of tea?"

I considered shooting *her* with my Taser.

"Oh, I'd love to, but I better keep moving."

Thank goodness. I let out the breath I was holding.

Etta's face fell. "Well, that's a shame. Let me walk you out, seeing as Izzy can't with her busted leg and all."

I thanked him again, hardly believing my luck, and watched them leave together. I wouldn't have let Etta go, except somehow after seeing Mr. Black blush, I was more worried for him than I was for her.

My heart was still bumping along faster than it should be, so I limped over and put the kettle on. There's something calming about the routine of making tea.

When it was ready, I decided to take the steaming mug outside and enjoy it on the "balcony." Something I hadn't done since I'd been shot. Using a single crutch to support me, I dragged a dining chair out there and sat down next to my dead cactus.

For the first time in weeks, I didn't have to worry about

anyone coming for me. Albert and Josh were in jail. My overdue payments were settled. My Corvette sat shiny and waiting for me on the street. And my new salary meant I could pay off the rest of the loan in about two years. Maybe two and a half if I supported my coffee addiction and flew home to visit my family once in a while. I sipped my tea slowly and basked in the California sunshine.

Twenty minutes later, the door to 3A opened and Mr. Black and Etta came out. His hair was wet and his shirt buttoned askew.

My jaw dropped. I almost dropped the empty mug I was holding too.

Etta escorted Mr. Black to the bottom of the stairs and waved goodbye. When she came back up, I pounced on her. Metaphorically speaking.

"Did I just see Mr. Black leave your apartment?"

"Yes."

"With wet hair?"

"Yes."

"But he said it was their ten-year anniversary recently. He has a daughter with a Disney Princess watch. He's supposed to be happily married!"

"I'm sure he is, dear."

I gaped at her.

"Oh, don't look at me like that. Nothing happened. He was walking away from our building when Mr. Winkle dumped a bucket of water on his head. Turns out Mr. Winkle was cleaning his fish tanks, but his drain was playing up, so he thought he'd toss it outside. I saw what happened and invited Mr. Black to shower and dry his clothes before heading home. No one wants to smell like fish water, you know. That's it. That's all that happened."

I stared, using every bit of the talent I'd inherited to try to read her.

A minute later, I broke eye contact and rubbed my face in resignation.

The woman before me might just be a greater mystery than the one I'd so recently solved. And I, super-detective-extraordinaire, had no idea whether she was telling the truth.

FROM THE AUTHOR

I hope you enjoyed EAT, PRAY, DIE. That way, I can rub it in my brother's smug face since he scoffed at me when I first started writing at the tender age of sixteen. If you want to help me make sure he gets his comeuppance, take a minute to leave me a review or mention this book to a friend who'll also enjoy it. That'll show him.

If you'd like to keep reading, the sequel THE HUNGER PAINS is available now. You can also get a free bonus scene in Connor's perspective below.

Want to know the jaw-dropping secret Connor's been hiding from Izzy since day one? Read this BONUS scene in his perspective and find out!

Grab your FREE copy at:
CHELSEAFIELDAUTHOR.COM/UNMASKED

ACKNOWLEDGEMENTS

Thanks goes to my number one fan, Rebecca, for cheering me on and stopping me from getting distract—SQUIRREL! What was I saying? Oh yeah, thank you to Tess and Morgan for your expertise in medicine and genetics, respectively, and to all of my beta readers: Tess, Katie, James, Rebecca, Sally, Mumsy, Naomi, Darren, John, Rosie, Melanie Cellier (author of *The Princess Companion*), Augusta (author of *A Dead End* under the pen name Keeley Bates), and Alex Brantham (author of *One Equal Temper*). Your feedback has been invaluable. Unless everyone hates this book, in which case, next time tell me the damn truth!

To my amazing developmental editor, Angela Brown, thank you for forcing me to add in a billion details (I counted). Because everyone wants to know what they ate for breakfast—since there's not enough of that sort of thing on social media. A huge thank you also to my line-editor, Julie from Free Range Editorial, who combed through the whole book twice and still pretended to find it funny, my proofreaders, Donna Rich and Leo Bricker, and my final pass editor Crystalle from Victory Editing. Anyone who finds a typo after all of that deserves a medal and a career change. Email me at chelsea@chelseafieldauthor.com and I'll see what I can do about the medal part.

Finally, thanks to my superhero husband (seriously, he wears his undies on the outside sometimes). And to God, for teaching me You have a sense of humor from an early age—like the day I was trying to impress a boy and borrowed my sister's T-shirt that read BRAIN DEAD; STILL KICKING, then busted my ankle falling down the stairs so I couldn't kick anymore. And for blessing my socks off. I assume that's why they keep disappearing anyway.

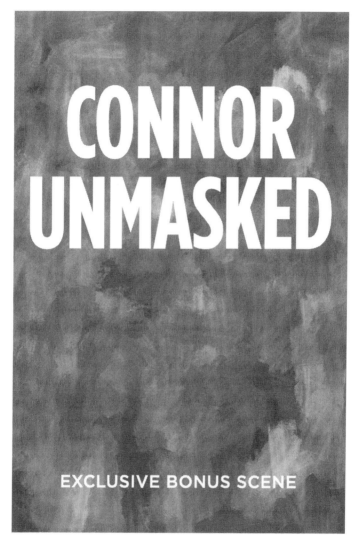

CONNOR UNMASKED

EXCLUSIVE BONUS SCENE

Want to know the jaw-dropping secret Connor's been hiding from Izzy since day one?

Read this BONUS scene in his perspective & find out!

For a full list of books by the author, please visit:
CHELSEAFIELDAUTHOR.COM

Printed in Great Britain
by Amazon